Gordon-Nash - New Hampton

P9-BYS-311

DATE DUE

JAN 24 2007	DEC 20 2011	
FEB 8 2007		
FEB 2 2007		
MAR 8 2007		
MAR 20 2007		
MAR 2 2007		
APR 24 2007		
JUN 9 2007		
JUN 20 2007		
JUL 2 2007		
MAR 25 2009	JUN 12 2012	
MAY 26 2009		
MAR 18 2010		
APR 21 2010		
JUL 29 2010		

TRAP DOOR

ALSO BY SARAH GRAVES

The Dead Cat Bounce
Triple Witch
Wicked Fix
Repair to Her Grave
Wreck the Halls
Unhinged
Mallets Aforethought
Tool & Die
Nail Biter

TRAP DOOR

A

Home Repair Is Homicide
Mystery

SARAH GRAVES

B A N T A M   B O O K S

TRAP DOOR
A HOME REPAIR IS HOMICIDE MYSTERY
A Bantam Book / January 2007

Published by Bantam Dell
A Division of Random House, Inc.
New York, New York

This is a work of fiction. Names, characters, places, and incidents either are the product of the author's imagination or are used fictitiously. Any resemblance to actual persons, living or dead, events, or locales is entirely coincidental.

All rights reserved
Copyright © 2006 by Sarah Graves

Bantam Books is a registered trademark of Random House, Inc., and the colophon is a trademark of Random House, Inc.

Library of Congress Cataloging-in-Publication Data

Graves, Sarah.
Trap door / Sarah Graves.
p. cm.
ISBN-13: 978-0-553-80429-4
1. Tiptree, Jacobia (Fictitious character)—Fiction. 2. White, Ellie (Fictitious character)—Fiction. 3. Women detectives—Maine—Eastport—Fiction. 4. Dwellings—Maintenance and repair—Fiction. 5. Female friendship—Fiction. 6. Eastport (Me.)—Fiction. I. Title.

PS3557.R2897T73 2007
813'.6—dc22
2006050139

Printed in the United States of America
Published simultaneously in Canada

www.bantamdell.com

10 9 8 7 6 5 4 3 2 1
BVG

TRAP DOOR

Over a long, successful career of killing people for money, Walter Henderson had never before snuffed out a personal enemy. He'd made a habit of keeping his private life and his business affairs separate, and planning to break that habit now aroused a variety of new emotions in him, none of them pleasant.

Anxiety, resentment, and the kind of bone-deep reluctance a lazy schoolboy might feel, facing a pile of homework . . . these were not sentiments with which Walter Henderson, a paid assassin, had any significant experience.

Thus as he sat waiting in his comfortable leather armchair for the inevitable to occur, he tried yet again to come up with some other way out of the situation in which he found himself. But he'd been over it all a hundred times in his head already and he'd found none.

Because there weren't any. So now here he was. *I'm not even supposed to be doing this anymore,* he thought irritably. With one exception—a loose end he meant to tie up very soon—he'd decided that his death-dealing days were history.

But apparently resolutions really were made to be broken, he thought. Then came the sound he'd been waiting to hear: stealthy footsteps on the gravel driveway outside, not far from his open window.

Walter looked up from the book he'd been pretending to read, in the warm pool of light in the den of his large, luxuriously appointed house in Eastport, Maine. It was late. The housekeeper had gone home to her own house, and his teenaged daughter Jen was already in bed.

Or so she'd tried hard to convince him as she'd headed upstairs an hour earlier: clad in pajamas, carrying a glass of milk and a handful of cookies, and yawning elaborately.

Smiling with affection, thinking how pretty she was with her golden tan, strong athlete's body, and sun-bleached blonde hair, Walter had bid his daughter a fond good night. Then he'd built a fire in the enormous granite fireplace that formed one whole wall of the room, piling it with chunks of aged driftwood so it flamed extravagantly before settling to a fierce red glow.

After that, with a scant two fingers of Laphroaig in a chunky cut-crystal lowball glass to keep him company, he'd sat down with his book to wait. Despite the chilly spring evening the fire let him keep the window open, admitting salt air and whiffs of wood smoke along with the distant, varied hoots and moans of the foghorns on the dark water a few hundred yards distant.

Now Walter sat very still, listening to the sound of cautious movement outside, a whispery crunching on stones that someone was trying to minimize.

To no avail. That you couldn't approach the house without traversing an expanse of pea gravel was not an accident, any more than the elaborate alarm system, heat-and-motion detectors, or closed-circuit TV cameras that Walter had installed when he'd had the house built.

All turned off now, of course. Walter didn't want any record, electronic or otherwise, of what transpired here tonight. Just to be sure, he'd had an old buddy of his run up from the city a week earlier to disarm the devices, taking care to make it appear that the central controller circuits had silently malfunctioned.

In the unlikely event that anyone checked. Walter listened a while longer to be certain it wasn't only a wild animal out there, a deer or raccoon or maybe even a moose. There were plenty of them on the island where Eastport was located, seven miles off the coast of downeast Maine and another thousand or so from the neon-lit nightlife Walter Henderson was used to: pimps and hookers, loan sharks and dope addicts, pushers and grifters . . .

All in the past now, he reminded himself without regret. And from the sound of it, tonight's visitor was indeed human. A glance outside confirmed this; there was a light on in the barn, faintly illuminating a high square of window.

Which there hadn't been the last time Walter looked. He waited ten deliberate minutes, then laid his book aside, got up, and removed the loaded pistol from its usual place in the upper right-hand drawer of his desk. Placing the gun in his sweater pocket, he padded from the room, pausing in the dark hall but not bothering to go upstairs to see whether or not Jen was really asleep.

He knew she wasn't, that the yawning and milk getting and elaborate expressions of tiredness had all been an act. For the past few weeks, ever since she'd graduated and come home from the exclusive New York boarding school where she'd spent her high school years, she'd been sneaking out via those same back stairs nearly every night to meet a boy.

And not just any boy. Walter knew it was that worthless little helper the carpenters had brought with them last summer when they arrived to rebuild the barn. Which by itself was okay, bringing along a useless helper. He understood that. People had expenses to cover and sometimes they resorted to methods.

Charge high, pay low . . . it was how the world worked. Probably the contractor got a cut of the materials, too, in an arrangement with the supplier. All standard business practice and all right as rain as far as Walter was concerned, as long as nobody got too greedy.

The kid, though. The kid was something else. Because when the barn job was done and the carpenters had all gone, the kid kept coming around. Doing another kind of job now, wasn't he? On Walter Henderson's daughter.

The thought stopped him in his tracks: Jennifer. His pearl, the only person he knew of in the world who hadn't somehow been contaminated or befouled. The idea of some mangy little nobody with grimy fingernails even thinking about touching her . . .

Well, but it *wasn't* thinkable, was it? That was the whole point. Back in the city he'd have snapped the kid's neck with his two hands, and that would've been that. Dumped him in a landfill or in the trunk of an abandoned car; if push really came to shove there was a sausage factory in Paramus that would take the kid, no problem.

But Walt couldn't do any of those things here, not without screwing up his plans for finishing off that other loose end. And now it seemed no matter what else he tried, he couldn't get rid of the kid.

Padding quietly in the plush moosehide L.L. Bean moccasins Jennifer had given him for Christmas, he slipped down the hall to the silent kitchen, past dimly gleaming appliances and the wall-mounted panel for the alarm system.

The panel's bulbs glowed green, meaning the system had been armed. But according to Walt's gadget-literate buddy, "on" commands weren't reaching the devices the system controlled.

Walt hadn't told Jen about that, though; no need. For all she knew, the alarms worked as they always had. Thinking this, he continued along the dim passageway past the utility room where a pair of Irish wolfhounds stayed when he needed them to be out of the way.

A low *wuff* came from inside the room as he went by. The dogs' nails clicked on the tiled floor as they paced uneasily, alerted by the sound of his presence. Warning growls issued from their throats.

Walter made a face. Ideally, the two expensively bred guard animals should have remained utterly silent. But he hadn't been able to stomach the severity of the aversion training required to accomplish this.

Or to make them bite, either. Yet another sign that he was getting soft, he decided. He'd retired at the right time. But not too soft to do what needed to be done this evening; dogs were one thing, snot-nosed little daughter-molesting punks quite another, he reminded himself without much effort.

Quite another, and not much effort at all; like riding a bike. "Easy, guys," he murmured to the dogs as he let himself out the back door, easing it shut behind him. He paused on the flagstone terrace overlooking Passamaquoddy Bay.

Across it the windows in the houses along the distant shoreline of Campobello Island glowed distinctly. Below them the emerald green lights nearer the water marked harbors and jetties, while to the north the white beacon of the Cherry Island light swirled slowly, strobing the night.

He stepped from the terrace to the lawn, wincing at the icy breeze. April may be the cruelest month, he thought as he made his way downhill toward the squarish dark shape of the barn outlined on an even darker moonless sky, but in Maine at night you could pretty much count on May being a mean bastard, too.

The light in the barn had gone out. Pausing, he hefted the gun in his pocket as easily as other men might handle jackhammers or drive heavy equipment; tool of the trade. When he slipped inside the barn the scent of the new wood mingled with the sweet, grassy smell of the straw bales piled in the loft.

But then came a hint of Jen's expensive perfume, faint but enough to send fresh fury coursing through him. For an instant he imagined the two of them up there, visualized them freezing together in fright at some slight sound he made.

The thud of his heart, maybe, or the grinding of his teeth. Or the hot slither of the muscles in his forearms as his fists clenched and released.

Clenched and released. The boy shriveling, Jen scrambling to cover herself . . . Walter pushed the thoughts away, smelling now the sharp reek of gasoline from the big lawn tractor in the corner. Behind it on hooks, although he could not see them, were gardening tools, the curved scythes and heavy shears, cutting and chopping implements. All with their blades freshly sharpened.

Walter moved soundlessly in the utter blackness, needing no light once his predatory instincts kicked in. He knew how to do this, and he knew his way in the dark. To his right were the loft steps and behind them an area under the loft, originally meant for open space.

But Walter's housekeeper, a habitually silent and thus thoroughly satisfactory employee he'd brought with him when he moved here from the city, had surprised him by suggesting that the area be enclosed to form an office. That way whoever Walter hired to oversee the grounds and the animals wouldn't end up tramping in and out of the main house. So a room had been built there, unused as yet and with the loft's original trap-door opening still piercing its ceiling.

Guy ever needs to escape out of his own office, he can go straight up, Walter had thought with grim humor. If he can jump that high. Unlikely, though, that the kid Walter was after tonight had gone *down* into the office space.

Because the jumping part was no joke; it was a good fifteen feet from the loft to the concrete floor below. And the office was locked; if you got into it from above, there was no way out.

Walter felt the tight smile vanish from his lips. *No way out for me, either.*

Or only one way. And damn it, the whole thing was really all his own fault, wasn't it? He'd been firm enough in forbidding Jen from seeing the boy, all right, just not sufficiently clear about the consequences of disobedience.

And he knew why. Raising the child by himself after her mother's death, Walter hadn't wanted Jennifer to be afraid of him. He couldn't bear seeing the knowledge arise in her eyes—as it had in the desperate, imploring eyes of so many others—that he was dangerous. Thus he had failed to confide in his daughter certain important details about himself.

Such as what he did for a living: that he solved problems for people. Serious problems, ones so difficult and unpleasant that they could be taken care of only by force.

But that wasn't the kind of thing you told a little girl who idolized and adored you: that her father was maybe the most respected and feared professional killer on the whole east coast. And later . . . Well, the time had just never been right.

So at the outset of this whole business, Walter had merely asked Jen if she didn't think a town kid with no money and no prospects was maybe a little beneath her.

"Oh, Daddy," she'd responded indulgently, looking up from the magazine she was reading. "What an old-fashioned way to look at things!"

Yeah, it was. He was an old-fashioned father. And his daughter's answer had told him her reaction to his comments, too: she wasn't taking the hint.

That had been in the winter when she was home for holiday break. As soon as Jen returned to school, he'd arranged to have the kid prosecuted for stalking; an easy task, since maybe the local yokels didn't know who Walter Henderson was but the state yokels certainly did. Enough of them, anyway, to get accomplished what Walter required.

The kid's public defender, a jug-eared bumpkin with a boil on his neck and dandruff on his suit, had looked appalled at the sight of Walter's expensive legal team, the courtroom equivalent of a tank full of piranhas. Jennifer had come home for only a single day to testify, and despite her furious resentment she'd said exactly what he told her to say.

Or else. He'd been clear enough about that. And even if she didn't know the nature of his employment, she knew he controlled the purse strings: her tuition, pocket money, clothing allowance, car, all the rest. She was a smart girl, his Jennifer.

Just not quite smart enough.

The verdict, predictably, had been guilty. Disposition: the defendant was out on bail until the sentencing hearing.

Which, Walter recalled as he stood very still on the barn's main floor, was tomorrow. But his pending court date apparently hadn't deterred the kid in the slightest.

Walter turned slowly in a half circle, feeling the concrete beneath his moccasins, sensing the bulk of the timber-constructed loft in the shadows above. Silence. Except for . . . What the hell?

Suddenly he was all business, both hands on the pistol grip, feet planted like an athlete's. Gun up in a practiced stance, his eyes scanning the darkness, he swung to the left and right.

No one there, although he still had the strong impression of *someone* very near. Silent, or *almost* silent . . .

Calm down, Walter ordered himself. Cat-footed, he eased forward, feeling his pupils dial out to take advantage of any stray gleam. But . . . nothing.

Puzzled, he moved stealthily back out to where the barn's massive rafters rose high above his head unseen. The darkness up there was cavernous. The sound he'd heard had likely been just a barn beam creaking. Or a mouse.

Then annoyance at the stab of fright he'd felt hit him: Goddamn it, why hadn't the kid just given in?

Although Walter's own infrequent court dates had never had much effect on him either. None, actually, he recalled as he approached the loft stairs again. Because like anyone else in his business he'd accepted that sometimes you took one for the team, sometimes you didn't.

But once upon a time Walter had *had* a team, an organization in which his own place was secure and unquestioned and to which his loyalty had been supreme.

This kid didn't. This kid was either too stupid to know he was going away or too foolish to care.

If he *was* going away. Walter took another step. If instead the little punk didn't end up with a suspended sentence. Because a guilty verdict was one thing but a sentencing decision was another. And unless a judge was securely bought and paid for, you never knew what one would do.

Doubt over this was one reason why Walter was out here in the dark, sneaking around his own barn in the middle of the night with a gun. He padded toward the row of pine-board enclosures already made comfortable with straw bedding for the next bunch of animals he planned to acquire when the weather got warmer.

He already had sheep paddocked in their own shelter at the other end of his property. He meant to add goats, maybe a llama. After all, a man couldn't be a country squire without livestock. The idea amused him. But his smile faded swiftly once more at the memory of his final encounter with the kid, only a week earlier.

One last chance, he'd decided, which by itself was uncharacteristic of him. And he'd already known that it probably wouldn't work, that if the court's order *and* a felony conviction wouldn't stop the kid, then nothing else would.

Only one thing would stop him. Still, for Jen's sake, Walter had made it his business to run into the boy in front of the hardware store down on Water Street in Eastport's tiny business district.

"Sure, Mr. Henderson, I understand," the kid had replied when Walter, in reasonable tones, had explained his concerns. Jen had a future, college and a career to look forward to. Jen had a life.

Unlike you, he'd wanted to add. The kid had a pretty face and curly blond hair like an angel's, but that was the only even faintly angelic thing about him. His smile was mocking—that alone would have gotten him killed back where Walter came from—and he wore torn dungarees, ratty sneakers, and a T-shirt that said *The Liver Is Evil and Deserves to Be Punished* on the back.

"I sure am going to miss her, though," the kid added slyly. His inflection deliberately left no doubt about just which of Jennifer's many fine qualities he most would regret losing.

You know nothing of regret, Walter had thought clearly. "I'm sure you will," he had replied, his own voice gone soft. Back in the city, men who heard that tone out of Walter generally reacted by soiling themselves in terror.

But the kid just stood there grinning impudently at him. Walter yearned to tear the T-shirt off his back and ram it down his throat, preferably in front of the smirking gaggle of friends who hung back a little ways listening.

"Tell Jen I said so long, though, will you?" the kid added. "I mean, since I'm not going to be seeing her again."

All the while his snotty expression and his eyes, alight with ignorant malice, conveyed another message entirely: *Get stuffed, you stupid old fart. I'll see her if I want to see her. Do anything else I want to do to her, too.*

Then the kid had turned and swaggered away with his sniggering pals—also clad in T-shirts, though the temperature was a bare fifty degrees—into the hardware store, leaving Walt out on the sidewalk watching his reflection in the store's front window as he ran a hand over his short silvery hair.

Smiling to himself because Walter now knew what the score was, which the kid so clearly did not that it was pitiful. That conversation was the other reason why if the kid was out here in the barn tonight, Walter was going to kill him.

And he was here, no question about it. Being very quiet. But with senses sharpened by thirty-plus years at the top of a human food chain so brutal it made jungle man-eaters resemble tenants of some particularly benign petting zoo, Walter could feel it.

Smell it, too, as if the new creatures he meant to acquire for his estate were already inhabiting and fouling the place. Walt's nose wrinkled involuntarily as he took another step into the darkness.

And . . . that sound again. *Creak-creak.* Was it a beam? In its faint regularity it summoned the mental picture of a boat tied to a pier, moving with the gentle swells of the sea, a rope rubbing against wood. *Creak . . .*

Creak. Only not quite. Familiar, but he couldn't place it. He knew the smell, though. He hadn't been expecting it, not yet, but all at once its identity came to him.

The smell of death. *Oh, Christ . . .*

Jen. *No . . .*

Dropping the pistol as a rush of ice-watery terror poured through him, Walter Henderson scrambled back to the barn door, its window a rectangle of deepest marine blue against the darkness of the wall.

Had the kid killed her? He fumbled against the particle-board panel to the right of the door, where the new circuit breaker box and the light switches were hung.

Had he? Walter's breath came in painful gasps. Oh, sweet Jesus God in heaven, had the stupid little son of a bitch done that?

"Jen?" he shouted, all possible need for stealth evaporated. Never mind the kid, who could and most certainly would be dealt with later. All Walter wanted, all his every shrieking brain cell required absolutely right now, was to see . . .

His frantically searching hand found the light switch and flipped it. White light flooded the barn's interior, from the fluorescent panels hung on chains beneath the rafters.

Half blinded by the sudden brilliance from above, Walter turned in a helpless circle, feeling as if he'd been impaled on an icy spike.

"Jen? Goddamn it, Jenny, I know you're in here."

Frantic, he flung himself at the loft stairs, the gun all but forgotten as he tossed heavy straw bales aside.

"Jenny?" he gasped. Then a bright scrap of cloth caught his eye. It was one of her silk scarves. She had a drawerful of the things, a tumble of them in jewel-toned colors like a sultan's riches.

Snatching the scarf up in both hands, he pressed it to his face, inhaling the perfume he'd smelled earlier, drunk with it as he turned. "Jenny!" he bellowed.

No answer. Staggering forward, he peered over the railed edge of the loft, down the side wall of the unfinished office room and across the barn floor.

Silence again. Hope pierced him; maybe he'd been wrong. Maybe this time she hadn't been lying to him. Maybe she'd been upstairs in her bed all along. Asleep, safe . . .

Then he felt it through the thin soles of his moccasins, up through the loft's floor. An odd vibration; slow, rhythmic, and occurring in time with the sound he had heard.

Was still hearing now. *Creak* . . . It came to him all at once, what the sound was. What he would find when with trembling, sweat-slick fingers he grasped the big iron handle set into the top of the loft's closed trap door.

Nearly weeping, Walter strained at the heavy thing, hauled it up and fell to his knees at the opening's framed-in rim, the sweet-smelling silk scarf still clutched between hands pressed together as though in prayer. Below him through the square trap door opening lay the office room: dark, enclosed, silent.

Or almost silent. "Jen?" Walter whispered. The soft perfumed folds of her scarf caressed his cheek. "Jennifer, honey, are you down there?"

Creak . . . The sound slowed, stopped. Steeling himself, the most respected and feared professional killer on the whole east coast bit back a whimper.

And peered over the edge.

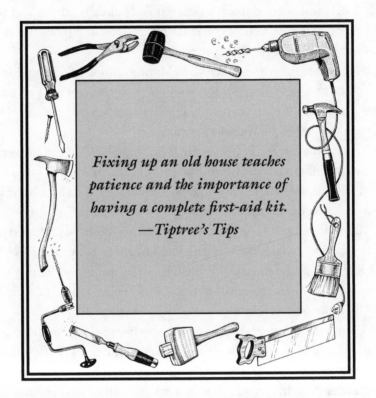

Chapter 2

*Fixing up an old house teaches
patience and the importance of
having a complete first-aid kit.*
—Tiptree's Tips

My name is Jacobia Tiptree and when I first moved to Maine, the last thing I expected was for my dead ex-husband Victor to end up haunting my house. My idea was to repair the ramshackle old dwelling and live happily ever after in it.

Which right there was absurd. I no more knew how to rehabilitate an antique house than I knew how to jump off the rooftop of one and fly.

Soon after I moved in, for example, I found a springy spot in the hall floor. And springiness, I'd heard, meant weakness. So I jumped energetically on the spot in order to test just how weak it really was, whereupon my foot went through and the rest of my leg followed, all the way to my hip.

And there I stayed. I couldn't pull my trapped leg up past the broken floorboard, whose sharp splintered ends already threatened several of my favorite arteries. I couldn't go down, either; the floor around the hole felt solid as concrete.

So I waited: one hour, then two. Monday, my black Labrador retriever, came and sniffed me, then went away again, bored. The trashman came, and the meter reader. Neither heard my shouts, and the mail carrier passed by without stopping.

Finally my son Sam came home from school and found me there, furious and humiliated. "Mom," he said gently, looking down at me and taking in the whole sad situation. "You know, I think maybe the next time you decide to make a hole in the floor . . ."

Right. *Cut it with a saw.* Although at the time I'd have preferred just using a bomb, and if it blew me up, too, I might not have minded very much. Because the alternative was repairing the house, which as a personal-injury generator was already showing itself to be (a) efficient and (b) murderously creative.

Meanwhile, my ability in the happily-ever-after department looked doubtful as well. For instance, back in the city I'd just finished divorcing a guy whose idea of faithfulness consisted of leaving his wedding ring on his finger while he slept with other women, an activity he pursued so regularly you'd have thought he'd entered a contest, and if there'd been one for most commandments broken in a single marriage, Victor would have won it.

And I had Sam, whose idea of sobriety was . . . well, I'm not sure what my son's notion of sobriety consisted of then. Before we moved here he was mostly too drunk, too stoned, or too strung out to think much about it at all; at age thirteen, his liver most likely resembled a pickled herring, his eyes were so bloodshot and frantic that they looked as if they belonged on a cartoon character, and as for his brain, I preferred not to imagine its probable condition.

And I wasn't feeling so good myself. Until coming to Eastport, we'd lived in Manhattan in a building so exclusive, it took genetic testing to get approved to move in. Afterwards, though, the standards of behavior in the place were so trashy—fights, screaming, howled threats to actually *cut up the goddamned charge cards*—I thought they should have parked junk cars out front and set up a broken washing machine in the lobby beside the potted palm.

But never mind, it was a roof over our heads and it's not as if I didn't have plenty of trashy troubles of my own. Victor's girlfriends, for instance, had gotten the idea that I was their pal, a sort of comrade-in-arms in the sordid little romantic tragicomedy they shared with my husband, instead of a person who badly wanted to bash all their heads together.

Victor liked girls who were dewy-eyed and innocent, ignoring the fact that by the time he got through with them they'd be such bitter harpies, the only way to get near them was with a diamond bracelet dangling at the end of a long, sharp stick.

Often they called me weeping, two or three of them at a time—one of the girls, I gathered, had sounded out the words in the phone book where it gave instructions on how to make a conference call, and she'd taught all the others—complaining about what an awful son of a bitch Victor was.

Like maybe I didn't know that. I felt like asking them, since he made no secret of the fact that he was married, who the hell they had been expecting, the Dalai Lama? That maybe by some miracle he wouldn't leave them twisting in the wind the way he'd left me?

I mean unless he needed something: his good shirts sent to the laundry, say, or a button sewn on. Then he'd stay home just long enough for me to start believing that this time, everything might somehow miraculously manage to turn out hunky-dory.

After a while I started sabotaging those buttons, getting up in the wee hours to hide in the utility closet with a flashlight and cuticle scissors, snipping half the threads on each one from behind where it wouldn't show. That's how desperate I'd become: hotshot money manager by day, button snipper by night.

Oh yes, I had a career, too, mostly based on the same variety of freakish inborn talent that produces perfect pitch, double-jointedness, and the ability to win at poker by memorizing all the cards and the odds. In short, at the time I was the kind of money management magician who could make a nickel walk smoothly across the tops of my knuckles, and by the time it got to my little finger it would be a silver dollar.

Too bad the folks for whom I made fortunes were the kind I'd have preferred not to spend much time around; not unless I'd drenched myself with holy water and equipped myself with a mallet and wooden stake. Because let's face it, my clients were the kind of individuals for whom the term "ill-gotten gains" was invented.

Say, for instance, that you were a person who just happened to be skimming the profits off a chain of specialty clothing stores. Before I came along, you could invest your loot in strip clubs or in other shady establishments known primarily for their habit of burning down regularly. Alternatively, you could pack the cash in a satchel and bribe or threaten some poor fool to carry the bag to Puerto Rico for you.

You can't do that anymore; the security noses at airports have gotten better at sniffing cash. Instead you can . . .

But on second thought I'm not going to give details. I don't want to screw it up for whoever's doing my old job now; honor among thieves, and all that. To make a long story short, though, back then I helped introduce what's commonly known as the underworld to the concept of investing on Wall Street.

Legitimately, I mean, as opposed to their usual way, which was called the pump-and-dump. And no, I'm not going to tell you how to do that either. The point is that on a referral from a friend I took on a few shady clients; next thing you know, I was money manager to the Mob.

In the end, however, I chucked it all, dumped Victor, and moved out of Manhattan in a sad, last-ditch effort to salvage my pathetic life. And to save Sam, who by then was very little more than a walking sickness. Extracting my son from the city was like pulling a rotten tooth: no matter how bloody, painful, or disgusting the process may be, you've got to maintain your grip.

Which I had. So fast-forward a few years to me and Sam still living in Eastport, a city of about two thousand on Moose Island, seven miles off the coast of Maine. The house I'd bought wasn't all fixed up yet, but it hadn't fallen down either; over time I had come to regard this as a glass-half-full situation since if I thought of it any other way I would spend every minute weeping.

And not only on account of the vast, yawning money pit . . . er, I mean lovely, historic dwelling I'd come to call home. For one thing, Sam had grown up into a handsome, strapping twenty-year-old but his substance-abuse woes hadn't resolved quite as permanently as I'd hoped. And for another, about three months after we buried him, Victor began haunting the place.

The entire island, I mean, not just my little piece of it. Although on the pleasant morning in May when what we later called the Trap-Door Fiasco began, it was my house that my deceased ex-husband seemed happiest to have learned the trick of infesting.

●　　●　　●

"Hex screws," my friend Ellie White said, checking this item off our list. We were sitting in my big old kitchen with its tall bare windows, pine wainscoting, scuffed floor, and antiquated appliances, getting ready to start on a building project.

Behind me the refrigerator rattled and hummed as if the ice maker were running. But it didn't have an ice maker; not unless you counted the way the inside of the freezer frosted up solidly every week or so.

"Lag bolts, nuts, and washers," I said; Ellie checked the list again.

I'd spent the early part of the morning outdoors, trying to fix rust spots already bleeding through the nearly new paint on the house. Note to self: Next time you sand vast amounts of old paint *off* 175-year-old clapboards, try to remember to rust-block the equally old iron nails in the boards before putting new paint *on*.

"And the battery-powered screwdriver," I added, glancing over to make sure this indispensable item was plugged into its charger on the kitchen counter. It was, and with any luck the little green light on the device meant it really was charging, not just pretending to do so.

Victor stood—transparently; what a show-off—a foot or so to the left of the counter, his smile fading and reappearing like some especially obnoxious version of the Cheshire Cat's.

I ignored him. "Chain saw," said Ellie.

Or I tried. Turns out that a dead ex-husband is even harder to ignore than he was when he was alive. "Check. I already put it in the bed of the pickup truck."

Ellie smiled. "Jake, you're so efficient," she said, marking it too off the list of essentials.

With pale green eyes, red hair, and tiny freckles like gold dust scattered delicately across her nose, my best friend, Ellie, resembled the kind of impossibly fragile fairy princess who flutters around laughing musically and granting people's dearest wishes with a wave of her magic wand.

But appearances were deceiving; despite her looks, Ellie was about as fragile as a Mack truck. When a task needed the chain saw, she started it, ran it, and sharpened its chain when that turned out to be necessary, too; she was a downeast Maine girl born and bred and took no backchat from machinery.

"Foolishness," my housekeeper, Bella Diamond, grumbled from her usual place at the soapstone sink. She stood at it so often that there would have been a pair of footprints on the braided rug in front of it if she had tolerated footprints.

Which she didn't; now with her shirtsleeves rolled up past bony elbows she was washing in hot steaming soapsuds and rinsing with scalding water every plate and cup we owned, none of which had been dirty in the first place.

Letting Bella wash clean dishes was better than the alternative, though, because she was a clean freak and right now it was spring-time, which around here meant a housecleaning so thorough even the skeletons in the closets got polished. So it was either boil salad plates or dip all the lamps in the house in sterilizing solution, to get rid of the many germs which Bella swore gave off toxic vapors when sizzled to death by lightbulb heat.

"You two girls up at the cottage all alone with all o' them sharp tools and big, heavy lumber and who knows what-all, tryin' to build a dock," Bella said disapprovingly.

That was the project we were planning. And theoretically we could actually do it. Victor's smile winked on and off like a flashing neon sign: *Hi! Hi! Hi!*

"One o' you," Bella went on darkly, rinsing yet another cup in a torrent of steaming water, " 'll ampertate a hand."

She'd turned up the thermostat on the water heater when she came to work for us. So nowadays before taking a shower we had to calibrate "hot" and "cold" with the delicacy of someone working the controls on a nuclear reactor.

"Band-Aids," Ellie said, taking the words out of my mouth. She looked up from the list. "Okay, then, if the thermoses are full of coffee and the cooler is packed with sandwiches . . ."

"Done," I confirmed, already looking forward to these. I'd packed them but she'd made them: ham salad on fresh homemade bread with real mayonnaise, sweet pickles, and lettuce out of the cold frame she'd constructed from old storm windows in my backyard. Sometimes I thought I'd have tried building the Great Wall of China with Ellie, just for the lunch.

". . . then I think we've got everything," she finished. The lumber and other miscellaneous dock-building items were already up at the cottage waiting for us.

"Hmph," Bella snorted skeptically again, which was when I noticed that despite being dunked nearly to her armpits in water that was (a) hot enough to cook lobsters in and (b) soapy enough to clean the Augean stables, she didn't appear to be in (c) very good spirits.

"Something wrong, Bella?" I asked.

She shoved a limp hank of henna-purple hair out of her face. With bulging green eyes, big bad teeth, skin the color of putty, and the rest of her hair pulled so tightly into a rubber band, it made her look as if she were walking into a wind tunnel . . . Well, let's just say most of

Bella's many virtues were on the inside. "Yes," she snapped miserably. "There is."

Which gave me pause. I already knew from experience that when Bella was unhappy the house got so clean people couldn't even live in it. Animals, either; from her place atop the refrigerator Cat Dancing meowed uneasily, tail twitching at the unwelcome notion of our housekeeper on a hygiene binge.

Cat hairs, for instance, might easily come under attack, even ones still attached to the cat. Uttering a feline oath, the big cross-eyed Siamese streaked from the room; Victor vanished simultaneously, the air around him twinkling mischievously in his wake.

"Everything okay?" Ellie asked, noting the look on my face.

"Yeah, fine," I lied, trying to sound convincing. It wasn't the first time Victor had been seen around town since his death the previous winter. I had it on good authority that he'd shown up in the IGA where he bought two tomatoes, paying the cashier with what appeared to be real money although the till was short $2.79 at the end of the day.

Soon after that he'd made an appearance at the Peavey Memorial Library on Water Street. There he stuck around for most of a lecture on Native American petroglyphs before departing, leaving in the air a brownish stain that lingered worrisomely.

But it was his first time here at my house. I should count myself lucky, I thought; twelve weeks was a lot longer than he'd ever let go by without annoying me, back when he was alive.

"What's wrong, Bella? Come on, now. Out with it," I said.

Because Victor was bad enough, but if I didn't get to the bottom of this Bella difficulty I might come home later to find the whole inside of the house washed and waxed, including the pets. Looking around the kitchen for the possible source of the difficulty, I saw only Bella's puzzle books—she was a demon for anagrams, acrostics, and crosswords—still in a canvas satchel.

Ordinarily by this time of day she'd have finished off two or three of them, with the devilishly difficult *Bangor Daily News* Sudoku thrown in as an afterthought. These she did in her head, glancing first at the grid with its few numerical clues, then filling in the rest as she went by with a scrub brush, a mop, or the sharp hooked dental tool she used to clean out the grooves in the stove knobs every morning and evening.

So whatever her worry was, it was already throwing her off her routine, I realized uneasily. Just then the dogs—Monday the Labrador retriever, and Prill, our big red Doberman, waltzed in from the parlor. Ellie got up to find biscuits for them; she was a sucker for animals.

Luckily the Doberman had a soft spot for her in return, as well as for any other human beings to whom she'd been properly introduced. But strangers Prill didn't like so much; we'd saved her from life on the street where her trust had been eroded by the hardness of stray-dog experience, we guessed.

And she was getting worse. Not biting, nor any suggestion of it. But the more familiar and confident she became with us, the worse her barking and growling with visitors got.

"Bella," I said. From behind me Victor's gaze seemed to linger wistfully, but that was surely just my imagination.

I hoped. "No kidding," I said to the housekeeper. "I mean it, now. What's going on?"

She turned reluctantly. "Miz Tiptree," she began, her tone implying that whatever the story turned out to be, I was dragging it from her.

I wasn't. Bella had engineered this moment and we both knew it. She didn't like asking me for favors, so she worked it around until I made her do it.

"Jake," I corrected. Getting her to call me by my first name was an ongoing battle, too. But I kept trying, knowing that if I ever gave in she would be disappointed in me.

"I'll put the rest of these things in the truck," Ellie said diplomatically, gathering the screwdriver and its power pack from the counter and placing them in their carrying case.

For our project today she wore frayed denim coveralls, yellow boots, and a yellow turtleneck shirt under a red hooded sweatshirt.

Her red hair was tied back with a purple scrunchy, her boot laces were red-and-green plaid, and dangling from her ears were a pair of lime green ceramic M&Ms.

"You," I told her, "look fabulous."

She shot me a smile that could've lit up a football stadium, standing there with her arms full of tools and the excitement of a coming adventure on her face.

We just didn't realize yet how much adventure. If we had, we'd have probably put the tools away and gone back to bed.

"Thanks," she said, and when she'd gone out I faced Bella again. "All right, what's this about?" I demanded a final time.

Cat Dancing had already returned to the refrigerator top and gone back to sleep, and having devoured all their biscuits the dogs had departed as well, to take up once more their usual places in the best chairs in the parlor.

If they'd had thumbs they'd have turned on the television. And Victor was still gone, which was perhaps the best omen of all, though I already feared not a permanent one.

"Friendship," Bella uttered sorrowfully. She stripped off her rubber gloves in a despairing gesture and tossed them on the dish drainer. "And Miz Tiptree, I'll tell you I'm right torn up over it."

My heart sank further. When Bella got right torn up it was a cinch we were in for a decontaminating extravaganza. Soon she'd be grabbing the toothbrushes from our hands, peering suspiciously at them before dipping them into an exotic brew of antimicrobial fluid before the toothpaste even got scrubbed off our teeth.

"Okay, lay it on me," I said, wishing someone else were here to help absorb her aggrieved outpourings. My current husband, Wade Sorenson, was out on the water at the helm of one of the enormous freighters he regularly guided into our port—the deepest natural anchorage in the nation, second only to Valdez, Alaska—for a living.

It was the price for tying a cargo vessel up in our harbor that you needed local help to do it. In the wild currents, strong tides, and harshly unforgiving granite channels of Passamaquoddy Bay, getting in at all was like guiding a rodeo bull through a needle's eye. But

Wade had been Eastport's harbor pilot for years, and I had it on good authority that he made the freighters perform as obediently as lambs.

Sam wasn't here, either. He had his own place now, a small frame house that had once been Wade's down on Liberty Street overlooking the water. And having managed by the skin of his teeth to finish up his winter semester of community college, I guessed that today he was either (a) lining up a summer job at the boatyard out on Deep Cove Road, or (b) sitting with his pals in front of one of their computers here in town, playing Grand Theft Auto while getting drunk, stoned, wired, or some even more toxic combination of all three.

The boatyard job, I felt sure, wasn't even on Sam's radar this morning. And the only other person capable of managing Bella Diamond was my father, but he was already occupied on the roof of my old house trying to find all the places that needed patching, after a winter of so many leaks that living in it had been like camping in a melting igloo.

If I listened hard I could hear his boots scraping around up there, which was at least some comfort since it meant I probably wouldn't see him sail down past the kitchen window anytime soon. So for now it was just me and Bella, who still stood by the sink wringing her hands.

Sighing, I poured another cup of coffee and prepared to hear her out; fifteen minutes later, she'd unloaded the whole story on me. And at first I was pleased because hey, I was trying to avoid a housecleaning apocalypse here. But it wasn't long afterward that I began wishing with all my heart that I'd left well enough alone.

● ● ●

Hauntings in Eastport's antique houses were so common that hardly anyone even talked about them. Only occasionally would an Eastport newcomer who'd recently bought one of the old places appear pale and shaken in the library or grocery store, mentioning with embarrassment—*are they going to think I'm crazy?*—what had happened in the attic, the pantry, or the half-bath newly installed under the stairs.

Or in the cellar, where my own house's early disturbances originated.

The strange manifestations that began as soon as Sam and I moved in—
an icy spot on the stairway, a scuttling in the hall, other things at once
less obvious and more deeply unnerving—had dissipated once the cellar's foundation got excavated and a strange book was removed from it.

Leather-bound and inside a wooden box, the odd volume had apparently been hidden when the house was built, as the granite stones
of the cellar walls were being hauled in by oxcart and piled atop one
another. Changes and repairs had nearly uncovered it a few times;
most notably a water main put in when the house first got plumbing
pierced the foundation inches from the thing.

Then when a pipe burst the box resurfaced, rescued from the
flood by my father, a stonemason whose nosiness was equaled only by
his stubbornness. Whereupon a really weird thing about the old book
was revealed: my name was in it. Handwritten in ink in an elegant
cursive full of old-fashioned flourishes, it appeared at the end of a list:
all the occupants of my house from its very first tenant in 1823 right
up to—and including—*me*.

Which if you think about it was pretty inexplicable right there.
Next, the haunting stopped; not all at once but gradually, like an infection subsiding. It was as if with the discovery and removal of the old
book, the house had the equivalent of a bad tooth pulled and the rest
of its system could settle.

That is, until Victor showed up. Now I wondered uneasily if just
possibly the earlier disorders had left a vacancy, a place he could move
into the way the missing-tooth spot may breed new unpleasantness if
you're not careful.

So after I'd finished hearing Bella Diamond's tale of woe that
morning, I dashed off a follow-up letter to some fellows in Orono that
Ellie had recommended, specialists in dealing with old Maine manu-
scripts and their forgotten authors. The two men had worked for her
father, Ellie told me, and I could trust them, so after some introduc-
tory correspondence and a few phone chats, I'd sent them the strange
book itself about three weeks earlier.

Now I felt impatient, unnerved by Victor's appearance and wishing at least to have one mystery solved. My last name, after all, is so

unusual I can only think someone in my past must have made it up to cover his (or her) own past misdeeds. And the question of how it could be accurately listed in a book hidden nearly two centuries earlier was, you will admit, a curious one.

Some of this I mentioned again in my letter to the Orono fellows, but mostly I just gave them a little nudge. Could they update me, please, on anything their examination of the volume might so far have uncovered? As I didn't mean to rush them but I was of course very interested in what they had to say.

Sincerely, et cetera. I put my return address and a stamp on the envelope and dropped it in the mailbox on the back porch for the carrier to pick up.

After which, given what turned out to be the eventfulness of the next few days, I forgot all about it.

● ● ●

Soon after I mailed the letter, Ellie and I were in Wade's pickup truck, ready to go. Or anyway I hoped we were ready:

Tools, check. Sandwiches and coffee, check. Work clothes, hip boots, unbridled optimism entirely out of proportion to our experience with the task at hand . . .

Yeah, we were down with that, as Sam would've put it. Never mind that building a lakeside dock was about a gazillion percent more challenging than anything I'd tried before in the planning-and-construction department. Until now I'd stuck with the small-scale fixes on the Key Street house; bashing out any walls was beyond my ken, for instance, and probably always would be.

Not that I hadn't tried. But that's an important thing an old house teaches you if you let it: don't bite off more than you can chew, and especially not out of a structural beam. Everything looks easy on those do-it-yourself TV shows, wood floors gleaming under fresh polyurethane while a glib home-repair guru squares up new bathroom tiles with mathematical exactitude.

My efforts were more like some old slapstick comedy film: teetering atop a ladder, paint pail upended and brush swinging wildly. On the other hand, probably no one expected much out of the Brooklyn Bridge either while it was still on paper.

Speaking of which: "Right here," I replied when Ellie asked if I'd remembered to bring along the drawings we'd made of our planned dock. I pulled the notebook out of my satchel and she pulled the truck out of the driveway. She was driving, because when I did it she claimed I turned into a wimp—this was true, but only because other Maine drivers so emphatically weren't— whereas when she got behind the wheel she mysteriously began channeling Evel Knievel.

"I hope we can make some headway on the dock," I said as we headed down Key Street toward the water. "First barbecue of the season in a couple of days, you know. Wade's excited."

Glancing back, I spotted my father sashaying along the roof ridge of my house, proceeding with all the verve, casual vigor, and general foolhardiness of a man half his age.

"Mmm," Ellie said. "We'll see. About the dock, I mean, not the barbecue. That I'm totally up for."

On the roof, my father stuck out a crowbar and pulled back a wide swath of old shingles, exposing equally ancient tar paper. Also it was *shredded* tar paper, so even from a distance I could see the rotted wooden sheathing lurking beneath.

Presto, instant leak-source discovery. I'd sent a pair of roof professionals up there a couple of years earlier, but what I'd had done to it then turned out to be whistling in the dark.

In fact what I'd had done then *did* whistle, every time the wind blew hard. Now my father stood frowning at it, snapping the red suspenders he wore over a blue work shirt, blue jeans, and boots. With his stringy gray hair tied back into a leather thong and a tool belt around his waist, he wore no safety harness and was not hanging on to anything.

"What was Bella so upset about?" Ellie asked, partly to divert me from the sight of my father playing Walking Wallenda.

"Missing person," I answered distractedly. "Friend of hers has a kid gone AWOL. Big kid, though, nearly Sam's age. Took off on his own, probably, on account of some trouble he's in, she didn't say what. Not an abduction or anything like that."

My house was an 1823 white Federal clapboard with three full floors, three redbrick chimneys, forty-eight double-hung windows each with a pair of forest-green shutters, and a drop from the roof beam to the ground of about seventy-five feet.

"He'll be fine," Ellie said reassuringly, meaning my father. And probably she was right. Being on the FBI's Most Wanted list for so many years after my mom was murdered had given him a knack for surviving an astonishing variety of precarious situations.

He hadn't, by the way, killed her. But after she died and he went on the lam, I'd grown up thinking he had; only recently had he been cleared of the whole unfortunate business.

"What did Bella want you to do?" Ellie asked. On either side of the street more old white houses gleamed freshly in the spring sunshine. New green bumps of bulb foliage pushed up through dark bark mulch in tulip beds; painted picket fences glistened with moisture that the day's weak warmth couldn't dispel.

Springtime, I thought distractedly, wishing that this year the sense of sap rising didn't somehow remind me so strongly of strangling vines, creeping vegetation gone wild.

"I'm not sure," I said. "Missing kid's mother is worried and she asked Bella to angle around about it with me, maybe see if we could be persuaded to get involved. But," I added firmly, "we can't." Which I'd told Bella before she'd even had a chance to fill me in on any more of the details; no sense giving her false hope.

Ellie stopped at the end of Key Street overlooking the bay. Out on the waves a small green fishing boat puttered, gulls circling its wake. Beyond, the Coast Guard's orange Zodiac vessel sped in circles, throwing up gouts of white spray as a new class of fledgling Coasties practiced handling her.

"No, of course we can't," Ellie agreed placidly. She turned left onto Water Street and drove past the flower shop and the redbrick library with its tall arched entry, leaded-glass windows, and a War of 1812 cannon bolted to a slab on the lawn out front.

"For one thing, we're not hooked into the teen scene anymore, are we?" Ellie added. A few years earlier we could have gotten Sam to find out things for us, ask around among his buddies and learn where a local teenaged runaway might be headed. But now . . .

A pang of sorrow hit me as I thought about Sam now. "Yes," I replied. "And besides . . ."

Besides, we weren't in the snooping business anymore either. When I'd arrived in Maine, just about the first thing Ellie and I had done together was solve a nasty murder; her local knowledge and my damn-fool stubbornness had turned out to form a surprisingly effective investigative team.

"We've given all that up," I concluded as Ellie guided the pickup toward the harbor past the Happy Landings Café. Its awnings, tables, and umbrellas were stacked out on its deck awaiting warmer weather. Next came the police station, located in the old brick-Italianate Frontier Bank Building, and after that the Mexican restaurant, La Sardina, with gigantic geraniums and jade plants thriving in the big plate-glass front windows.

"Yes," Ellie said firmly as we drove by Wadsworth's Hardware store. Decades ago the store had been located on a wharf across the street, but the great storm of 1976 had blown it into the bay and the wharf right along with it.

"We *have* given it up," Ellie repeated as if convincing herself. Her daughter Leonora was a year and a half old now, and needed more of Ellie's focused time when she wasn't in day care. Not that Ellie begrudged it—the time or the focus. Lee wouldn't have gone to the day-care place at all if she hadn't refused to eat or sleep when deprived of her posse of baby buddies.

"Hey, who's that?" Ellie wondered aloud suddenly. We were passing the fish pier with the two big tugboats, the *Pleon* and the *Ahoskie*, snugged up against the pier's black rubber bumpers. Under the pier loomed the forty-foot wooden pilings, thickly draped in seaweed and encrusted with generations of barnacles, that kept the pier's deck dry at the highest of tides.

Today at the pier's far end a man stood, staring out at the water and, to judge by the movement of his lips, saying something to it. I recognized him as Bert Merkle, a crusty old character who regularly reported seeing UFOs among the junk cars, rotting boat carcasses, empty metal barrels, and bundled newspapers that formed a vast wasteland in his backyard.

But that wasn't who Ellie meant. On one of the green park benches across from the pier sat another fellow; not a local guy, and it was still a little too early in the season for tourists.

"Don't know," I told her as we drew nearer. But I'd been eyeing him too, because . . .

No, it couldn't be. The guy had thinning hair, dark horn-rims, a white shirt with an open collar and the sleeves rolled up, and a nice pair of flannel slacks.

His oxblood loafers had tassels on them. "Oh my God," I said softly, feeling my heart pound. He took the horn-rims off and his profile without them was the giveaway.

"That's Jemmy Wechsler."

Ellie knew the name; I'd talked about him enough over the years. But she stayed cool, not doing anything until she knew what I wanted.

"Turn around," I said at last, so she made a neat three-point reversal against the curb in front of the Moose Island General Store's corner doorway and we went back.

When we reached the fish pier parking lot, Jemmy was on his feet waiting for us. As we pulled alongside he swung up into the pickup's backseat as calmly as if murderous mobsters hadn't been hunting him practically forever, hoping to collect the price on his head by the simple method of delivering it on a plate.

"Jemmy," I began, "what the hell are you . . . ?"

Back in the city, before I married Victor and had Sam and became a hotshot money professional, Jemmy and I were pals. In fact, I owed everything to him, since if he hadn't taken me under his wing when he did I'd be dead.

Because sure, I was a cautious kid. You couldn't grow up the way I had—in rural hill country with my mom's folks, who always looked as if they were sucking on sourballs and whose family life was the equivalent of a sackful of rabid cats—without learning that.

But when I ran away at fourteen I still had very little idea of what to be cautious about, which in a nutshell is why the life expectancy of even the wariest young girl on her own in the city is measurable in weeks. ". . . doing here?" I finished lamely.

Jemmy smiled. He'd had extensive dental work, bright white choppers replacing the stained, crooked originals, and now I saw he'd undergone some facial surgery, too. Cheeks, chin, even hair implants . . .

"Jake," he said, ignoring my question. "How are you?"

Close up, I couldn't even have said what it was that I'd recognized so surely and almost instantly; something around the eyes, maybe, a look of amusement mingled with a clear-sighted awareness that the world's a perilous place.

It was what had made me trust him back when I was a teenager and Jemmy was an experienced, twenty-eight-year-old man of the world: that unlike any of the other adults I'd met since stepping off a Greyhound into the concrete jungle, he never even bothered pretending any differently.

"When did you get here?" The last time I'd seen him was a couple of years earlier. He'd been racing away from Eastport on a boat, until the boat blew up. The event saddened me greatly but not long after it I received an e-mail from him, suggesting that rumors of his death in the blast had been exaggerated.

Faking his own death had been his only option. The problem was an enormous sum of money that he'd stolen from some guys who hadn't exactly been known for their forgiving natures.

Or for faulty memories. So if Jemmy was here now all of a sudden, it meant that somewhere else must've become terribly unsafe. And *that* meant . . .

Trouble, Ellie's eyes said as she glanced briefly sideways at me. *Big trouble.*

Jemmy didn't answer. "See that guy?" he asked.

We were passing a new, small bookstore started up by recent transplants from Portland in one of the old two-story storefronts on Water Street. Called Mainely Murder, the store looked tantalizing and I planned a session of browsing as soon as possible.

But right now another sight was even more interesting to me. In front of Mainely Murder stood Eastport's police chief, Bob Arnold, a plump, pink-cheeked fellow with thinning blond hair, an amiable expression, and rosebud lips, wearing a cop uniform.

With him was the guy Jemmy had pointed out: fiftyish, gray hair clipped short on a bullet-shaped head, a no-nonsense look about him that I happened to know he deserved. "Sure, Jemmy, I see him. That's—"

It was Walter Henderson, Eastport's lowest-profile but perhaps most controversial Person From Away. A year earlier Walter had blown into town and immediately bought up the best of Moose Island's remaining shorefront. Then he'd built himself a McMansion on it, huge and ostentatious as hell.

Or so I'd heard; I hadn't seen the place myself. "Uh-huh," Jemmy agreed quietly.

"Ellie, pull over." She looked questioningly at me but did as I asked, into the tiny gravel parking lot of the Snack Shack. Inside the low metal Quonset building, Bodie Wanamaker hovered behind the counter displaying today's newspapers.

It was damp at the cottage this time of year, and without fresh newspaper it would take an age to get a decent fire going. Besides, I suddenly wanted a few words with Bodie; that is, in the unlikely event that I could get more than one.

"Morning," he uttered unsmiling, his gnarled hands spread flat on the counter between the cash register and the lottery ticket machine.

"Good morning, Bodie." I picked up one of the papers while trying to think of how to wangle an answer out of the store's famously silent proprietor.

"Nice day," I tried. Bodie was somewhere in his eighties, with a bald freckled scalp and wattled neck, but without any of the mellowing that great age is said to confer on people. Wade said that somewhere under all that dour Yankee flint beat a heart as warm and tender as a hockey puck.

No answer from Bodie. "I see Bob Arnold's taking complaints on the street nowadays," I hazarded.

More silence greeted this. "I wonder what Walter Henderson is complaining about," I tried again, angling my head toward the harbor. "Down street," I added, that being how the locals would've described the direction I was indicating.

Bodie eyed me, unpersuaded by my stab at the local lingo. His thin pink lips, pressed tightly together like two slices of unidentifiable lunch meat, parted reluctantly.

"You a-goin' to buy that there newspaper,"—*pay-pah,* the Maine way of saying it—"or just stand there a-maulin' it with your fingers?"

Fing-gahs. "I'm going to buy it, Bodie," I gave in. So much for a little advance notice of what was on Walter Henderson's mind this fine morning.

Although I already had a feeling I might know. "You're Ellie White, aren't you?" Jemmy was asking her when I got back in the truck.

She nodded at him in the rearview while she took the turn onto Washington Street. "You're as pretty as Jake told me," he offered smoothly.

"Mm-hmm" was her unimpressed reply. We passed the massive granite-block post office building, the Arts Center comfortably housed in the old Baptist church—the congregation had a modern new building now, and an acre of parking on the edge of town—and headed uphill on our way off the island.

Behind us in my mind's eye Bob Arnold went on listening to an obviously unhappy monologue being issued by Walter Henderson, who hadn't so much as glanced at us as we passed. But . . .

Jemmy's gaze remained mild. "Ellie, can you drive faster?" he inquired casually.

He didn't have to ask twice.

Horace-Langley Rare Books & Papers
21 Livermore Avenue
Orono, Maine 04058

Professor David DiMaio
Miskatonic University
Providence, Rhode Island 03666

Dear Dave,

Just got a hurry-up note from the Eastport woman and I'm not sure what—or how much—to tell her. Still recovering from opening the parcel and seeing the old book, actually. I know we always said there was a chance of this happening, that under the proper conditions real physical evidence might've survived. But to see the thing, hold it in my hands—!

Unless—could it be a forgery? Some sort of elaborate hoax? It would take a lot of doing and she doesn't seem the type, but I've enough sad experience in that department to wonder. Anyway, drop a line when you can. I know finals and graduation probably still have you hopping, but once things calm down Lang and I would love to see you.

And—Dave, take pity on me and let me know what's what with that damned book. It's making me nervous.

Best!

Horace

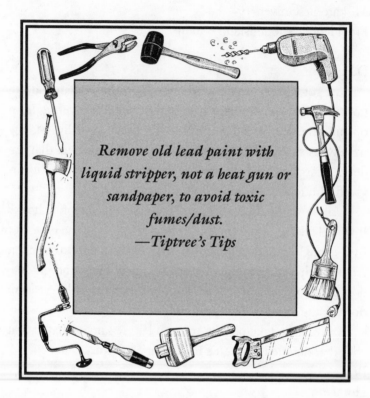

Remove old lead paint with liquid stripper, not a heat gun or sandpaper, to avoid toxic fumes/dust.
—*Tiptree's Tips*

Jemmy rode quietly as we sped over the curving causeway toward the mainland, with Passamaquoddy Bay heaving deep blue and whitecapped on our right and the calmer, paler sand-and-water expanse of Carryingplace Cove to the left. It was low tide. Gulls swooped and flapped among smaller, delicate-legged terns moving in flocks on the gleaming clam flats.

"You look different," I said to Jemmy.

"Yeah, I've been transforming myself. No disguise like a surgical disguise," he added matter-of-factly. Glancing into the rearview mirror, he ran a hand over his shiny forehead.

"Next time they're going to give me more hair," he added with a lilt of anticipation.

He'd started balding in his twenties. "Will you look at that?" he said, eyeing himself admiringly. "Joan Rivers'd kill for that jawline, wouldn't she?"

He'd always been vain. But also realistic: "Someday I'll go back, though, have the surgeon take out the implants and put it all the way it was before," he went on. "In a heartbeat I'll look like that guy in the story about the painting, that Dorian Gray."

He laughed then, just making conversation; about himself of course. He'd always been that way, too easily entertained by his own cleverness. The thing about Jemmy, though, was that he made you feel clever right along with him.

Except sometimes. Like now, for instance. What the hell was going on? "Sorry to hear about Victor," he said in a completely different tone.

I didn't know how he'd heard about Victor. But Jemmy had his methods. Must have, to stay alive this long. Also, he'd despised Victor.

"Thanks," I said. "It was very fast." My ex-husband had been a brain surgeon and he'd died of a brain tumor so virulent that it belonged in a horror movie.

"Not that it felt fast when it was happening," I added. For the thousandth time since his death I averted my thoughts from what Victor had been reduced to in those final days.

"Yeah. Well. He must've had his good points," Jemmy conceded generously.

This was so transparently not what Jemmy had ever thought of Victor that I laughed aloud, and the mood lightened.

Mine did, anyway. Ellie just kept driving, as fast as she dared through the speed trap just over the causeway, then faster, her gaze fixed stonily on the road ahead. When we got to Route 1 she waited for a log truck to pass, then turned north.

"So," he began as she stomped the accelerator again; the truck took off as if supercharged.

I shut up, hung on, and let Jemmy talk. "So listen, Jacobia, I hate to put you to any trouble but the truth is, I need a place to hunker down for a while," he said.

As if I hadn't come to that conclusion already. "Guys who're looking for me got a whiff of me back where I was before," he added.

By "whiff," he could've meant anything from "I had a funny feeling" to "a slug from a .38-caliber automatic made a whizzing sound as it passed through what's left of my hair."

The road wound through the forest, deep evergreen mingled with stands of gray-trunked hardwood and thorny bramble thickets. The leaves weren't out yet, so the undergrowth looked deceptively penetrable. But even now, any more than a dozen or so yards off the pavement and you could get lost so badly you might never find your way out again.

Another eighteen-wheeler, this one loaded with pulp from the paper mill twenty miles north, roared by in the opposite direction on its way to the loading docks in Eastport. Six inches of clearance between our fender and its massive spinning tire was apparently regarded by Ellie as plenty; she didn't flinch.

But in the truck's buffeting backwash she spoke up. "How'd that happen? Them getting a whiff, I mean."

Jemmy shook his head ruefully. "Electronics. Guys who want me, they've got these programs, watch the e-mails to and from all a person's contacts."

That was so clearly and massively a crock, I didn't bother commenting. First of all he didn't use e-mail anymore; he wasn't stupid. And second, he didn't have any contacts. In the past couple of years he'd become as isolated as an asteroid in space.

As lonely, too, probably. But I'd learned long ago that Jemmy would tell me the truth when he was ready, or as much of it as he ever did. Now he opened his mouth to spin more of his goofball story, got a glimpse of my face, and decided against.

We pulled out of the woods and into the hilly headlands of the St.

Croix River tidal basin. Below the cliffs edging Route 1 on our right, the crisscrossed nets of herring seines hung from long, slender poles, their reflections forming wavery X's on the moving water. A trio of seals gorged themselves on the catch in one of the seines, getting in their morning meal before the net owner showed up with his rifle.

Across the bay the red-tiled gabled roof of the hotel at St. Andrews spread grandly, the cream brick building at this distance like a castle in a fairy tale. We zoomed through Robbinston, a bayside settlement consisting of a Grange hall, a boat landing, several churches, two motels, and a cluster of houses pulled up tightly to the road as if eager to observe whoever went by. A pickup hauling a boat trailer backed expertly toward the water as we passed, the driver casually turning the wheel with one hand.

"What's Walter Henderson got to do with it?" I asked. Jemmy was not, I noticed, carrying any kind of bag, which meant he'd gotten out of wherever he'd been last with just the clothes he was wearing; ye gods.

He examined his fingernails. Ahead the road widened and improved, acquiring decent pavement and a discernible shoulder as we approached Calais, the nearest market town to Eastport.

"Well," he said at last, "Henderson's got the contract. On me, that is. So I figured . . ."

To kill him, Jemmy meant. As punishment for stealing the money. "Walter Henderson?" I repeated, letting a surprise I didn't feel creep into my tone.

Jemmy didn't know the identities of all my old clients back in the city. He nodded again as Ellie glanced significantly at me: so Henderson was a hit man. This to her would ordinarily have been big news all by itself. But . . .

"Wait a minute." I was still unsure I understood all of what Jemmy was telling me. "Just one contract? I thought whole squads of guys were after you."

"They were. Only the rest have all given up and gone on to other things. I have," he added, "managed to collect pretty good info on that." He grimaced. "Henderson, though. He's a whole different breed of cat. He's had subcontractors, bad guys in a whole bunch of different cities, beating the bushes."

Which was, I recalled, a technique for driving an animal into a trap. Jemmy saw me thinking this, smiled wanly at me with his surgically altered face.

"So anyway, now you're here." Ellie's tone conveyed just how welcome he was in her opinion; i.e., not very.

"Yeah. And if you want to know the truth, I'm in kind of a fix."

"The mind," she agreed acidly, "boggles."

Mine certainly did. It had been a long time since I'd had to take seriously any similar situation, up close and personal. Back in the city sometimes a guy would visit my office wanting to put all his possessions in his family's name, and by the way could I sign him up for a brand-new, hideously expensive life insurance policy, too?

Not worried about the size of the premiums, usually paying the first one right across my desk in cash. That's when I'd know I wasn't going to see the guy again, and pretty soon nobody else would either.

And that the guy knew it, too. I stared at Jemmy, who made a silent "what can you do?" shrug but didn't elaborate.

After a few more miles, Ellie took the unmarked turn onto the lake road, which devolved in a hundred yards to rutted gravel and finally to dirt. While we bumped between trees barely budded into pale springtime nubbins, I found my voice.

"But he's expecting you here, Jemmy. He must be." Because I was here. And wherever I was, Jemmy always showed up sooner or later.

"Yep," he agreed. "Laying back in the tall grass waiting for me, no doubt."

Ellie kept driving over rocks and through the potholes with which the lake road was so plentifully furnished. The trees on either side were young hardwood—poplar, maple, and white birch with its papery bark curling off in strips. We passed a turnout where the local kids came to fool around, beer cans littering the tire ruts in the soft earth.

Without being asked, Ellie stopped; I hopped out, grabbed the cans and other trash—fast-food wrappers, mostly—and tossed them in the bed of the truck for later disposal at home. Once upon a time I got angry when I did this; now I just thought they'd learn someday.

After all, if I had, anyone could.

"That's why this is the only place I finally can take care of the situation," Jemmy went on when I got back in. " 'Cause this is where *he* is. For now, though, I just need a spot to lie low."

We cut through a swamp where ancient black stumps hunkered among the yellowed stalks of last year's cattails, then followed a narrow track through the trees. Past tall pines and charcoal-gray mounds of enormous granite boulders jutting along the lake's shore, the trail cut between a pair of pin oaks.

It continued through an old iron gate I had to unlock, then past a pair of hunter's huts each with its woodpile, outhouse, and spark-guarded metal chimney. *Trail's End,* said the rough sign on one. Jemmy smiled as we took the final turn into the last clearing.

"Perfect," he breathed. We got out into the silence broken only by the occasional *chuk-chuk-chuk!* of a kingfisher on a branch somewhere over the water, waiting for an unwary perch. The air smelled sharply of last autumn's fallen leaves soaked by recently melted snow, and of the ice-cold, intensely mineral-laden lake.

Jemmy turned in a slow circle to take in the pristine forest scene. Trees, water, sky . . . directly ahead stood the cedar-shingled cottage with blue-checked gingham curtains tied back at its windows, dwarfed by the big old trees.

The curtains were made of cloth that had been sold off for pennies when the local weaving mill went out of business years ago. A scarred chopping block made out of a chunk of rock maple stood nearby, wood chips scattered thickly around it. Stepping past Jemmy, I unlocked the door and we went in.

"Nice," he observed, looking around. The whole downstairs was a single pine-paneled room with a woodstove, plus a small kitchen area equipped with a gas stove, a primitive icebox, and a hand pump over the sink. "This is excellent."

Furnished with mismatched chairs brightly painted in primary colors, sofas covered with crocheted throws we'd bought at thrift shops, and bentwood tables each bearing an oil lamp and a book of matches, the cottage was so authentically Maine-woodsy you half expected a moose to be standing outside the window looking in.

Which many mornings there was. "I'll get a fire started," said Ellie, taking my newspaper and gathering sticks of kindling from the wicker basket under the stairs.

Her voice sounded odd, as if something unpleasant had occurred to her. I waited for more but she merely crouched by the stove with her back turned, crumpling up news stories.

Jemmy stepped out onto the deck, a rustic affair of graying lumber bolted together atop concrete footings. Silently he gazed at the nearby lake's edge. A look of puzzlement spread on his face.

"Didn't there used to be a pier right down there?" he asked. I'd brought him here once. "And is it just me, or is the water a little . . . ?"

"Higher, yes," I replied, stepping out to stand on the deck beside him. After the spring melt of the record snow we'd endured over the previous winter, the lake was a good deal higher even than it had been last fall.

"Three feet since you saw it last, as a matter of fact," I told him. "We've had a lot of rain."

Better than drought, which had turned last summer's grass yellow-crisp and dried up people's wells. But in autumn the skies had opened, and they'd stayed that way right on through February. The rocks that had once lined the water's edge, serving us as diving platforms and sunbathing perches, were now completely submerged.

"It's why Ellie and I are here, to build a new dock. Because the other one floated away."

As I spoke I watched him carefully. He never did tell me everything right off the bat, preferring to ease into things. But it was clear already that he meant to confront Walter Henderson somehow.

"How come he's still after you?" I asked.

Jemmy blinked, as if the thought of the pickle he was in was the furthest thing from his mind. "You mean when all the rest have quit?"

Yep, that's the part I meant. Ordinarily those guys were so single-minded, you practically had to drive a stake through their hearts. But when one stopped they all did, usually.

He smiled, crinkling the smooth, taut skin on his new face. "Because Henderson's the best. And the best gets paid up front, see? The whole enchilada. So even though there's no one else still around to care anymore . . ."

The real old-guard Mob fellows, I knew, had almost all died by now, either murdered or from natural causes. If you thought breathing your last behind the walls of a maximum-security prison counted as natural, that is.

I didn't. "Got his money, means to finish the job," Jemmy concluded. "Matter of pride, that kind of thing. So I've got to do something about him."

He turned earnestly to me. "Because, Jake, he's not gonna quit. Those subcontractors of his won't come after me here—this's his own private territory, you see, and nobody fools with him. He doesn't want any big dogs but him runnin' around in it."

I understood; if you don't want a fight, don't mix with critters who're inclined to. And don't let them come around where they might be tempted to start one with you.

"He's got no organization behind him anymore; nowadays he flies solo," Jemmy continued. "That just makes him worse, you see, 'cause he takes it all so personally. Thing is, he's not a have-gun-will-travel kind of guy anymore either."

Oh, I don't know. I'd thought Walter Henderson looked like he could still move pretty fast when he wanted to. And my guess was that he probably still did want to; just glancing at him this morning as we passed him on the street, I'd gotten the impression of a snake striking.

Potentially striking. Jemmy went on, "So it's just him and me. And I can't go on this way," he admitted reluctantly.

"Sure," I said. I understood that, too; spending all his time staying one step ahead of a hired killer couldn't be much of a life. And Jemmy was no spring chicken anymore, not for that kind of thing.

But being that it *was* him—brilliant, feckless, given to wild schemes that might or might not work out as he hoped—what he was saying now didn't only spell trouble, as Ellie had already intuited.

Instead it could spell disaster, like a few other situations that were already fairly high on my bad-stuff list. A ghost in the kitchen, a leaky roof, a son with a booze problem, Bella's cleaning binge, and now . . .

Jemmy, arrived to confront an old enemy and resolve an old conflict for good. That most of all made me want to shoo everyone else away and stay here alone at the lake myself.

Still, Jemmy was my oldest friend and long ago he'd saved my life. I mean literally saved it: off the street, into a job and then into school . . .

"You can bunk here for a while," I said. "For as long as you need to."

"Great. I'll help you with the dock," he offered cheerfully. "Least I can do, lend a hand."

The only nails he knew anything about were at the ends of his fingers: clean, manicured. As for running any power tools . . .

"No," I told him. "After lunch you're going to Calais, to the stores there. Buy yourself some supplies. Boots and warmer clothes, for instance, sweaters and a hat and a down jacket."

"I imagine it still gets plenty cold at night out here," he agreed.

I eyed his thin shirt and slacks. "Yes, it certainly does."

He had no idea. "Get ready to keep that woodstove stoked," I advised. "Also you'll need food, drinks, reading material, and so on. Assuming you like reading by lamplight. Or flashlight."

The summer before, Wade had decided the primitive conditions here weren't as charming as he'd originally thought. So he'd set up a solar generating system for the cottage: collecting panels, a charge controller, a deep-cycle marine battery, and an inverter to transform the direct current to AC. He'd spent a weekend just figuring out the schematics, then putting it all together.

And it had worked like a charm. Eureka! I'd thought, turning on an electric light after dinner instead of stinking the place up with lamp oil smoke. But now after the long winter the storage battery was uncharged and the solar panels were safely wrapped up in the toolshed, waiting to be remounted on the roof.

Another thought hit me. "You have any money?" I asked Jemmy. One way and another what he'd stolen hadn't lasted long. "Because if you need some, I . . ."

His smile of appreciation cut me off. Even through all the face work he'd had done, you could still see the old Jemmy shining through; amused, calm even in the face of catastrophe.

Which this wasn't; not yet. "Don't worry about a thing," he told me.

He pulled a cigarette out and lit it without offering me one. He remembered how I took my coffee, too, I was willing to bet, and that I liked yellow mustard better than gray, loved the smell of new Crayolas, and couldn't abide anchovies or most horror films but loved *Blair Witch*.

He changed the subject suddenly. "Remember that day in the diner right after I first met you? We pretended we were boyfriend and girlfriend? You were a skinny, tough-talking little thing and you were wearing a plaid skirt. You looked like you were about eleven."

"Yeah." Despite my misgivings about his presence here, I had to laugh; we'd had fun. "All the mushy stuff we faked, and the waitress glaring at us until we ended up having to get out of there before she called the cops."

I'd never been his real girlfriend, though. Not even close; yet another reason I'd trusted him. And still did, sort of.

His tone turned apologetic. "I know it's a surprise, me showing up here. And I'll understand if you—"

"Don't be ridiculous," I cut him off swiftly, and went back inside, where by now Ellie had gotten the woodstove radiating, its waves of warmth nearly visible in the room, and was unwrapping the ham salad sandwiches at the kitchen counter.

Luckily she always made extra. "Why don't you unload our stuff from the truck?" I told Jemmy as he followed me in. "There isn't much, just the cordless drill and a few other gadgets."

Ellie looked up, her eyes still full of whatever it was she wanted to say to me. But for the moment I ignored her.

"We'll eat," I told him as she poured steaming coffee from the thermos into thick white china mugs, "and figure out what you need. Then while we work on the dock, you can supply yourself for remote lake-side housekeeping."

And that's what happened: first the unloading of our tools—Jemmy had plenty of energy, even if it was only nervous energy—then lunch. Ellie's ham salad was as smooth and mellow as pâté, her fresh baby lettuce leaves ruffling out over the edges of the homemade bread. She'd made fresh lemonade, too, and run it through a seltzer bottle to give it fizz.

Later, with input from me, Jemmy made a list of items required for his survival in a no-plumbing, no-electricity wilderness environment. And when I finally handed the keys over, he started Wade's old truck and muscled it into gear competently. Maybe this will turn out all right, I thought, watching him go.

But Ellie threw a look of undiminished dislike at him as he bumped away down the road, disappearing among the spring-green trees.

●   ●   ●

"You're making a big mistake," Ellie said as soon as Jemmy was gone. "Why did he have to bring all his troubles around here, anyway?"

Scowling, she grabbed up her canvas carpenter's apron and wrapped it around her waist. "It's like he's got his own personal bull's-eye painted on him," she added, "and now you're going to have one, too."

I tightened a leather tool belt around my own middle. In its many loops and pockets hung everything I needed: hammer, tape measure, socket wrench, and the heavy-duty fasteners we'd bought for putting the first section of the dock together.

"You know I can't refuse," I replied. She'd heard all about my run-away youth.

Almost all. "Besides," I went on, "Jemmy's not planning anything that'll cause me any problems. He'll probably just try to set up some kind of a meeting with Walt Henderson. Pay him off or something. Buy out the contract so he's *not* wearing a bull's-eye anymore."

Well, a girl could hope. "I mean guys who kill other guys for money, they've got no loyalty," I told Ellie. "They always switch sides and go to the highest bidder."

I couldn't believe I was discussing such things way out here in the Maine woods. "Or Jemmy might stay for a while and take off again without anything happening. He has before."

Well, except for that boat explosion. "And either way it's not like I'm involved. Not if I don't want to be," I added resolutely.

Ellie shook her head. "If you think that, maybe you don't understand the situation," she pronounced as we got to work.

We'd prepared the concrete mix in big plastic basins a week earlier, moistening the powdery stuff with lake water we hauled up in buckets. Stirring it thoroughly with hoes and trowels, we'd poured it into two square wooden forms made out of scrap lumber to create the base blocks for the dock pilings.

While the mixture was still wet we'd also set a big bolt head-down into each of the blocks' centers so that the bolts' threaded ends stuck up straight. Now Ellie used a clawhammer to knock the wooden forms off the blocks, each eighteen inches square and a foot tall, while I centered six-inch-square metal brackets on the bolts and wrenched nuts onto them, securing the brackets.

"Remember Bella's friend? The one with the missing kid?" she asked as she hammered away.

"Mm-hmm." I began ratcheting the nuts tighter onto the bolts until they would turn no farther. When I was done, each concrete block had a metal frame bolted to the top of it.

"But what's she got to do with anything?" I asked.

"I'm not sure yet." Ellie hauled six-inch-square pine posts over to our work area. We'd already cut them to nearly the right length using the chain saw; later we would need to perfect our measurements to make the dock's surface level.

But we couldn't do that until after we got them into the water, and found out how far they stuck up out of it. "I know who Bella's friends *are*, though," Ellie went on.

I didn't. Like Walt Henderson, I too was a Person From Away, and regularly missed whole layers of Eastport nuance as a result. By

contrast, Ellie had known the area's whole complex family and social
network by heart before she could even talk.

"—and one of those women has an eighteen-year-old son," she concluded grimly.

"Well, then, Bella's friend has even more of my sympathy," I replied, tightening down the final bolt with a last twist of the ratchet tool.
Because if you think a toddler can fray your lone surviving nerve, try
listening to the old 'Mom, I'm not a kid anymore' routine two million
times.

Then try it when the kid is staggering drunk. "But I fail to see . . ."
I added as Ellie positioned the first post carefully atop a concrete
block, forcing it tightly into the bolted-on metal frame.

We'd had to shave the post ends a little to make them fit. "I know,"
she replied. "You *don't* see, Jacobia. *And* you don't know the rest of the
story."

She stuck a galvanized nail through one of the holes in the metal
frame's sides, banged it in, then did the rest *bing-bang-boom,* two nails
per side for a total of eight. That fastened the wooden post to the concrete block. And we were using galvanized nails—that is, rust-proof
ones—because the block would be underwater soon, if everything
went right.

"So, since you're obviously not up on the background info,
I'll give you the high points," she said. "First, based on who Bella's
friends are, if the runaway kid she's so worried about is the one I think
it is—"

It was. Ellie was never wrong about things like this.

". . . his name's Cory Trow. He had a court date this morning, supposed to show up at the courthouse in Machias. Whole town knew
about it."

Except me. Between Sam's drunken antics and a roof so leaky you
could strain spaghetti through it, I'd had my hands full. So I hadn't
heard about all this.

"And," she continued briskly, "the court date he had was for a sentencing hearing." Never a good thing. But I had a feeling worse was to
come, and I was right.

"Because he got convicted on a stalking charge. And the complainant . . . wait for it . . . was Walter Henderson's daughter," she finished.

Ye gods. "So you think he took off. Blew off his sentencing hearing, which means he'll get a . . ."

"A prison term, yes. If and when he ever does show up again. Alive," she added darkly.

Which was when I caught on. "But that's not his big problem, is it?" I said slowly. "His problem is—"

"Walter Henderson the hit man," Ellie finished for me. "Bingo. Who is here in Eastport at all, I gather, because your pal Jemmy has a habit of coming up for air in your vicinity."

She gestured for me to help her hold the second post, then hammered the nails in just as she'd done with the first. Now we had two concrete cubes, each with a six-by-six wooden post sticking up from it about four feet.

Too bad that at the moment the cubes were also sitting fifty yards from the water's edge. And since docks are most usefully positioned *in* the water, not fifty yards from it . . .

"And what do you want to bet our buddy Mr. Henderson's going to feel like doing some *recreational* killing," Ellie said, "when he finds out that the town boy who's been bothering his daughter isn't in court where he belongs?"

She took a deep breath. "That instead Cory Trow's on the run, maybe even planning to bother Mr. H's precious little girl *again?*"

The memory of Henderson conversing earlier that morning with police chief Bob Arnold popped into my mind. "Probably he already knows," I said.

It was what Henderson had been chewing Bob's ear about, I was willing to bet. "How little is she, anyway?" I asked. "The daughter?"

To move the huge concrete blocks, we'd invented a transport vehicle consisting of a wooden pallet, some styrofoam blocks I'd managed to beg from the guys out at the boat school, and the wheels from Ellie's baby daughter Leonora's stroller.

It was a lovely little item with blue trim and white padding inside, and Ellie had adored it when Wade and I showed up with it as a gift for Lee's first birthday. But Leonora hated it. She'd bawled when she was placed in it.

So Ellie and I had cannibalized it. To keep it from rolling downhill uncontrollably, we'd tied a rope handle to the rear end and bolted a wagon handle to the front. The completed cart resembled one the Little Rascals would build, and we hadn't had a test run.

But our choice was between trying it or toppling the blocks end over end down to the water, a process we thought might bode ill for the eventual integrity of the whole dock structure.

And for our own. So together with much grunting and groaning we hefted one of the concrete blocks onto the cart. The stroller wheels bulged with its weight but didn't collapse.

"Jen Henderson's a teenager," Ellie said, eyeing our cart doubt-fully. "The tall, blonde, athletic type. I've seen her, and so has every male human being in Eastport over the age of two."

We centered the block by rocking it back and forth; once we got rolling, any instability could lead to an upset.

"Jen takes the whole golden-girl thing to extremes, though," Ellie elaborated as together we gave the block a last centering wiggle.

"She looks . . . oof! . . . like a Barbie doll on steroids. Not that I think she uses them. At her age she doesn't need them, to look the way she does. Protein shakes, maybe."

By that time I was gasping. Ellie wasn't even breathing hard but we still looked at each other with trepidation, wishing we'd brought along someone who regularly ingested both steroids *and* protein shakes. Loaded, that cart was *heavy.*

But there was nothing left for it but to tie the block to the platform, start the whole thing rolling and hope for the best. "So the bottom line is, you think this kid took off to avoid being sent to jail for girl trou-ble," I said.

The rickety little contraption, loaded with a concrete cube massive enough to anchor a fair-sized motorboat, stood poised at the top of the slope leading sharply down to the water. And to make the whole proj-ect even more of a challenge, the path to the water's edge was bumpy.

Very bumpy: rocks, exposed roots, ragged jounces and jogs, any one of which could tip the cart. "But now he's in a worse fix because the girl's dad has a habit of blowing guys' heads off. Or whatever it is," I amended, "that Henderson does to the targets of his professional assignments."

"Yup," Ellie said. "And none of it would be happening at all if *you* weren't here."

Oh, terrific; now *I* was the cause of the whole mess. Or my habit of attracting Jemmy was to blame, anyway. So in a way I was responsible for the girl being here, too; the entire subject was starting to make my head hurt.

"Are those wheels strong enough?" Ellie asked dubiously, her brow furrowed as she eyed the setup. "Because once it hits those bumps on its way downhill . . ."

I spread my hands in a "who knows?" gesture. A shove would get the cart going and we'd learn the answer fast. Stopping it again would be another matter, but the lake would do that.

We hoped. "Grab the rope," I said.

The plan was to control the cart's speed by hauling on the rope handle from behind. And from in front I hoped I could also control its direction, since a concrete block careening wildly off into the forest wasn't what we had in mind.

No point imagining the negative possible outcomes, however. For one thing, there were too many to think about all at once. I lifted the wagon handle. "Okay, push it."

The vehicle began rolling, slowly at first and then faster. A lot faster; the spokes in the little blue wheels blurred. Ellie planted her feet in the gravel of the path to try slowing it down from the rear but the bright yellow boots she was wearing skidded ineffectually through the stones.

"Hey," she protested. I leaned hard against the handle from below, also without much result.

"This hill," I muttered as the makeshift cart built up even more speed, "is way steeper than I . . ."

Suddenly the little red wagon handle snapped off with a loud *crack!*

and then the rope broke when Ellie's feet hit a protruding root, stopping her abruptly.

Holding the rope's end, she sat down hard on the path while the cart careened away from her. "Jake!" she cried. "Look out!"

Gripping the broken handle, I lost my footing on the path and hit the ground, too, as the loaded cart trundled straight at me with the massive concrete block wobbling and bouncing on it.

"Jake! Get out of the way!"

"I'm trying. . . ." Scrambling aside as the murderously heavy vehicle rumbled past, missing me by centimeters, I landed in what had once been a thicket of old elderberry bushes. We'd cut them down the previous summer so that someday we could stack kayaks and canoes on the spot.

Now the whole area with the cut stems jutting up from it was about as comfortable as a bed of nails. Also our cart was still rolling, jouncing, and bumping while we sat staring.

At the water's edge it bounced gaily over a boulder, two wheels exploding outward, their spokes and plastic parts flying in all directions, concrete block still perched miraculously atop the platform. And . . .

And then it *soared*. Out over the water it hung in thin air for a moment while Ellie and I watched openmouthed. Next with a dramatic *splat!* it splashed flat onto the lake's surface, bobbled a bit . . .

And *floated*. The top-heavy post tipped the pallet platform precariously. But the block's weight prevailed and the post at last straightened as the platform steadied itself bravely, small waves rippling around it.

"The styrofoam worked!" I cried, jumping up to dance around deliriously while Ellie still frowned at the thing.

"Genius!" I exulted, heedless of the cuts and scratches on my hands and arms and the many bruises, unseen but certainly not unfelt, in the process of developing on my legs.

"I am a genius," I chanted as the pallet platform proceeded out onto the lake. Because the idea for the wheels had been Ellie's, and she had supplied them. But the floating element of the project had been mine.

All mine. And it worked. I just stood watching it, grinning and reciting: "I am ab-so-lutely, a complete and thorough . . ."

"Jake," Ellie said as the pallet went on floating away from the shore with our post and block on top of it. "Don't you think we'd better . . . ?"

Suddenly I stopped chanting. Dancing, too. Because Ellie was correct. The thing was floating, all right.

Just as I'd hoped. But it was also moving fast, captured by a sudden offshore breeze whose force sent it speedily across the waves right out into the middle of the lake.

Where it flipped over and sank.

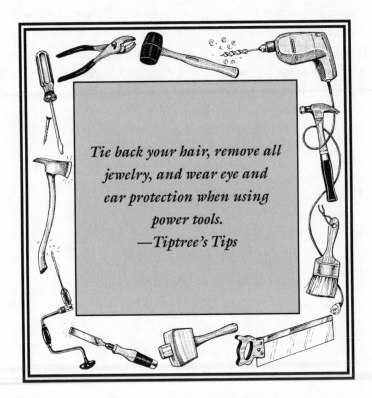

Chapter 4

Tie back your hair, remove all jewelry, and wear eye and ear protection when using power tools.
—*Tiptree's Tips*

Maybe I should try talking to Henderson," I said. "Before he gets a chance to do something to Jemmy."

It was midafternoon and we were on our way home from the cottage, Ellie at the wheel again as we zipped hair-raisingly down Route 1 toward Eastport.

We'd already stopped at the gas station near the turnoff to the lake so she could call Bella. The conversation had confirmed her suspicions about who the missing boy was.

Now Ellie spoke as if she hadn't heard me. "If Cory Trow doesn't show up on his own and *we* don't find him, Walt Henderson might. And if Jemmy's right about what Henderson's like, he *might* kill him."

After the sinking incident we'd hauled a pair of kayaks out, paddled to where we thought the cart had gone under, and dropped a buoy attached to a weighted line over it to mark the spot.

Then Jemmy had returned with the pickup truck's bed full of his purchases—including three six-packs of imported beer, a gasoline generator, and a portable TV—have I mentioned he was a city boy?—and once he arrived Ellie made it plain that she wanted to get out of there pronto.

"If something bad happens to her friend's kid and we haven't even tried to stop it, Bella will blame you," she pointed out now.

Yes, and after that Bella would develop such a housecleaning mania, we'd all be lucky to escape with our skins. But for all I knew, Cory Trow might've returned home by now, ready to face the music.

Besides, Cory wasn't my big problem. Jemmy was. And while we'd struggled with the cart I'd had plenty of time to absorb the true precariousness of his situation.

"Maybe Henderson didn't see Jemmy downtown this morning," I said. "But maybe he did. And he could've even followed us to the cottage turnoff."

After that if he was in a car we'd have known he was there; you could hear a vehicle's tires on the dirt road from miles away in the lakeside silence. Still . . .

"Never mind that Jemmy's in the deep forest," I added. "You feel so safe out there, you know? Like all of civilization is on another planet far away and you don't have to worry about it. But a guy like Walt Henderson doesn't care. He'll crawl through the teeming jungle with a knife in his teeth to finish off the fellow he's after."

"So what would you do? If you did get the chance to talk to Henderson, what would you say?" Ellie asked, steering sharply to avoid a deer that had suddenly appeared in the roadway in front of us.

Because it wasn't enough in Maine to watch out for the other drivers, many of whom apparently had trained at the same place where

they teach people how to get shot out of cannons. You also had to ne-
gotiate through the animal kingdom.

"I'm not sure," I replied as the deer faded into the trees and Ellie
returned the truck to the proper lane with casual ease; my heartbeat
only stuttered a couple of times. "But if it came right down to it I'd
think of something."

After all, I used to talk men in Henderson's line of work into a lot
of things. Health insurance, for instance; even in those days a major
surgical procedure could wipe out a fortune, ill-gotten or not. I'd persuaded a couple of them into legitimate business careers, too; why
work in an industry where a gunshot wound is a common cause of oc-
cupational injury when you can have a snazzy suite of offices on the
fortieth floor of a major downtown landmark building?

While, of course, remaining just as crooked as ever; where do you
think all those lost pension funds in the early nineties went?

"We're assuming Jemmy's assessment of Henderson is correct?"
Ellie asked. We were approaching the causeway to Moose Island. A
cop in mirrored sunglasses appeared to ignore us from behind the
wheel of his parked squad car, the words *Pleasant Point Police* lettered in
black on the side of it.

I felt his eyes on my neck like a couple of insects as we went by. "It
is correct," I said, then added, "Jemmy may be a tad flaky but he's always been reliable on the topic of who wants to kill him."

"Okay, then." We passed the Quoddy Airfield with its freshly
paved runway and bright orange airsock, then the Bay City Mobil
Station, the firehouse, and the IGA.

In the parking lot the high school kids were holding a car wash,
some holding up hand-lettered signs while the rest squirted each other
with hoses. "In that case . . . ," Ellie began.

She swung the steering wheel unexpectedly, taking us down
County Road toward the south end of the island. "No time like the
present," she declared.

Five minutes later we were at the end of a road that terminated
suddenly in a gravel turnaround. Beyond that a massive rock wall

loomed like the perimeter of a fortress, sharp-tipped black iron spikes jutting from the wall's capstones every couple of feet.

"Henderson's place," Ellie told me. "You'll talk to him while I wander around keeping an eye out for Cory."

She frowned at the rock wall. "Not that I really think he's here. If he's got any sense it's absolutely the last place he'd go. But that way we can tell Bella we at least tried to find her friend's fugitive son."

Because you couldn't lie to Bella. She sniffed fibs with the same unerring skill she used to ferret out household dirt; Victor used to say her first cranial nerve was overdeveloped.

"Kill two birds with one stone, huh? Good idea," I said.

Assuming the dead birds didn't turn out to be us. Bearding the lion in his den seemed a more apt description for what we were doing; privately I wasn't so sure about Ellie's notion.

Still, letting Henderson know I was aware of his plans might be enough to make him change or at least postpone them. And if I did nothing and something happened to Jemmy, I would never forgive myself.

So my choice was clear. *Private,* a sign announced from the closed iron gate. No one answered the intercom box mounted on it. I climbed back into the truck.

"Okay, you've had all the good ideas so far. Now what?" The property was a wildly scenic compound overlooking the whole bay. I didn't know much about it but Ellie had spent her whole childhood on the island, and did.

"Now," she said with determination, "we take the direct approach. Before he put this wall up there was a picnic spot on the water side of the property. Dirt road leading partway in."

Great, another dirt road. She put the truck in gear and began nosing it down a barely visible track, parallel to the wall and away from the gate.

Sixty yards later she stopped again. This time we both got out. Ellie marched away from the truck; I followed, my misgivings increasing.

"And unless he also built a wall on the water side, which I don't see why he would . . . ," she continued as we pushed through some bushes, then came out on the other side of them.

No kidding, and I wouldn't exactly call the approach direct. The wall ended but what replaced it worked equally well; coming to an abrupt halt I reached back reflexively for a steadying handful of those bushes, all that kept me from a plummeting next step.

"You're kidding," I managed, though Ellie appeared unfazed. We were looking at a cliff with about an eight-inch path running along the edge of it. To the left, another massive rise of sheer granite swooped up, dizzying me; to the right was an apparently endless expanse of breathtakingly empty air.

"Nobody even knows you can do this except kids who grew up around here," Ellie said blithely, stepping onto the path, which to me looked approximately as wide as a tightrope. I closed my eyes, decided that was a bad idea, and hastily opened them again.

"Remind me again why we can't just come back when someone's here to let us in?" Gulping, I crept forward.

If for some insane reason you wanted to invade Walter Henderson's place, you'd be better off landing a helicopter on the back lawn.

"Because maybe they won't let us in." She moved limberly ahead of me, no hesitation at all; to her this was nothing. "And then we might not get to look for Cory Trow. You want to at least say we have, remember? And do it with a straight face?"

She stepped quickly away from me. "Besides, I want this Jemmy nonsense over and done with as soon as possible."

Okey-dokey. I put my foot out. In response, my heart traded places with my tonsils. Crumbs of loose granite fell rattlingly away. "But once we get past this part we can just walk along the back end of the property and up to the front door," Ellie called over her shoulder cheerfully.

Yeah, this part. A seagull sailed by, his beady eye fixing me contemptuously. Out over the water, ducks skimmed, wings whistling.

"What, then we ring the bell and say 'Avon calling'?" In defiance of any possible inkling of common sense whatsoever, I shuddered a tiny bit farther out along the narrow cliff edge. A big chunk of granite broke off under my feet and tumbled to the rocks below.

Far below; a hundred feet or more to where deep water moved sullenly. I averted my eyes, battling a sudden attack of vertigo. Part of the trouble was that in my case vertigo usually won. The other part, however, was my current actual position on the planet, commonly known as Too High Up.

"I don't know what you'll tell him," Ellie replied with a grin as her foot slipped; nimbly she recovered her balance. "You said *you'd* think of something."

Me and my big mouth. Meanwhile the farther we got along the cliff's edge, the less sure I felt about what had turned suddenly into an extreme hiking adventure. On the other hand, I was not going *back* over that awful path; not without a parachute.

And a life raft; even if I were to survive the fall, the water below looked deadly. So I forged ahead, we reached the end of the trail at last, and after a further ten minutes of bushwhacking through brush thick enough to repel battle tanks, we approached the house.

It was a big, modern-looking octagonal structure of cedar and glass, with the emphasis on glass. My first thought was that calling it a McMansion was inaccurate; this wasn't the crap people built when they had more money than God but no taste to go with it.

This was the real thing, a house so perfectly proportioned and in keeping with Maine's bold coast that it looked as if it had grown there. Plantings of box hedge, rhododendron, and bay laurel increased the serenely organic feel of the place. Even the pea gravel in the driveway somehow managed to look naturally deposited.

The cedar steps led up to a free-form deck. There, more huge plants stood in massive unglazed clay pots. The only sound came from a heavy-looking set of wind chimes tuned to produce a low, vaguely Asian-sounding series of hollow clunks, a far cry from the jangly sour-note clangers I usually despised.

There wasn't so much as a single dead leaf on the driveway. Imagining my own place, all I could think was that keeping this one so pristine took lots of maintenance, probably professional; I couldn't imagine Walter Henderson doing much raking. But it seemed nobody was here; I hoped Henderson wasn't already out hunting Jemmy.

Maybe he'd given all the help the day off, I thought, but at a sound from behind me I turned and revised my opinion abruptly. Because two very helpful-looking Irish wolfhounds were indeed on the job; helpful, that is, if you wanted someone torn limb from limb.

"N-n-nice doggies," I managed through a sudden clog of fear in my throat. They'd come around the side of the deck in silence like a pair of trained assassins until the click of their toenails betrayed them.

Big toenails, to match their big bodies. And big teeth. Slowly the animals advanced, one step at a time, blank-eyed and deadly. From the corner of my eye I saw Ellie's hand reach very slowly for the door. "Get ready," she said.

Yeah, get ready to die. *Grrr,* the dog on the left said with menace unparalleled in canine history.

Urr, the dog on the right agreed gutturally, and then *wuff!* Which I guessed translated to *Let's get 'em!*

"Go!" Ellie cried, yanking open the screen door, shoving the inside door open and flinging herself past it. I scrambled after her, feeling the unmistakable tug of teeth on the cuff of my right jeans leg.

The moment lasted forever while a set of madly munching canine incisors chomped their way up toward one of my calves. But luckily those pants had been sent through the washing machine a million times and the amount of bleach Bella used on clothes of all colors was enough to rot wire mesh.

So I got in while the cuff of my pants stayed out, a trade I was delighted to make under the circumstances, and Ellie slammed the door. "Oh . . . my . . . God," I exhaled slowly while she leaned on the stairway banister, panting.

Silence from outside. "Good thing it was unlocked." My heart thumped in my rib cage as if trying to escape. Then came an awful thought: "You don't suppose they can get *in* here, do you?"

Because we wouldn't necessarily hear them coming if they did. Around us the floors were mostly covered with the silky-soft Persian carpets that always look so excellent on polished wood, while muffling stealthy footsteps with such superb efficiency.

"I'm not sure," Ellie replied nervously. "I'd better look around for dog doors."

The beautifully crafted Thomas Moser furniture and framed Diane Arbus photographs weren't half shabby either, nor were they reproductions. Back in the city I'd had a client who collected such stuff, and under his expert tutelage I'd learned to tell the difference.

An antique brass clock under a glass bell ticked softly on the inlaid mahogany serpentine sideboard, built maybe around 1710—yeah, that client again—in the stunningly beautiful black-and-white-tiled hall. It led back to the kind of kitchen featured on home-decorating shows whose budgets run into seven figures. I glimpsed the gleaming brushed stainless-steel side of a Sub-Zero refrigerator tucked between custom-built cherry cabinetry and granite countertops.

In short, hit man Henderson had the decorator from heaven; that, or his own perfectly flawless good taste plus the fortune to indulge it. "Hello?" Ellie called into the silence.

No answer. No canines appeared, and neither did anyone else.

I crept hesitantly into the formal living room, where pale blue and gold upholstery contrasted gorgeously with the marine tones of the carpet. The cream floor-length curtains were the kind you can see in palaces everywhere, sumptuous in fabric yet decorously restrained in their cut and design.

No frills. No doodads. Nothing but the best. It gave me a bad feeling, because Walter Henderson hadn't gotten all this by being lousy at his job, had he?

Not on your tintype. "Jake, look at this."

I followed Ellie's voice down the tiled hall to the den, a low-ceilinged, pine-paneled wonderland of casual comfort whose imaginary entry placard might just as well have read *Things Guys Like*.

There was a large but not overly humongous television and a good sound system, stacks of DVDs—Henderson was big on Humphrey Bogart, John Wayne, and Duke Ellington—soft leather chairs and sofas each equipped with a well-positioned brass reading lamp, a laptop computer on a desk, and the pièce de résistance, a massive stone fireplace that occupied one entire wall of the room.

You could have roasted a whole pig in the fireplace. I wanted a stiff belt from the Scotch bottle in the glass-fronted drinks cabinet, too. But we didn't have time. The two hounds from hell could be creeping up on us.

Or someone else could. "There's a back door in this place," Ellie said. "To a terrace. Come on."

"But won't the dogs be . . . ?"

"Yep." She nodded grimly. "They're still on the deck, and the terrace is attached. But I looked into the refrigerator," she went on as I followed her to the kitchen of Julia Child's dreams: double ovens, six-burner gas stove, copper pans over a butcher-block-topped workspace big enough to fix meals on the *Titanic*.

"Housekeeper's out doing errands," said Ellie. "We must've just missed her but she'll be right back."

She gestured at the evidence for this: a damp-looking dishtowel, a few drops of water in the brushed-steel sink, and most compelling of all, a note on the refrigerator saying that someone named Erma was out doing errands and would be right back.

"Without locking the door?" I remembered the keypad mounted by the entrance we'd come in. At the time I hadn't thought much about it, being more interested in not having my leg turned into mincemeat. But now . . .

"Why d'you suppose the alarm hasn't gone off?" I asked.

Ellie had opened the refrigerator. She rummaged around, then took something from it. "Maybe it's a silent alarm," she replied.

Not a pleasant thought. Then, without waiting to discuss her next move with me, she stepped out the back door.

"Here, doggies!" she called, waving a porterhouse steak. At the sight of it my heart practically seized up in terror.

"Ellie, that's not going to . . . urk!" I hurried out after her as the dogs charged slavering around the corner of the deck at us, apparently in a race to see which one of them could reach and devour us first. She tossed the beefsteak confidently at them.

"Ellie!" I squeaked. The dogs ignored the steak, secure in the knowledge that we were meatier and there were two of us. Jaws gnashing, the animals *flew* at us.

It was another thing I'd learned from that old client with all the money: guard dogs are trained not to eat any of the tasty things intruders might toss at them, as the treats might be laced with strychnine.

Still there needs to be a command that will *get* the dogs to eat, since obviously they must be able to. For one thing if the creatures get hungry enough but *can't,* they might just decide to abandon *all* their training and consume their owner.

This whole sequence of thought raced through my mind along with the realization that I hadn't had my last will and testament updated lately. As the dogs crouched to leap, lips drawn back over teeth that looked as sharp as surgical scalpels, I summoned up the simplest command I could think of.

"Eat!" The dogs stopped in mid-lunge, looking confused. Then they turned, spotted the steak, and began playing tug-of-war with it, sort of the way a pair of lions on the veldt might toy with a hapless gazelle.

But once they polished off their appetizer they'd still want Ellie and me for the main course. And now they were between us and the door. So while the animals were still licking their chops, we scurried downhill through a long fenced pasture, under barbed wire sharp enough to inflict ritual scarring, and across a field leading to a big old barn.

A barn with—thank God!—a door we *could* open, since the gruesome twosome had indeed made quick work of their snack and were hot on our heels again.

We fell inside and Ellie slammed the door shut, leaning on it. "Good . . . heavens," she gasped.

"Yeah," I wheezed sourly. "Safe at last. If you call being trapped here with no way to get out, *safe.* Why couldn't we wait inside for the housekeeper to get back?"

Outside, the dogs snuffled ravenously. "Jake, what do you suppose Bella would do if she found people in *your* house?"

Suck them up into the vacuum cleaner, probably, I thought. "Call the cops," I said.

After that, the next thing you knew Bob Arnold would be out here arresting *us,* or at least making our lives miserable. And that was definitely not in our game plan.

Ellie waved a hand tiredly at me. "Let's just take one bad thing at a time." She flopped down onto a bale of straw. "At least the dogs didn't eat us."

Light from the windows above carved shafts of brilliance high in the gloom, but they didn't reach the floor and otherwise the place was as dark as the devil's pantry.

"I don't suppose there's a phone in here," I groused. And of course I hadn't brought along a cell phone, reception at the lake being pretty much nonexistent.

"Hmm," Ellie said, getting up. "That's a thought. I'd have one out here if this place were mine."

She was right. No wires led to the barn but if they existed they were probably buried. Walt Henderson liked things neat if the rest of the place was any indication.

I peered around. "Is there a lightbulb, maybe? You'd think there'd at least be a . . ."

Hmm. Stalls to the left, their shadowy shapes distinct. A big lawn-mowing tractor; I could smell it even before I glimpsed it, sharp reeks of gasoline and engine oil.

And something else. I turned slowly. Another smell hung in the air, not very nice. Ellie muttered in annoyance as she groped around for a switch. "You'd think it'd be here by the . . ."

Squinting around as my eyes adjusted to the gloom, I made out the corner of a room built into one end of the barn, under the loft. The room had a tiny window and as I pressed my face against it, hoping to spot a phone beyond the Sheetrock walls and locked wooden door, I spied a shape.

A longish, didn't-belong-in-there shape. "Ellie," I said.

"Got it!" she uttered triumphantly, and the barn's interior flooded with white light.

Along one wall of the room ran a flight of rough stairs, just a pine stringer and steps with a two-by-four railing to the loft above. "Ellie, grab that sledgehammer, will you?" I said.

She did, bringing it to me from the tool rack on the barn's far wall. Moments later I had the office room open; the lock was strong but the hollow-core door someone had set it into wasn't.

Inside, the not-quite-right shape floated hideously. Above, the square of brilliance silhouetting the shape was an open trap door. A rope led down through the trap door, stretched tautly from an old iron hook.

Hung by the neck from the rope was a man, face purple-black, head lolled sideways at an impossible angle.

What I remembered later was the way his curls haloed around his head, golden in the light from above. But at the time, for the space of an awful heartbeat, I just thought it was Sam.

In the next moment I realized it wasn't. The man wore brown trousers, a sweatshirt over a stained white T-shirt, and a pair of running shoes so ragged, the uppers seemed held to the worn soles by only a couple of shreds.

His fingernails, I noticed, were grimy but unbroken, and the skin of his neck—what I could make out of it through the awful discoloration there—bore no scratch marks.

So at least it had been quick. "Oh," Ellie said, sorrow and horror mingling in her voice.

I nodded, observing the slim wrists, the tanned backs of the victim's hands, and the soft-looking white skin covering the hip bones, still slender and sharply childlike, where the beltless waistband of the trousers had slipped a little.

"How long do you suppose he's been here?" Ellie asked.

"No way of us telling. Medical examiner'll have to do that. Poor little idiot," I added, suddenly angry.

Cory was his name, I remembered. Cory Trow. Because surely this was him, and after another glance at him Ellie confirmed it.

"Lost his girl, maybe facing a prison term. Guess he figured his life was over, might as well go ahead and put the punctuation mark on it," I said.

And do it here, so no one could miss the significance of the act: *See? See what you made me do?*

It was the selfish cry of a petulant child. God forbid that any of it was *your* fault, I scolded the young man silently.

God forbid he should suck it up, take a dose of unhappiness for his mother's sake if not his own. But then I saw something on his hand, a tiny shred of dark material.

Was it—please, no—a bit of bloody skin? Had Cory's death not at least been as swift and merciful as I'd at first thought?

Maybe he'd messed that up, too, ending by clawing at the rope around his neck when it was too late. The thought made me shiver.

"Found the phone," Ellie reported from a far corner of the barn where a sheet of plywood on file cabinets made a makeshift desk.

I stepped out of the room. The phone hung on the wall. Next to it leaned a wooden stepladder. "Wait a minute," I said. Ellie's hand was already on the receiver. "Can you bring that ladder over here first?"

Reluctantly she set the phone down. I put the ladder under the open trap door near the dangling body.

"Steady it for me, will you?"

"Jake, I don't think . . ." But she held the thing anyway as I took a step up, then another.

I've never enjoyed stepladders, and the nearness of a dead guy didn't make me any fonder of this one than usual. But at last I reached the second step from the top.

Nowhere to steady myself. Just me, eye to eye with a hanged man's hand. To which clung that little shred of something . . .

Gingerly I reached out. I drew the hand into the light coming down through the open trap door.

Below, Ellie sucked in a breath. "Are you sure you should . . . ?"

"Touch him?" I replied a little too sharply; gosh, this was unpleasant. "Why not? He's a suicide. And even if he wasn't, it's not as if there'd be fingerprints on him."

Or as if they'd do anyone any good even if there were; TV dramas may be one thing but real life is another, especially in rural areas. Nobody was going to investigate this kid.

His skin was cold, fingers rubbery-feeling. As I drew his hand farther out into the light, the body rotated toward me; I glanced up at the face again and wished I hadn't.

The shred of fabric clung in a hangnail on his right index finger. Blue; the fabric, I mean, although the finger was a sort of dusky slate color by now also. Tiny, delicate threads; silk, maybe.

Meanwhile the one thing missing from the scene was a "goodbye, cruel world" note. Then I spotted that, too.

From my perch on the ladder I could see at an angle through the trap door above. The rope was tied to a hook usually used, I supposed, to haul up those straw bales. In the loft lay more of them, mostly stacked but a few pulled down and shoved together to form what looked like a makeshift couch.

Or a love nest, a voice in my head suggested speculatively. On one bale rested a flashlight, its lens turned toward me, unlit.

Under it lay a sheet of paper. Following my gaze Ellie saw it, too, and let go of the stepladder, headed for the loft.

"Ellie, wait . . ." But it was already too late. When she released her grip on the ladder it wobbled the tiniest bit. Not enough to shake me off, but I have the kind of equilibrium that turns a wobble into a lurch and the lurch into the kind of motion generally reserved for major seismic events.

Released from my grip, the dead man's hand swung back and forth in front of my face as if trying to hypnotize me. From it fluttered the shred of cloth, little more than a few threads.

"Oh," I said mournfully as the fabric floated away and vanished. I scrambled down from the ladder and bent to search the floor for it, unsuccessfully.

For the one tiny bit of hard evidence, I mean, suggesting that perhaps Cory Trow hadn't really committed suicide.

That instead he'd been murdered.

"Here it is," Ellie said, coming down the loft stairs with a sheet of paper in her hand. Blue-lined and ordinary, it could've come from anywhere. Mindful of a hanged man still dangling a few feet from me, I peered at it.

Printed in pencil, a couple of lines gouged into it. THIS IS WHAT YOU WANTED. I HOPE YOUR ALL HAPPY. F*** YOU. CORY

"So can I phone Bob Arnold now?" asked Ellie.

"Sure." Interesting, I thought while she dialed, that Cory had used a kind of paper so unlikely to be traceable, and printed his suicide note in pencil. From someone who was getting ready to do something so permanent, I'd have expected ink.

But that was grasping at straws. "What's wrong?" Ellie asked after speaking into the phone and hanging up.

"Nothing. A piece of something was stuck to his fingernail, is all." I described the delicate fabric.

"Oh," she breathed, looking around for it just as I had but with no more luck. Moments later the wail of a siren cut off and voices approached outside, one of them familiar: Eastport police chief Bob Arnold's. The other was Henderson's.

". . . crank call," he was saying, sounding irritated. "You're welcome to check, but I guarantee you there's nobody in that—"

He must've come home after Ellie and I left his house. The barn door opened and Walter Henderson stopped on the threshold, looking from me and Ellie to the body behind us, its dangling legs framed by the doorway of the small room. He said nothing as Bob Arnold appeared behind him.

"Jake," Bob said, his tone annoyed. "Ellie."

A line from an old TV classic echoed in my head: *Lu-cee, you gotta lotta 'splainin' to do!*

But there was nothing comic about the way the barn's owner absorbed what he was seeing. No emotion showed on his face, not even surprise; suddenly I felt glad I hadn't wasted time trying to decide what to say to him. Because it was even clearer to me now than before that the idea of reasoning with Walter Henderson was ridiculous.

Silvery brush-cut hair, small neat features, pale lightly freckled skin. And those eyes, the color of sapphires, with all the human warmth of the gemstones.

"Nice place you've got here," I said when they turned on me again.

"Hello, Jacobia," Walter Henderson replied. "Yes, it is beautiful, isn't it?"

He smiled; not a pleasant expression. "In fact I've had some people tell me they'd kill to be in my position."

• • •

When I got home Bella Diamond was making coleslaw. This time of year, when we were all so hungry for fresh stuff, she put everything but the kitchen sink into it, broccoli and carrots and in prudent doses even slices of raw cauliflower.

She'd assembled the slivered vegetables and begun adding the dressing, a high-end bottled brand to which she added plenty of celery seed. After that she put in her secret ingredient, its identity so closely guarded by her that even I hadn't been able to discover it.

"Now," she recited to herself as she always did at this stage of the proceedings. "Right before we serve it we'll pour off some of the liquid and add a dab more cabbage. That way most of it'll be limp and creamy, but not floppy. Just," she finished, "the way we like it."

Snapping the top onto the plastic container, she placed it in the refrigerator. The round-shouldered old vintage model hummed and clattered in response to having its door opened even briefly. Then she confronted me.

"That boy ain't home yet," she said, brushing cabbage shreds from the cutting board into the palm of her hand.

"No, Bella, he's not. And I'm afraid he's not going to be. Ellie and I found Cory in Walter Henderson's barn a little while ago. He's dead."

Bella's face fell, and her eyes searched mine penetratingly.

"Oh," she said at last. "Then I imagine things around here are going to get somewhat"—*summat*—"complicated."

Yes, I imagined they were.

Dave DiMaio
Miskatonic University

Dear Horace,

Still a few tests left to run but they'll only confirm what we both suspected. Age of ink and paper, chemical composition of the glue, stitching thread analysis and that "leather" binding— all consistent. Let me finish up and I'll give you a full report. Then we can decide what to tell the book's owner; needless to say, in this case the unvarnished facts might not be appropriate.

Speaking of which, perhaps coincidentally—though I think not—I got a call from Bert Merkle yesterday. "Just keeping in touch," he said. I've heard he's claiming he's from Harvard now. Guess our halls aren't ivied enough for him. But he asked about you, which seemed odd since you were never friends. He's living in Eastport; odder still, don't you agree?

Bert always did have a nose for news. I wonder what set it sniffing? Brilliant, of course, and naturally talented. Trouble is, I'm never completely sure which side he's on.

So—word to the wise, Horace. If Bert comes snooping you might want to give me a call. My love to Lang—is it too paranoid of me to suggest that you two take a little vacation somewhere together?

Cheers,

Dave D.

Chapter 5

*A creaky stair tread makes a
pretty decent early warning
system. Think before fixing?*
—*Tiptree's Tips*

My beloved 1979 Fiat Sport Spyder convertible had rack-and-pinion steering, double overhead cams, five speeds forward, and a professionally applied apricot paint job on a jazzy little Pininfarina body, plus black leather bucket seats and a black cloth top.

It was a thing of beauty and a joy for about as long as it had taken the original owner to drive it from the showroom; after that it had started living up to its acronym, *Fix It Again, Tony*. But I still treasured it.

Too bad that a few hours after Ellie and I found the body in the barn, the car sat in a ditch where my son Sam had put it, on a side road near the tiny mainland town of Cooper, not far from Eastport.

"I'm sorry, Mom," Sam said, for the fifth time. "But honestly, there was nothing I could do. The guy was crazy, he came right at me. For a minute there I thought he was trying to hit me."

It was one A.M. and pitch dark; cold, too, with the kind of icy chill you can still get in Maine at night even in mid-May. I wrapped my sweatered arms around myself.

"Okay," I told Sam through gritted teeth, trying to keep them from chattering. Since finding Cory's corpse that afternoon, I'd been afflicted with a kind of free-floating anxiety that made me feel as if I were chewing on broken glass.

A car crept by, the driver's face a pale featureless blur as he rubbernecked us. We'd set emergency flares a hundred yards down the road both ways, though, and we were lit up pretty well right around our vehicles, too.

"I understand," I said. Working in the floodlight mounted on the rear of his truck cab, my husband, Wade, put a chain around the Fiat's front axle, then hooked the other end to his tow bar.

But Sam wasn't satisfied. He still thought I was angry. Or he was protesting too much as he sometimes did when he really was guilty of something.

"It was like the guy was trying to run me off the road on purpose," he complained as Wade swung into the truck cab and put it in gear.

Sam looked sober. Sounded sober, too. And as far as I could tell out here in the chilly fresh air, he even smelled sober.

Unfortunately, in Sam none of that was any guarantee that he actually was sober. "Mom," he said, reading my expression, "I haven't had a drink in a week."

That either. "Okay," I replied as the truck pulled forward slowly and the front end of the Fiat emerged from the saplings and brush it was stuck among. From what I could see, the car was a little scraped up but essentially undamaged, and Sam said he hadn't hit anything hard on the way off the pavement.

"You're sure you're not hurt?" In the harsh light from the flares his face looked ghastly.

"Yeah." He'd been coming back from an AA meeting in Machias, or so he'd gone on insisting. It was why I'd lent him the car at all; he'd owned it for a while but when he couldn't afford the maintenance he'd given it back to me.

"Little shaken up, I guess," he added. Wade set the brake on the pickup and jumped down from the cab, got the chain off the Fiat, and stowed the tow bar in the truck bed, one efficient move after another.

"Scared me, was all," Sam said. "You want me to . . ." He waved at the Fiat.

"Drive it home?" Somebody had to, assuming it would drive at all. I still didn't know what kind of mess the trees and brush might've made of the car's undercarriage. My first impulse was to let Sam ride with Wade and drive the vehicle home myself to check it out.

But if I said no, it would mean I really did think Sam was intoxicated, and that would start a whole big controversy.

"Sure. If you feel up to it." Since his dad's death Sam had fallen hard off the wagon a couple of times.

More than a couple. He got in the Fiat; it started fine. "You go on. We'll follow," I said. "Just in case."

He grimaced, then realized I meant in case the car died on the way home, or wouldn't steer. Not *in case you really do turn out to be too sloshed to stay on your own side of the road.*

Because this time at least I thought Sam really was sober. When he'd gone Wade and I collected the road flares in silence, not speaking until we were in the truck.

"Good thing you answered the phone," Wade said mildly as he turned toward home.

"Yeah." Because when it rings at midnight your average mom knows it's probably not the Prize Patrol, calling to say she's won three million dollars. After the crash Sam had walked to a nearby house and gotten the people there to summon me, then waited in the cold and dark.

But I didn't want to talk about Sam; over the past months it seemed Sam was all Wade and I discussed. "Wade, are you really sure it's okay for Jemmy to stay at the lake?"

Because maybe I'd acted hastily; the camp had originally belonged only to Wade, after all. He should say who got to use it, I thought, or at least have a vote. But he didn't seem concerned about that.

"Oh, yeah," he answered easily, slinging an arm around me. With a sigh so deep it felt as if it had come up from my shoes, I let myself relax against him.

"Hey, you're my girl," Wade said in the same deep, calm voice that had captured me back when I first met him. "And he's pulled your irons out of the fire a few times, hasn't he? Only fair, help him out in return."

I nodded, feeling Wade's muscular shoulder against my cheek. When I first met him I thought he was a man's man, the kind who went hunting and fishing with his buddies, no girls allowed. He'd be the type who on Sunday afternoon watched endless football, getting up at halftime only to work on his truck, and who thought men's jewelry was silly with the possible exception of the Timex.

And I'd been right; Wade was all that. In the dashboard's pale glow his short blond hair gleamed, his eyes scanning the road ahead competently.

" 'Bout a week, though, the mosquitoes are going to drive him out of there," he reminded me. "Or suck him so dry he'll need a blood transfusion. Blackflies, too."

"I hadn't thought of that." But it was true, man-eating tigers would be preferable to the insects at the lake once the weather got warmer, especially the blackflies; the biting swarms hadn't been locally dubbed "defenders of the wilderness" for nothing.

I hoped Jemmy wouldn't be there that long. We took the turn toward Eastport, Sam's taillights glowing steadily ahead of us in the dark.

"Wade . . ."

He glanced down at me, a smile crinkling the skin around his eyes, and gave my shoulder a squeeze.

"Never mind," I said at last.

I'd already told him about seeing the ghost of my ex-husband in the kitchen—if that had been what it was, and not some goofy imagining of mine—and about the reason why Jemmy had come here at all, and about the hanged kid.

Now I wanted to say I thought I might be in a mess, only I didn't know what kind yet. But there was nothing anyone could do about any of it tonight, so instead we went home to bed. Wade, who'd been up for work at four the previous morning, was asleep before his head hit the pillow.

I lay awake beside him thinking about Cory Trow and Sam. They were nearly the same age; I only hoped they wouldn't end up similarly, hanging being just a quicker way to get where Sam was headed if something substantial didn't change soon.

Then I did sleep, tumbling into a nightmare: Sam, my father, Victor, and the hanged kid dancing on my roof, each with a noose end dangling in front of him like a loose necktie.

Until they all vanished through trap doors, each soft-shoe routine ending suddenly in a short, sharp drop, a terminal snap.

● ● ●

"Suicide, my ass," Bella Diamond declared skeptically the next morning.

Perched atop the washing machine, where I was tearing thick plastic sheets down from the windows—in winter my old kitchen was so cold that on some days the inside of that ancient refrigerator was warmer—I turned in surprise.

Ordinarily my housekeeper wouldn't say a bad word if she had a mouth full of them. "Cory Trow no more killed himself than I'm the Queen of Sheba," she insisted while scrubbing feverishly at the kitchen sink.

Bella was so emphatically not the Queen of Sheba that it was tragic. But I wanted that sink to retain at least a little of its remaining enamel.

And what she'd said was what I thought, too. So I climbed down from the washing machine, took away her scrub rag, sat her at the table, and put one of the blueberry muffins she'd just baked plus a fresh cup of coffee in front of her. "How can you be so sure?"

Morning sun glared in through the suddenly naked windows, covered all winter with those plastic sheets so heavy-duty they resembled waxed paper. I wasn't even sure they kept the place any warmer, but at least they made me feel I was doing something to plug drafts.

"Don't take no genius," Bella said scornfully. Then she told me why, whereupon I very nearly choked on my own muffin.

"Married?" I repeated in disbelief. "And . . . a life insurance policy?"

She nodded. "Boy like that, who'd a thought he'd have a care for the end of his life? *Or* have a wife an' child?"

But it seemed Cory Trow had. "Even his mom never knew he got married," Bella told me. "His pals knew, though, an' one o' their moms called *his* mom last night, dropped the big bombshell on 'er in the middle of her grief."

I gazed at the windows, wondering if next winter *two* layers of plastic might . . . but no. Beautifully old-house-atmospheric as they were, the antique windowpanes had the thermal efficiency of tissue paper. And one of these times when I climbed up on top of that washing machine, I was going to break my . . .

"But wait, there's more," Bella pronounced, polishing off the rest of the muffin. "That policy won't pay if he killed himself, his mom says. Because it's too soon after he bought it."

Just then Ellie came in with her own child under one arm and a large ham under the other. Both were suitably wrapped, although from Ellie's harried look I wouldn't have been surprised to see a pair of toddler-sized coveralls pulled onto the pork and a sheet of aluminum foil fastened around Leonora.

But I wasn't finished with Bella. "How does his mother know the insurance policy won't . . ."

"Jake, you've got to help me," Ellie exhaled.

I ignored her for the moment. "How's she even know so fast that there *is* a policy? The friend wouldn't have known it and it's too soon for the insurance company to have—"

But my question was cut off. My father and the dogs came in behind Ellie, each canine competing with the other for who had the most sheer animal energy and which one could demonstrate it most disruptively. Dropping their leashes, my father made his escape, headed for the cellar and his tools while they bounded around, all gummy grins and clicking toenails, greeting us slobberily and demanding to have their breakfast.

"Coffee urn," Ellie said a little desperately as I got up to feed them. "A sixty-cup coffee urn, a good-size sheet cake, fifty sandwiches, and paper plates. By," she added in naked appeal, "eleven-thirty tomorrow morning."

Lee chose that moment to open her mouth wide; at once, most of the unhappy sounds in the world began coming out of it.

"Cream," Ellie recited, ignoring her daughter's wails, "and sugar. And lemonade, I suppose, for the children. And . . ."

Loud sounds from Leonora. Simultaneously, a stream of water began leaking from beneath that vintage refrigerator.

"Ellie, what in the *world* . . ." I began. But then through the din— Ellie's husband, George, said that in an emergency you could set Leonora up on the firehouse roof and use her for a siren—I realized: "Cory's funeral?"

Ellie slid her daughter unceremoniously into the playpen we kept in the kitchen for her. As Leonora's plump, padded bottom hit the playpen's cushioned floor, her mouth fell shut with a nearly audible snap.

"Goo-goo," she uttered happily; she adored the playpen.

"Yes," Ellie replied. From atop the refrigerator Cat Dancing observed the baby, then leapt down into the playpen beside her.

"Well, not a funeral exactly," Ellie amended. "A gathering to commemorate his life. Because you can't very well have a real funeral without a body, and *his* body . . ."

Was by now on its way to the state medical examiner's rooms in Augusta, where it would be autopsied as was usual in nearly all unattended deaths in Maine. "*Prutt,*" said the cross-eyed old feline as the child gripped her tail.

"That cat," said Bella Diamond balefully, "will suck all the baby's breath out of her."

But the cat didn't; soon Leonora turned to counting her own toes. "One, one, one, one, one," she said accurately.

Next Bob Arnold came in, surveyed us, and spotted the platter of muffins; since Bella had begun baking them regularly, my kitchen had started resembling Grand Central Station in the morning.

Although not smelling like it. You could practically see the baked cinnamon-sugar aroma grasp Bob's nose, leading him along irresistibly. "You ladies missed a trespassing charge by the skin of your teeth yesterday," he informed us.

"Um. Yeah. Thanks for your help," I said, meaning it.

"I told old Walt you were just a harmless pair of town do-gooders, putting together a survey on local library usage," our police chief said. "Got past the two dogs onto his porch by dumb luck, I told him, and then had to run for it."

Which was close enough to the truth to make me wince; the dumb part, anyway. Not that Henderson had believed it; his look as he'd greeted me still made me feel as if a set of crosshairs was centered on me.

"Don't like the cut of that guy's jib, never did since he moved here," Bob said, looking sour. "Henderson's got more pull than a team o' Clydesdales when he wants something, I don't know why."

He finished his first muffin, washed it down with coffee. "Look at the way he got that big house o' his built there. Land was s'posed to be in a nature trust, all of a sudden he's gotten himself a mansion on it," he said, taking another.

"*I* heard he also had something to do with the Trow boy being convicted on stalking," Bella said. "Payoffs or something."

Or maybe just the right lawyers. Either way . . . "Henderson's shaping up to be quite the steamroller, isn't he?" I asked. "Where his interests are concerned."

I didn't like what I thought that meant for Jemmy. I'd driven up to check on him that morning, watching all the way to be sure I wasn't being followed by anyone, but I hadn't been and Jemmy was okay.

So far. "What did Henderson want yesterday morning?" I asked Bob. "When he was talking to you on Water Street? He looked upset about something."

Bob nodded. "His lawyers'd already called him to say Cory Trow hadn't showed up at his sentencing hearing in Machias. So of course Walter came charging downtown to find me and let me know in no uncertain terms that I'd better do something about it toot sweet."

His face conveyed what he thought about that, the rosebud lips twisting as if instead of sweet blueberries he'd encountered a lemon slice. "He asked about you," Bob added.

"Walter Henderson did? But I thought you told him we were just . . ."

"Not at the barn," Bob clarified. "Before, when I was with him on the street and you both were driving by with that guy in the backseat of Wade's truck."

It was a useful trick of Bob's and one of the traits that made him such an effective day-to-day police officer in Eastport, his ability to seem fully engrossed in one thing while at the same time observing every single pertinent detail of another.

But I had the feeling Walter Henderson knew the trick, too, and five would get you ten it wasn't me or Ellie who'd drawn his attention as we drove by.

It was Jemmy, even hidden behind his new face. Bob finished the muffin. "So do you want to let me in on what you were really doing out there?"

Yeeks. Rushing in where angels fear to tread, was the honest answer. In this case honesty probably wasn't the best policy, though, because Bob was another reason Ellie and I had exited the snooping business.

The last time we'd done anything in that regard, Bob had been quietly in favor, but by the time it was over, Ellie and I had nearly gotten killed. So afterwards he'd reversed his policy.

Bella spoke up. "They were trying to find Cory. His mom asked me to ask 'em. So they did," she defended us stoutly. "And as for this suicide nonsense . . ."

"Bella," I intervened quietly as Bob got up. She looked at me and fastened her trap.

"All right," Bob conceded. "Kid bein' such a damn pest with runnin' after the Henderson girl, guess maybe it was reasonable thinkin' he might be there."

This of course hadn't been our only errand. But there was no sense telling Bob about Jemmy, either. He turned to Bella. "But the boy did hang himself, you know. They'll probably find booze or marijuana in the blood test, too, maybe even some pills."

Heading for the door, he threw over his shoulder: "Guess I might want a ration of chemical courage myself if I decided to do what Cory Trow did. Anyway, autopsy'll cover all the bases."

Guilt needled me. I remembered that there was another base, one Bob didn't know about. I thought of revealing to him what had happened to the shred of cloth on the boy's fingernail, decided again not to. After all, what possible good would it have done?

Besides getting me in a heap of trouble. Something in my silence must've alerted him, however. "I'm going to have a word with the workers at Henderson's place," he said, turning and eyeing me curiously. "See if they saw anything. Even though Horner says the kid likely died Sunday night when none of 'em were around."

Harold Horner was the county deputy medical examiner, the one who'd have referred the death to the state's medical examiner. Bob held my gaze a moment longer. "Either of you think of anything else interesting, call me," he ordered on his way out.

"Ellie," I said when he'd gone. Bella had already washed his cup and was hovering impatiently for mine.

But she would have to wait a little longer. "Ellie, why do you suppose a kid like Cory Trow would buy life insurance, then kill himself before the suicide clause expired? And why *didn't* Henderson's alarms go off? Heck, a place like that, he might even have more high-tech stuff installed, maybe even outdoor motion detectors."

"Well," she theorized reasonably, "it was the middle of the day. People going in and out, the housekeeper doing errands and all, you wouldn't want to be fooling with alarms all the time. Maybe he only turns the alarms on at—"

"Right. Okay, maybe he only turns them on at night. So if they were on, on Sunday night, how'd Cory Trow get in there? And how did he get past the dogs? Unless someone *let* him in . . ."

Our eyes met. "Jennifer," we pronounced together.

Walter Henderson's teenaged daughter, the one Cory had been headed to jail for stalking, might've turned off the alarms and penned the dogs up if she was expecting a nighttime visitor. And once the alarms were off, I supposed there was the barest chance they might not get turned on again until the next night, when it was likely that someone would've made a habit of checking them.

"Maybe she and her father didn't agree on Cory's undesirable status," I speculated. "In fact, his being forbidden fruit might just have made him *more* desirable."

"You think?" Bella inquired sarcastically, wiping furiously at a kitchen counter that was already so clean, a new white glove would've contaminated it. "From what I heard, that Jennifer girl was all over Cory like scales on a mackerel, right up until the minute *he* put his foot down."

Henderson's foot, she meant. Just then my own father came up from the cellar again and caught the end of the conversation. "Jen Henderson?" he said as he opened a work-roughened hand so I could see what it held.

Nails. Old ones, rusty and useless. "Out of the roof," he explained as Ellie turned to him.

"You worked on the Henderson place for a while, didn't you? Last summer when they were putting in that . . ."

"Barn foundation," he agreed. Smiling, he crossed to the playpen and bent to offer Leonora a calloused finger. "Baby," he crooned tenderly at her, and she babbled deliriously in reply.

"I didn't know that," I said. But there was plenty I didn't know about my dad, including where else he worked and what he did when he wasn't here at my house, laboring to keep the whole place from collapsing.

"That girl had Cory right around her little finger, his mom says," Bella sputtered indignantly. "And all the time he had a wife and baby over in St. Stephen, Canada, not forty miles from here, that he was keeping a secret."

"Sounds right," my father said, straightening. "Part about the Henderson girl, I mean. Hate to say it but from what I saw, she's what we used to call a man-eater."

He dropped the old nails into the wastebasket by the sink and I didn't protest. I used to save ruined parts of the house just out of sentiment, but as soon as I discovered how vastly they outnumbered the working parts, all the bloom went off that rose.

"Fellow with a blood pressure and a toolbox risked his life just walkin' onto the property, seemed like to me," he remarked, just as Ellie's husband, George Valentine, came in and made a beeline for the now pathetically diminished pile of muffins.

"What'd you think of 'er?" my father asked him. "Henderson girl. You were out there too last summer, I seem to recall."

George was a pale-skinned, compactly built fellow with a bluish five-o'clock shadow always darkening his stubborn chin. From the glint in his eye you could gather the strong notion that getting on his bad side might be unwise, and you would be correct.

But George's sense of humor was even quicker than his temper, and longer lasting. "Oh, please don't throw me in that briar patch," he chuckled in reply. "I could get in a whole heap of trouble making remarks about that."

But by the way he seized Ellie around the waist and hugged her, we all knew he couldn't. "Hey, girl," he said, gazing into her eyes.

"Get along with you, now," she said, flustered, and pushed him away, blushing. She thought George walked on water, and for her he'd have given it a try. "Just answer the question."

"Jen Henderson," he repeated thoughtfully, tucking another muffin into his overall pocket for later. In Eastport, George was the man you called for sparks in the fuse box, bats in the attic, or trees that had once been vertical but now were horizontal on your front lawn.

"Let's just say in a choice between her and a trap full o' quicksand, I'll take the quicksand," he said.

Bending to kiss Lee, he shot Ellie a look full of romantic promise that made her blush even more deeply than before. "Later, babe," he told her sweetly, and went back to work.

"Startin' to look as if we might have to do something fairly radical to that roof of yours," my father said when George had gone.

But I already knew. When nails got as bad as the ones he'd just shown me, the roof they'd been taken from was ready to blow off in the next stiff breeze.

Or fall down into the attic. "Just be careful," I told him as he strode out to resume laboring on it, wrapping his stringy gray ponytail into its leather thong and whistling as he went.

"Anyway, if Jennifer let Cory in, it answers one question," I said, finally relinquishing my cup to Bella, who bore it to the sink as if it carried plague germs. "But it raises some others."

Such as, how'd a love scene turn into a death scene so fast? And meanwhile there was still the problem of Jemmy.

Seeming to catch my thought, Ellie looked up from the list she was making for Cory Trow's memorial. "Jake, just stop trying to bamboozle me about that guy, will you?"

"Who?" I replied, trying to look innocent.

She made a face. "Oh, come on. For years you've been talking about Jemmy Wechsler as if he's some cuddly old uncle."

In the playpen Leonora sang softly; Bella had gone upstairs to make the beds. "Well, not an *old* uncle," I objected, knowing I wouldn't win this argument.

"So harmlessly entertaining," Ellie went on, deliberately not hearing. "But I got a look at him. Listened to him, too."

She hesitated. "Jake," she said gently as if delivering bad news. "Jake, that man's a sociopath."

But that was no secret either. "Yeah," I said, giving in. "You're right, he doesn't have as many personal feelings as other people do."

Or any feelings, actually. "When he first latched onto me," I said, "years ago, I thought he was working on me as a project. Rescue a kid off the street, you know, give himself some kind of personal merit badge for it."

But later I realized I had it backwards. Jemmy was the project. He was trying to like someone, investigating different aspects of human emotion and figuring out how they might work.

"What made you catch on?" I asked Ellie. Because nowadays he had the human-being act nearly down pat.

"His voice," she replied promptly. "With him in the truck behind me all I could think of was piano wire," she said, shivering expressively.

Yep, that was Jemmy. "So let's not pretend he's harmless or I'll get cranky," Ellie said.

"All right," I agreed as yet another swath of tar paper fell past the kitchen window. Then Bella hustled in with a mop in one hand and a bucket in the other; wordlessly she shoved the bucket under the hot-water tap and Lysol fumes billowed into the air, pungent as chlorine gas.

When she'd departed once more, Ellie said the other thing I was thinking. "If Henderson learned somehow that Cory really didn't intend to go to jail after all, that instead he'd decided to run away, and then Walter *found* Cory . . ."

"And forced or lured him into that barn . . . but how?"

"Don't know. But if it did happen that way, Henderson might have killed Cory and fixed it somehow to look like suicide."

"So when we saw him talking to Bob Arnold on Water Street yesterday, he'd have already known Cory was dead."

"Mm-hmm." Ellie folded her list and tucked it into her pocket. "He could've turned those alarms off, too. And written the note."

Suddenly I wished I could ask a lot of questions of a lot of different people, and then it hit me.

I mean that I was about to get the chance. "It's why you did it, isn't it?" I asked Ellie. "Set the memorial for tomorrow and volunteered the two of us to arrange the refreshments. So we could . . ."

"Get a look at them all," she agreed. "Maybe learn something useful. Cory wasn't exactly a pillar of the community, so I'm not sure who'll come. But you never know."

In the playpen the baby and Cat Dancing dozed peacefully together, Lee's chubby arm around the animal's neck. If anyone else had tried it, that cat would've performed major surgery on them.

"The mother, the wife, the girlfriend, and his other pals," Ellie recited. "It's easier if you get them all together in one place. Assuming we can," she added. "But if we don't do the food, even *we* don't have a reason to be there."

She lifted Leonora from the playpen, settled the sleeping child on her shoulder. Meanwhile the leak from the refrigerator widened inexorably into a puddle; all the newly exposed kitchen windows rattled.

Pretty soon I would need to haul roof-repair shingles for my dad, too; lots of them. *Up* the ladder and *down* the ladder; repeat until your legs fall off.

Or you do. And at the lake there was a dock to finish. "Um, remind me again why we're doing this at all?"

Ellie pointed upstairs where my housekeeper ran the vacuum cleaner furiously over the hall carpet. Next she might pull apart the plumbing to be sure all the pipe interiors were spotless; the last time Bella's engines got revved she'd decided the insides of our ears were a serious source of filth and spent a day chasing after Wade and me with a whirring device like a miniature Roto-Rooter.

"Then," Ellie went on, "there's Jemmy." And when I looked blank: "Well, if Walt Henderson murdered Cory Trow and we could prove it . . ."

"Oh!" I said, understanding suddenly. "He might go to jail. And behind bars, Henderson couldn't try to kill Jemmy anymore, could he?"

Because as Jemmy had said, Henderson flew solo; there was no one on the outside to do his bidding. His subcontractors wouldn't return to the job either, since he wouldn't be around to pay them. And as Jemmy had also pointed out, no one else cared.

"But we don't know for sure what happened and we're a long way from finding out," Ellie concluded. "And right now it's time for me to take Lee over to preschool."

Leonora's eyes popped open. "Kids!" she screeched gleefully. Ellie's answering smile was beatific despite the painful eardrum injury she'd undoubtedly just suffered.

"Jake," she told me, "why don't you start by clearing all your other chores up today so you'll be free for tomorrow?"

She eyed the refrigerator leak meaningfully. I could have called a repair person but for what that would cost I could also have bought Greenland, kept all our frozen food up there, and had it flown in by private jet.

And it wasn't the first time that refrigerator had sprung a leak. In fact I already had the necessary replacement part; all I needed was to install it.

The breeze rattled the antique window harder and the pool on the floor enlarged. Then the phone rang and it wasn't the Prize Patrol calling any more than it had been the night before.

"Mom?" said Sam. Ellie waved and went out.

"Hey, Mom?" An ice cube rattled in his glass. It was ten o'clock in the morning.

"What is it, Sam?" I asked, feeling my throat close with the old, familiar sorrow. Upon reflection, I was still fairly sure he hadn't been driving drunk last night. But today . . .

"Listen," he slurred into the phone. "I got news."

Today he was fully loaded.

● ● ●

Sam wanted a visit from me at his house on Liberty Street, for reasons he seemed unable to articulate on the phone. But given a choice between confronting a drunken Sam and stepping in front of a high-balling locomotive, I'll take the train.

So after he hung up I dragged the refrigerator away from the wall. The trouble was with the drip pan that sits atop the rear compressor collecting humidity drainage. Meanwhile the compressor itself gets warm, evaporating the water.

Until the drip pan gets a hole in it, which in my experience happens only a few moments after the refrigerator is delivered. Replacing the pan requires a pair of pliers, a tubeful of gooey stuff called thermal mastic, and every single swear word you know plus several you will undoubtedly invent on the spot.

"Um, what are you doing?" Wade inquired thirty minutes later when he came down from his workshop in the ell of our old house. There when he was not being Eastport's premier harbor pilot, he repaired old firearms, reloaded shotgun shells, and performed other tasks closely related to the exploding of gunpowder in confined spaces.

At the moment I felt a lot like that gunpowder. Gritting my teeth, I used the pliers to give the nut on the bolt holding the drip pan down another half turn. It was all there was room for in the tiny space between the compressor and the refrigerator's myriad other internal parts.

This, I thought clearly, is why the repair people get paid the big bucks. "Fixing," I answered Wade, "this darned . . . Ouch!"

The pliers slipped off the nut suddenly, sending my hand yet again into the sharp metal corner of the drip pan.

"Oh," he said. And then, accurately sensing my mood, "Would you like help, or should I just go muck myself?"

Only he didn't say "muck." A rueful laugh burst from me just as the nut finally revolved off the top of the bolt.

"Thanks, but now that I've got it off I don't think I will need . . . Oof," I said, wiggling the loosened drip pan and frowning.

The bolt, permanently soldered onto the compressor, stuck up through the pan's middle. To remove the pan you simply lifted it off the bolt. Or you would if there'd been any clearance between the pan and the bolt's end.

Which there wasn't. I turned and tilted the pan first one direction and then another, yanking at it with increasing force. At one point I braced both feet on the refrigerator; this didn't seem likely to work but I was desperate.

Wisely, by now Wade had gone back up into his workshop where I heard him whistling, trying, I suppose, to drown out what was now becoming a really creative bout of snarling and cursing.

But finally Bella came downstairs and found me struggling with the appliance. "Missus," she said, taking in the futility of what I was doing.

The drip pan sat askew on the compressor top; I couldn't get it off, and now I couldn't get it back on again, either. "Jake," I corrected automatically, giving the pan a final yank.

"What is it, Bella?" If I couldn't get the darn thing off and I couldn't replace it properly, then . . .

"It's . . . the doctor's room," she replied hesitantly. That was what she called the small guest room we'd turned into a sickroom for Victor, the room that he had died in.

I sat up abruptly, bonking my head hard on the windowsill behind me. "What about it?" I demanded, rubbing the bumped spot with the hand I'd wounded on the sharp part of the refrigerator.

I hadn't seen Victor since the previous morning, and Wade had pretty well convinced me that *that* had been a hallucination, just as I'd been trying to tell myself.

"He ain't passed," Bella said, peering at the ravaged guts of the old appliance; I'd been working on it for over an hour. "Hand me a rag," she added, and I obeyed. Not that I thought she could do much about the situation, but it was dusty back there so I figured she just wanted to clean up.

"What do you mean, 'passed'?" I asked.

She merely spared me a glance of disdain while wiping grime off the compressor and the screw mounts holding its support frame tightly to the back of the appliance. "Screwdriver," she commanded.

Six minutes later she had the frame loosened and lowered far enough to get the old drip pan off and the new one on, all because she'd bothered to wipe the work area clean so she could see what she was doing.

And let that be a lesson to me, I thought. "Finished," she pronounced.

But when I plugged the refrigerator back in, awful sounds came from it, like something inside yammering to get out. Next I noticed that the spots I'd braced my feet against now resembled the impact craters of bombs. And that the big dents had what smelled like ammonia hissing out of them.

Only it wasn't ammonia; it was freon gas.

Poisonous freon gas. And then what with summoning the fire department and getting Wade, Bella, the dogs, the cat, and myself all outside before we could be gassed to death by my unfortunate repair attempt, Bella didn't get a chance until later—while we watched the firemen rush in wearing hazardous-materials masks—to finish telling me what she'd seen upstairs in what she called the doctor's room.

The doctor himself.

●   ●   ●

I spent the rest of the day resisting the strong temptation to drive back up to the lake and check on Jemmy again.

After all, I told myself firmly, unless I sat there guarding him myself with one of Wade's shotguns, there wasn't much I could do about him. And if I *did* go, Henderson might follow me and find out where Jemmy was.

If he didn't already know. So when I got done telephoning the helpful fellow at the appliance store, I turned to the job of rust abatement on the outside of the house. Like this:

Sand the rust off the nail head, tap the nail in with a nail set—like hitting a nail with *another* nail—put some paintable caulking compound into the resulting dimple, smooth it, and apply a burst of rust-inhibiting paint from a spray can.

Keep a brush handy to brush out any paint drips and continue until your shoulder seizes up from fatigue or all the rust spots are covered. I worked until I'd done two more rows of clapboards all the way around the house, then went in and helped Bella wipe off our cold food items before placing them into the new refrigerator.

Funny how a repair date takes days or even weeks to arrange, but a replacement appliance can show up in about twenty minutes; luckily Prill the Doberman had met the delivery guy before, so she didn't delay matters by threatening to snack on him. "Lovely," Bella pronounced it when we were finished, though by tomorrow she would be wiping out the vegetable bins with Windex.

Next came dinner, dishes, animal care, and a sad examination of my checkbook balance after the refrigerator debacle. Thus by eleven-thirty that night after a discouraging roof-repair update from my father—

Those rafters had enough rot in them to sink a schooner, and did I by any chance have any heavy-duty tarps to cover up all the holes he was making up there? Because as we all knew, sooner or later a major roof repair would trigger torrential rain. . . .

—I should've been out cold. But instead my eyes were as wide open as if they'd been propped that way on toothpicks.

Finally I went to bed. I thought Wade was asleep already but his hand slipped over to cover mine sympathetically.

"Sorry," I murmured. "I didn't mean to wake you."

"You didn't. Bad day, huh?"

"Not all of it. Just . . ."

"Yeah." I'd told him about Sam calling up drunk.

"Sometimes I think I spend half my time denying to myself what I know about Sam, that he's in real trouble. The other half I spend believing it. But I haven't the faintest idea what to do about it."

"Mmm. We could try another intervention."

If you ever want to re-create authentic medieval torture, try an intervention. "I guess."

Three months earlier, with the aid of a counselor from the health center, we'd gotten together to confront Sam. He raged, wept, apologized, and swore to us that he would try the rehab place we'd arranged for him. Then he'd eluded us all at the airport and gone on a bender that lasted weeks.

"Wade?" I said again a while later. But by then he really was asleep; I slid out of bed.

Monday and Prill danced happily at the foot of the stairs. "Come on, dogs," I said, pulling on a heavy sweater and leashing the pair of them. "Let's go out."

The night was silent, not a car or a footstep breaking the hush. Mist crept in the glow under the streetlights and the chilly air carried the perfume of buds fattening on the maple branches, sticky green sap-bombs getting ready to burst open.

The dogs romped ahead, snuffling at each stray scent as we climbed the Sullivan Street hill between the Quoddy Marine store and the weed-tangled ruins of what once had been a row of nineteenth-century houses, now reduced to concrete foundations half hidden among weeds.

Partway up the hill I paused to look back over the town, the gleaming black front windows of the shops on Water Street and the empty, sodium-lit expanse of the breakwater half surrounding the boat basin. At this hour I could almost believe Victor wasn't the only ghost wandering Eastport; in the dark with the long-gone dwellings looming invisibly around me, it felt more like we all were.

As I continued uphill, real, physically present dwellings rose from the fenced yards. A few lights here and there in the shaded windows suggested that I wasn't the only sleepless one tonight, either. Finally I stopped before a bungalow with a low sloping roof, enclosed front porch, and leaded-glass ornamentation in the windows. A small yard showed evidence of gardening: mulched beds and raised boxes heaped with new loam.

A light was on here, too, and a figure moved behind one of the shades. It was Henny Trow's house. Without pausing—I didn't want time to second-guess myself, for this was where without letting myself know it I'd been headed all along—I went up to the door and knocked.

The woman who answered was tall and slender, with frizzy dark hair cut short around a narrow, full-lipped face. Her dark brows arched questioningly when she saw me but her red eyes, puffy with weeping, showed no surprise.

"You're Jake Tiptree. Bella Diamond pointed you out to me, one time. She thinks a lot of you, you know." Henny stepped aside to let me in.

"The dogs—" I began apologetically, still not knowing quite what I'd intended. Prill eyed the woman doubtfully until I said it was okay, then relaxed.

"Never mind. Bring them along." Cory Trow's grieving mother walked away from me into a room furnished with threadbare rugs, messily heaped bookshelves, and chairs and lamps well arranged for reading. A big round oak table was covered with notebooks and papers.

I followed, the dogs panting and yanking in all directions in this new place. "Let them off the leash, why don't you?" Henny said without looking back. "It doesn't matter, there's nothing in here they can hurt."

She wore a black cowel-neck sweater, slim black jeans, and black leather slippers with little fake jewels on the uppers. A plain gold band gleamed on her wedding finger as she took a cut-crystal decanter from the sideboard and poured two drinks.

"I'm so sorry about your son," I said as she handed me one. Freed of their restraints, the dogs hustled around the room in an orgy of sniffing and wagging.

"Thank you. Please sit down." The upholstered armchair was as shabby as the rest of the furniture, but comfortable. And the drink was a good old single-malt Scotch; sipping it, I couldn't repress a small sigh of appreciation.

"I'm sorry to barge in on you. I was out walking, I saw your light, and . . ."

And ever since we found him, I wanted to say, *the sight of your hanged son has been with me, dangling from a mental rafter as if the only real haunted place is inside my head.* But I didn't say it; this wasn't about my feelings.

She drank from her own glass and set it down with a look of resolve as if she'd have preferred emptying the bottle.

"Yes," she said. "You saw that I was up, probably imagined me walking the floor in my awful grief, alone."

Close enough. But before I could say something to blunt the sharp edges of the image her words summoned, she went on. "Well, I'm alone, all right. Cory took care of that. But unfortunately there's a small problem with the rest of your scenario."

She took another swallow. "The problem is that my son was a thoroughgoing little shit."

The dogs settled by the hearth where a sulky wood fire was emitting more smoke than heat. To cover my surprise I got up and re-arranged the logs without asking permission.

She wasn't fooled. "Don't pretend you're not shocked. What a thing to say about your dead son, right? That he made your life a misery from the moment he was born. Ruined it, really."

I sat again. "Drove off anyone who tried to care about you. Did his best to break your heart," she added. "And now this."

A sob threatened her; she washed it down with the rest of her drink. "Now this," she repeated.

Time to cut to the chase. I didn't know how much the bottle had held when she started, but it was half empty now. "So you're satisfied that he killed himself?"

She didn't even pause at the suggestion that it might not have been suicide. "Oh, of course he did. Cory made everyone wish he'd never lived. And when he got done doing that, he decided to make me wish I never had, either."

I sipped cautiously at my drink, thinking one of us ought to stay sober and it wasn't going to be her. "But there must've been a more immediate reason . . ."

If Cory Trow *had* killed himself, there was no point pursuing it further. In reply, her strong features said the answer to my question was obvious. "He didn't want to go to jail, is all. And he was going to, he'd pushed that Henderson man to the limit." She met my gaze. "Cory was never much for realizing the long-term consequences of his actions."

I tipped my head questioningly. "Henderson's team of legal attack dogs made sure he was convicted," she explained. "Now it was time to finish him off. And running would only make it worse, of course, but Cory wouldn't have thought about that."

"And you asked Bella to ask us to find him because . . . ?"

Her dark eyes staring into the revived fire, she bit her lip before answering. "He was my son," she said at last. "He needed help and it was still my duty to help him if I could."

Her strong-boned face would've been ugly if it hadn't held a lively intelligence and the kind of emotional honesty that always trumps mere looks. Right now the raw anguish in it was as painful to me as if I'd stuck my hand in the fire.

I changed the subject. "How'd you know Bella, anyway?"

A smile curved her lips. "Oh, I'd hired her a few times. As you can see, I'm not much for housework. She took a liking to me, I can't imagine why."

I could. Bella had a soft spot for odd ducks, me included.

"I couldn't afford to keep her. But when Cory didn't come home I didn't know who else to call," Henny said bleakly. "Those horrible buddies he'd been running with were certainly no help."

"I thought you'd have someone here with you now, though," I ventured. "Relatives or . . ."

She laughed bitterly. "That would be nice, wouldn't it? But I don't have any. Parents gone, no siblings. My husband went off to the Persian Gulf six weeks after we got married and never came back. Jeep accident."

Thus the wedding ring. "But you were pregnant?" She nodded, then got up to refill her own glass, waving the decanter at me.

What the heck, it wasn't as if I had to drive.

"And," she went on as she poured, "he was the baby from hell. Then he became the kid from hell, and then the teenager from . . . oh, God."

Her hands shook; she regained control of them with a swallow of liquor. "Killing himself would've been another angry impulse, that's all. He had so many of them . . . but I tried. I really did."

I believed her. And once again I knew just how she felt.

"What about the life insurance?" I probed. "And this story I heard of him having a wife and baby . . ."

She sat up straight, nodding agreement. "In Canada. One of his friends' mothers called to pry, wanted to know if I knew I had a grandchild. Which I didn't, but she was thrilled to fill me in, of course." Her lips tightened. "The upshot is that what she told me is apparently true. Too much detail in the story for it not to be. But that's all I know. I haven't heard from the girl. I'm not sure if *she* even knows yet that he's . . ."

Her face crumpled. I cut in swiftly. "And the insurance? I'm not sure I understand why a boy like your son would . . ."

Would care if anyone benefited by his death. The unfinished sentence hung cruelly in the air between us.

But she took no offense. Harsh reality offered more reliable comfort than illusion, as we both understood all too well.

"It was part of a crazy plan he had to fake his death somehow and make a lot of money off it," she answered bluntly.

"May I see the policy?"

In response, she left the room; while she was gone I examined a small collection of Native American baskets she kept on a shelf, local artefacts made of sweetgrass and pounded poplar decorated with porcupine quills. At last she returned with a folded sheaf of boilerplate pages.

"He'd told me about it," she said as I scanned the thing. It looked correct—the no-pay-for-suicide clause was near the end, among the other perfectly proper exceptions—but now I had a new question.

Where'd he gotten the money for the premium payment? And who'd sold it to him?

"I don't know," his mother said. "I refused to participate and Cory stopped talking about it. That's what he always did when he knew I disapproved of anything."

She shook her head sadly. "But he must've bought the policy anyway. On the Internet, maybe? I found it when I was looking through his dresser, after the police . . ."

This time she did sob, pressing her fists to her breastbone. When the spasm passed, she continued. "With Cory it was always something. And this marriage . . ."

She looked up helplessly at me. "Maybe his wife paid for the insurance. Maybe that's why he married her, she has money. But as I said, I don't really know anything about it. Only what I've been told."

She reflected a moment. "The marriage, too . . . besides cash, he might've thought it was a legal way for him to get into Canada if he ever was in real trouble. With a wife and child there, the immigration people might . . ."

"Let him become a citizen? Well, maybe," I said doubtfully. I didn't know what the law said about that.

But maybe Cory hadn't known either. And maybe it didn't matter. If he'd killed himself before the suicide clause on his insurance policy expired, it suggested to me that he was big on schemes, not so much on the research required to make them pan out.

I gestured at the multitude of papers on the table in the dining area. There was a laptop computer there, too, and a pair of reading glasses. "Your work?"

Double doors from the dining area led to another room, smaller; a generous closet or possibly a sewing room. "I write newsletters and edit them," she said. "Freelance, mostly, for ad agencies, public relations firms, and so on. I started out in Boston when Cory was small, but once you've got clients you can do it long-distance if you're good at keeping in touch with them. And when he got older I thought . . ."

"A change of environment?" I could have told her it didn't work; not permanently. The geographic cure just put a brief gloss of novelty on everything.

But she knew that now, too.

Seeing me rise, the dogs scrambled to their feet.

"Thanks for coming in," Henny Trow said. "I didn't think I wanted company, but . . ."

"No problem. Call me if you feel like talking. But listen, if you don't mind one more question now . . ."

Her frizzy head tipped inquiringly. "Why there?" I asked. "Why d'you suppose he picked the barn on Henderson's property, of all places, to take his own life?"

And why that method? I might have added. There were easier ways. But she only shrugged. "To punish Mr. Henderson, I guess. To make it his problem. Cory was like that, he'd find your weak spot and exploit it if he could. But if that didn't work he got vindictive. And," she added, "it's where he'd been meeting the Henderson girl. It came out in his trial, that it was where they'd . . . get together."

A low light burned in the adjoining room, over a sewing machine with some fabric on it. She saw me looking at it.

"There's a woman here who designs clothing," she explained. "Special things, hand-dyed on silks. I do the sewing for her."

Eastport was full of hidden geniuses. "So you're a woman of many talents."

Henny shrugged. "An old hobby. I've always sewed in my spare time. My own clothes, and Cory's when he was little." Her eyes narrowed in pain again at the memory. "And writing's not exactly a big-money occupation, so I can use the extra cash."

She stepped back from the door. It was my cue to go. "Thanks for the drink."

The fabric was blue. I bent to leash the dogs as the door closed behind me and the light in the living room went out. But she was probably still in there, sitting in the dark, not going upstairs to bed on this first night after her son's death.

She'd be trying to make it last, this brief time when only a day still separated them. Breathing air he'd breathed, touching the things he'd touched, before it all whirled away into memory.

Before he was really gone. But there was nothing I could do about that. In the darkness the world tilted a bit under my feet: that Scotch. The night air cleared my head, though; by the time I finished climbing the rest of the Sullivan Street hill, I was awake and glad to be out of Henny Trow's too-warm living room.

And still thinking about that blue cloth. Which was why as a car sped uphill from behind me I didn't notice at first just how fast it was coming.

Its headlights brightened ominously as I reached the narrow part of the street, without sidewalks and bounded by granite outcroppings, hemming me in so there was nowhere to escape.

I drew the dogs nearer to give the car plenty of room. As if on signal it veered and roared straight at me, its headlights swelling to blinding disks.

"Hey!" Fright made me shout as I flattened myself against the granite. "Prill! Monday!" I yelled, yanking the dogs in tight as the car's lights dazzled me.

Pressing the animals to my legs, I leaned desperately into a niche in the granite, sucking in my breath as the vehicle sped by with mere inches to spare. Exhaust fumes billowed into my face and gravel flew, stinging as it hit me.

Then after what seemed like minutes but was really only a couple of seconds, the car roared away. A hundred yards distant it stopped briefly, brake lights brightening, and I knew it would come back.

Instead, with a shriek of tires it took the turn past the water tower and into Hillside Cemetery, engine howling as it sped toward Clark Street and the fastest way out of town.

Tightening both dogs' leashes I hurried us all to where the sidewalk resumed, then paused to listen. Nothing. Slowly I began walking home, the animals trotting ahead unfazed as if to say a little accidental unpleasantness was a small price to pay for the pleasure of an extra walk.

But I didn't think it was accidental. And given Sam's near miss of the night before, I doubted that it was coincidence.

```
From: hlrb@mainetel.net <Horace
Robotham>
To: ddimaio@miskatonic.edu <Dave
DiMaio>
Subj: Eastport book

Dave


   Thanks for the news on the old book.
Now that it's happened I'm uncertain
whether to be elated or terrified time
will tell, I suppose. I'll keep a weather
eye out for Merkle but doubt he'll come
```

around. I agree he's a weird duck, not to
be trusted.

I'm afraid I can't agree with your
thoughts re misleading the book's owner,
though. For one thing, she must decide
whether or not to go on living in the
house where it was found. I think we've
got to play it straight with her.

But all that is a topic separate from
what is to be done with the book itself.
One potentially good result of telling
the owner all we know about it might be
that she won't want it back.

Meanwhile Lang says nix on the vacation idea for now. He's deep in research—
sends bookishly distracted greetings.

Horace

Chapter 6

*A loose flap of stair carpet is a
potentially fatal trap. Tack it
down at once.*
—Tiptree's Tips

Y ou don't think *she* did it, do you?" Ellie asked the next morning.

I pretended to consider. "Killed Cory? Hmm, a professional killer with a fine personal motive versus his own mother."

There'd been no car parked at her house, and even if there had been, Henny hadn't had time last night to get into one and come after me. "Nope," I said.

I was perched on a stepladder smoothing patching compound into the holes created when I'd pulled the plastic down from the kitchen window frames a day earlier.

"And you're sure it was deliberate? Someone actually *tried* to hit you?" Ellie pressed me.

"Oh, of course someone did," I said crossly. The patching compound, a gray substance with the consistency of loose mud, had a habit of dripping off the putty knife before I could smoosh it into the hole. Some of the compound fell in a glob to the hardwood floor behind the washing machine. But I could remove it later—fortunately, patching compound cleaned up easily if you let it dry thoroughly—with one of the stray socks huddled together back there, too; so *that* was where my good gray argyle went.

"The car swerved all the way over across the road to get at me," I said, finally managing to get a small dab of the patching compound onto the woodwork, approximately where it belonged. Awkwardly I smoothed it in.

"If there hadn't been a big enough crevice in that granite along the street, I'd be as mushy as *this* stuff now," I added, waving the putty knife.

Not smart. Some of the patching compound flew off the knife and onto the windowpane, and the rest went in my hair. And hair is the one thing even dried patching compound doesn't like to clean up out of.

"Somebody knows we're snooping," I declared. What else could explain two recent attempts at vehicular homicide?

Careless driving, maybe; still, I thought odds were against a pair of such similar accidents so close together.

"Well then, have you told Bob Arnold about it? Because if someone's going around trying to run you and Sam over with cars," said Ellie, "Bob's the first one who ought to know."

"Sure, call the cops." I clambered to the floor under Cat's cross-eyed gaze. She'd adopted the new refrigerator without any hesitation; it was the looking down upon people she enjoyed, not a particular spot from which to do it.

"I should tell Bob," I went on, "that someone tried hitting me, *and* just by coincidence somebody did almost the same thing to Sam, only a night earlier."

Cat looked scornful. "And I should *also* tell him how sorry I am that no, I couldn't recognize the car again."

Its headlights had blinded me. "Nor did I get a look at the driver, and I didn't get a plate number, either, not even part of one. And neither did Sam."

In Cat's opinion, if you couldn't leap gracefully from things, then you shouldn't get up onto them. Helpfully she demonstrated the technique by launching herself acrobatically, landing on my shoulder with every single one of her sharp claws fully extended, and teetering there for an excruciatingly painful moment before exiting the room.

I let loose some of the curses I'd practiced while working on the old refrigerator. But there was no point to chasing her; if there had been, her nine lives would've been used up years ago.

"I don't know, though," Ellie said, packing oatmeal cookies into a plastic box. At the last minute she'd decided a sheet cake wasn't enough dessert for Cory's memorial, set to start in twenty minutes.

I wiped the thickest globs of patching compound out of my hair with a wet paper towel as she went on. "What if his mom got fed up with him, maybe decided she deserved payback for all the heartache he'd caused her, got him to Henderson's barn somehow?" she speculated. "It's an awful idea, but . . ."

Yes. It was. "But she *would* have understood the suicide limitation on the policy," I said. "Or assumed it. That kind of thing is common knowledge to most people, wouldn't you say?"

Just maybe not to a teenaged wise guy like Cory, with so little real-world experience or idea of how anything worked. "As for that fabric I spotted at her place, if it was the same stuff I saw on his hand, he probably got it snooping in her things, looking for money," I said. It was the reasonable explanation. "Hooked a scrap of it on his fingernail, it was still there when he went to the barn." Because he hadn't been in the nail-cleaning habit either, I recalled.

"I used to hide money from Sam all the time," I added. Although in the end my own wallet had been the best hiding place; after a while of finding only a few pennies for his trouble, Sam had stopped looking there. Even today I kept my walking-around cash in my pants pocket.

"You know," Ellie said, surveying my patch job on the window frame, "if you just smoothed that some more with the edge of the putty knife . . ."

"Yes, and if my grandmother had wheels she'd be a tricycle," I responded irritably, still rubbing my cat-scratched shoulder. And then I saw it, over by the sink where my dead ex-husband used to stand with a cup of coffee, criticizing me while scanning for tasty edibles he could pluck up and devour.

A Victor-ish shape. Resolutely I scraped patching compound from the putty knife into the wastebasket, and when I looked again the shape had disappeared.

"We should go," Ellie said. She hadn't noticed anything. "I'd like to get all the food on the tables before they start."

For the event she wore a lime green turtleneck under a denim smock, red-and-green-striped leggings that would've turned my calves into tree stumps but on hers looked divine, and blue suede clogs.

"Okay." I surveyed the kitchen. Cat Dancing had returned to the top of the refrigerator; thumping from above said my father was on the roof again, and the dogs snored in their beds.

And Wade was at work, while Sam was I-didn't-know-where: situation normal. "I guess I can leave for an hour without the whole house falling down completely in my absence," I said.

As if in reply a horrific crash came from upstairs, followed by a cracking sound, a much larger thump, and a string of profanity that put my refrigerator-inspired curses to shame.

All suggesting that my father had just fallen through the roof into the attic.

• • •

"Leave me alone," he groused minutes later as Bella dabbed blood from his forehead. "I'm fine. Damned rotten sheathing."

Luckily the attic had contained a pile of old mattresses some earlier tenant had thought too unattractive to use but too good to throw out. And he'd landed on them.

Mostly. "Hush up and sit still," Bella told him, inspecting the gash over his eye. "You look," she allowed reluctantly, "as if you'll live through the day."

"Hrmph," he growled at her. He was the kind of person who if he suffered a calamity and survived, all he wanted was for you to forget it.

But I was the kind who if he tore so much as a hangnail I had to keep an eye on him for an hour or so, to reassure myself. So over his grumpy protests we took him along to Cory's memorial gathering, where as usual he gravitated to the prettiest female in the room.

"My goodness," Ellie said at the sight of Walter Henderson's daughter Jennifer flirting shamelessly with my father. "Sociable, isn't she?"

The church hall with its white wallboard interior, low ceiling, and green tiled floor still smelled faintly of baked beans and dishwashing liquid from the fund-raising community supper held there the night before. The church ladies had helpfully left all the tables up, decorated with centerpieces of construction-paper spring flowers that the Saturday-afternoon Bible-study children had made.

"That's putting it mildly," I replied. Tall, blonde, and so tan that she made the rest of us look like we had blood diseases, Jen Henderson resembled an ad for vitamin supplements. Or surfboards.

Or both. She was wearing a pale blue cashmere sweater over a white wool skirt so short that I could have used it for a belt. While Ellie went to cut more cake for the memorial service attendees, I approached Jennifer; my father retreated tactfully.

"I know who you are," she said when I introduced myself and offered condolences on the death of her friend.

She wore unusual perfume, a faintly exotic-smelling blend of sandalwood and lime, and she'd inherited her father's eye color: cool blue sapphire. "You and that other one," she angled her head at Ellie, "you're who found him. But he was no friend of mine," she added. "Don't get the wrong idea about that."

Those amazing eyes hardened at some thought she didn't share with me as around us the few others in attendance—teachers from the high school, a gaggle of rowdy, dungaree-clad young men, a dozen other adults who I guessed might be schoolteachers' wives and husbands—mingled in quiet conversation. But no one looked as if she could be Cory's rumored wife.

"I don't even know why I came," Jen declared. "What a waste of time."

I was starting to think so, too. Some of Cory's buddies had begun engaging in horseplay near the refreshments table. My dad ambled over and with a few words urged them in the direction of the cake; sullenly, they complied.

Then another girl approached us: mid- to late twenties with a jaunty, confident way of moving and short dark hair done up in purple-streaked gel spikes.

"Hello," she began amiably, grinning at me. "I'm Ann Radham, Jen's hipster sidekick." She had multiply pierced ears, a tiny gold lip ring, and horn-rimmed glasses on her snub nose.

"Don't mind her," Ann added to me as Jen glowered. "She's irony-deficient."

"I want a drink," Jen Henderson declared in petulant tones, ignoring her friend's quip and looking around fretfully as if wondering why, now that her wish had been so clearly expressed, the beverage didn't appear.

"Later," Ann told her comfortingly. "Go and talk to people, now, like we said you would. Just make conversation. It'll look weird if you don't."

So that was the plan: social damage control. I wondered why either of them cared. But Jen obeyed her friend, her sun-streaked hair moving glossily on her shoulders as she turned away.

One of the teachers stepped to the front of the room and began reciting an earnest homily about "our friend Cory." But Cory's actual friends, a spray-can-huffing, video-game-addled bunch of knuckleheads if I ever saw any, stared as if a Martian had stood up and begun quacking incomprehensible syllables.

"Jennifer's feeling tense," Ann Radham said apologetically. "This has all been a shock."

"I suppose." I let skepticism creep into my tone. To shock Jen Henderson you'd need the large, economy-sized brickbat, I'd already decided.

Ann glanced at me. "Not everyone swims in the deep end of the pool," she said, acknowledging my unspoken assessment. "But Jen's a good kid. She just thinks everyone blames her now. For what happened to Cory."

I thought about that while taking in Ann Radham's remarkable costume: a pink Hello Kitty T-shirt and pearl-buttoned sweater, baggy painter's pants whose multihued stains looked deliberately applied, and turquoise jelly shoes. Her earrings, peeping beneath spikes of that eye-catching purple hair, were Betty Boop figurines, and on her wedding finger was a Captain Marvel decoder ring.

My own slim jeans, white shirt, and penny loafers suddenly felt terminally dowdy, especially with the patching-compound hair decoration I wore. "Should they?" I asked. "Blame her?"

Ann made a disparaging face. "Of course not. That's ridiculous. The criminal charges were all her father's idea, that whole stalking thing. She just went along with it because he told her to—I mean, he *is* her dad. As for Cory killing himself . . ."

Across the room one of the knuckleheads appeared at Jen's side and began talking to her, probably on a dare. Smirking, he bounced on sneakered heels while his pals looked on, elbowing one another, massively entertained. After a moment of this Jen turned coldly away, which to his pals seemed the most hilarious thing of all.

"Cory was a strange ranger," Ann said. "Jen just liked him for a while 'cause he thought she was so glamorous. Like a movie star, you know? And he thought she was smart."

At my look she went on, "Yeah, maybe Jen's no intellectual giant but just look at *his* friends. It's like the cast of *Dumb and Dumber* over there."

"You've got a point." While I watched, Ellie tried her luck at talking to one of the boys: no dice. Maybe if her voice had come out of an Xbox or Game Boy, they'd have paid attention to it. But otherwise, as they say, *fuhgedaboutit.*

On the other hand here was Ann herself: smart, friendly, maybe willing to converse in a little more detail about Jennifer Henderson.

I broached the subject delicately. "Come on," Ann replied, unfooled by my approach. "If you're thinking she had anything to do with . . ."

"To do with what?" Jen demanded, at my elbow suddenly. And without waiting for an answer, "I'm going to get the car, this is too boring. You can come or not," she added rudely to Ann Radham, "but I'm out of here."

Her good looks and long, athletic stride turned heads as she departed. "Do you know anything about the wife Cory's supposed to have had?" I asked Ann. "Or a baby?"

The growl of a sports car engine sounded outside, followed by an imperious-sounding horn toot, sharp as a summons. Ann wadded her napkin into her styrofoam cup, ignoring my questions. "Got to go."

"Duty calls, eh?" I said lightly, but putting an edge into it. One thing was already clear; Ann was second banana in this friendship.

If it was a friendship; something didn't mesh about the pair. Ann paused, eyeing me. "Like I said before, Jen's a nice girl. Going to college on a softball scholarship this fall; she wouldn't have been keeping in touch with Cory anyway once she got there. She's a pitcher, got a fifty-five-mile-an-hour fastball, if you can imagine."

I could; as a physical specimen, Jen Henderson rocked.

"And I don't know what you two are up to," Ann went on, glancing over at Ellie, "but she's a fun kid. And if you think there's anything else going on, you are so on the wrong track."

"Your loyalty is admirable." But I must have looked unconvinced. Ann shook her head; the Betty Boop figurines danced.

"I'll be at the Bayside later if you want to talk," she said.

Oh boy, did I.

• • •

At the time, the Bayside Café on Dyer Street was the place where Eastport's young smart set would meet to eat, drink, and socialize. An old tube-tired Schwinn bike leaned against the wall outside and a

poster on the door still listed the live music acts that had been sched-
uled for the previous Sunday evening.

To my surprise Ann Radham's name was on the poster. As I entered she looked up from behind what appeared to be all the percus-
sion instruments in the world, on the tiny stage tucked into one corner
at the front of the café.

Ranged within reach were base, snare, and tenor drums, crash and
suspended cymbals, maracas and gongs and what I thought might be
a set of temple blocks, plus more I didn't recognize.

"Jennifer get her drink?" I asked.

Ann nodded. "We went back to her place, she's got a stash of
those little bottles they give you on airplanes."

At my raised eyebrows she added, "I never get asked my age, and
I don't drink anyway, so I save them for her."

She picked up a pair of drumsticks and began tapping a rhythm
out quietly while I glanced around, taking in the casual, post-lunch atmosphere and the smell of fresh-baked chocolate brownies, a specialty
of the house.

"My bike outside?" she asked, and I indicated that the Schwinn
was still there; no sports car for Ann, apparently. The perks of friendship didn't extend quite that far.

The Bayside's tables and chairs were all old-fashioned wooden
kitchen sets, painted bright white and mostly occupied now by the café's
usual daytime crowd: laptop-carrying, alternative-music-listening young
consumers in the eighteen-to-thirty-five range, Internet-savvy and fully
aware that their tastes in everything from art to xerography now ran
most of the economy.

Over the past couple of years Eastport had become a magnet for
these young adults, their arrival mirroring the back-to-the-land movement here in the sixties, only with electronics. Just as pleased with
themselves about it, too, but not in an unpleasant way. It seemed part
of this group's collective persona in fact, that they were all so darned
nice; right now, for instance, a third of them were chatting amiably on
cell phones, not a raised voice in the bunch.

It made me yearn a little for the good old days of Johnny Rotten and the Sex Pistols, if you want to know the truth. And speaking of famous musicians, Ann Radham finished a muted but powerful minute-and-a-half solo performance that if you closed your eyes, you'd have thought it was Buddy Rich.

I was blown away and said so. "Thanks. That and a buck fifty will get me a cup of coffee," she replied, getting up from behind the drum kit.

She seemed at ease with me already, but why wouldn't she be? Ann Radham might be quirky but she was also clearly the kind of girl who'd had a good, strong sense of herself by about age two, I estimated admiringly.

"Come on, I gotta eat something," she declared, gesturing for me to follow her.

We crossed the well-lit room with its soft-drink bar, wide-screen TV tuned soundlessly to CNN, and open kitchen at the back. While she ordered I got coffee from the self-serve counter and took it to a table up front by the big window.

The place was decorated with movie posters from the forties and fifties, big living trees in tubs, and kitschy ceramic items: slinky panther planters, Smokey the Bear cookie jars, *Uncle Sam Wants You* mugs. In one corner stood a man-sized gorilla doll with a Red Sox cap on its head.

Ann received her order and looked around for me, hesitating for a moment as if she'd have preferred some other table. But she came over with her food: green salad, no dressing, a grapefruit soda. While she tucked into it hungrily, I asked a passing waiter to put it all on my check.

"Good salad?" I asked. She nodded, chewing. And after a sip of soda:

"Yeah. The sandwiches and cake at the memorial were pretty to look at. But my body's screaming for vitamins."

Mine was screaming to be stretched on a beach somewhere, no worries allowed; on my way here I'd detoured past Sam's house, found it locked and the shades drawn, a bunch of mail uncollected from the box.

"Not that grapefruit soda's going to supply any," she added with a guilty grin. "But I love the stuff."

Outside Sam's place the Fiat sat scratched and mud-streaked, looking as if it hadn't been moved in a while, windshield fogged from the inside.

"And a spoonful of sugar makes the medicine, et cetera," Ann concluded, forking up more greenery.

The car not having been moved was good, though, under the circumstances. Probably he was still out for the count following yesterday's binge, and after what had nearly happened to me on Sullivan Street, that was fine. I especially didn't want him driving until I'd had a chance to talk to him.

"So what's a hipster, anyway?" I asked Ann, not wanting to go at her too directly right off the bat.

She shook her head. "Who knows? Twenty-to-thirtyish, urban, with a certain ... um, shared sensibility. Certain clubs, certain music ... anti-fashion clothes, usually." She indicated her own garb, peered at me through the horn-rims.

"Overly self-aware, for sure," she went on. "But the bottom line is that if you're a hipster you can do pretty much whatever the rest of the world does, as long as you just kind of stay a little emotionally separated from doing it *while* you're doing it."

She tipped her head thoughtfully. "Like, these friends of mine were in one of those chain-restaurant steak houses the other week. The kind that once you're inside, you could be anywhere?"

I nodded to show I understood. We didn't have much of that kind of thing in downeast Maine; there wasn't enough population density here to make it profitable. When Ellie and I went to Bangor for shopping or whatever, we ate at an Olive Garden or an Outback Steakhouse just for the novelty value.

"So they had steaks there," Ann went on. "And the food was fine. I mean it has to be, right? That's the whole idea. But to them, all they talked about was what it meant to the culture, these, like, identical feeding troughs all over the country, all exactly alike." She devoured a pepper strip. "But when hipsters get old enough to be really running things, in like twenty years? *Then* look out. They think they're all about the individual, but what that really means is figuring out how to sell stuff that way."

A chunk of pickled artichoke heart followed the pepper strip. "Pretty soon there'll be a microchip under your skin, put there at birth, it knows what kind of TV you want to watch. Not what you say you do, but what you really do, deep down. Knows," she added, "what commercials to put on."

"Knows your secrets," I said, smiling as she shook her head at herself.

"Sorry," she said ruefully. "I tend to go off on tangents."

I didn't think so. More like a nice try at conversational misdirection, followed by the confession of a small personal flaw to make it seem as if the change of subject wasn't deliberate. I turned the talk back to my original purpose.

"Is that how you met Jen? In a club?" Because otherwise the pair of young women seemed to have come from different worlds.

"Mm-hmm," she replied reluctantly. Ann still didn't want to talk about her friend; she'd only agreed to meet me here because she'd realized that I would be persistent.

"She'd come down to the city on weekends from that fancy prep school she went to, we'd see each other around at different places," she recalled. "Got to be pals after a while. Jen's dad doesn't know about that, though, her partying in town. Thought she sat in the dorm on weekends, I guess, studying and painting her toenails."

Uh-huh. Sure he did. "Your music pay the bills?" I asked. I could play the game, too: back off, circle around, come back again a little later. "Because if what I've heard about that is right, it doesn't usually."

My chair rocked unsteadily as Ann nodded, chewing a mouthful of baby spinach. "You heard correct. I play with a group, a lot of gigs in lower Manhattan. You know, bars, basement social clubs, that kind of venue. Mostly downtown. At the start it was just open mikes; now they pay us. Well," she amended, "usually they do. More than they used to. But it's still not very much money."

I bent down to examine the wooden chair legs. The crosspiece between the front two ones had popped out of its hole, and when I put it back in again it still moved loosely.

"What do your folks think about that?" I asked, sitting up. "I mean the not much money. And . . . the lifestyle. I mean, it can be kind of tough downtown late at night."

Her gaze met mine. "They think I'm a big girl and I can take care of myself," she replied, her voice briefly steely. I got the sense that there had been a certain amount of family controversy associated with her independence.

And now it was over because she'd won, which didn't surprise me. "But no big disasters have happened to me," she went on, "so they know now I'm doing all right."

Again that sense of an obstacle overcome, something battled if not into submission then at least to a truce. "They're in Virginia, where I grew up. My parents are, that is. My dad's retired from government work," she added before I could ask. "Mom too."

Again nicely done; throw in extra, unasked-for information. Makes you seem forthcoming. "You go to school there?" I asked casually. "College or whatever, maybe music school? In Virginia?"

But even as I spoke I knew I was going too fast. Something new moved in her eyes at the flurry of questions, a flicker of shadow she wasn't quick enough to hide.

Some little item of her past that she didn't want to talk about, I guessed, thinking *Join the club.* Her cell phone's ringer thweeped, saving her from having to answer.

She checked it, flipped it shut. "Jen keeping tabs on me," she joked. "She makes a friend, she gives 'em a cell phone, that way she's never out of touch."

That way they're never out of her control, more like, I thought.

"Anyway, I've got a good place I live in with some other people," Ann added after another sip of soda. "Across the bridge in Williamsburg. They're cool, my roommates. Graphics designers, bloggers . . . you know the type."

I didn't. Except for the crew of young regulars at the Bayside, in

Eastport that kind of intensely media-and-information-rich life might as well have been happening on the moon.

But now wasn't the time to say that, either. "Was that how she kept in touch with Cory?" I asked. "Gave him a cell phone?" I was pretty sure he hadn't had one on him in Henderson's barn. Not on his belt or in his pants pockets, anyway.

A sudden flashback memory of the white exposed skin between the dead youth's sagging waistband and the hem of his rucked-up shirt made me wince; I banished it fast. "Jen gave him a cell phone?" I repeated.

Each of the tables held a cut-glass bowl of sugar and sweetener packets, salt and pepper shakers, and a cup of toothpicks. Ann ate a slice of tomato before answering.

"Yup. Don't know where it is now, though. Maybe he lost it." A slice of raw mushroom eluded her fork. She went after it, then popped it into her mouth. "So it's not like I'm just hanging out," she returned to her own story when she'd swallowed the vegetable. "I hustle like mad when I'm in the city, do a lot of stuff for the band. Stuff that if you're not a musician yourself you don't realize needs doing."

She tipped her head. "And lately a little acting in some off-off-Broadway productions when I have time, not that I have much. And not that anything's going to come of it, I know that. You think music's a tough business, try acting. You might just as well get in the cage with the lions."

I nodded, then bent to wiggle the chair's crosspiece once more. It wasn't broken, just needed regluing.

To do that you take the crosspiece out, tap a dowel plug in, drill the plug so the crosspiece end fits tightly into the new hole, then coat the hole and crosspiece with glue before tapping the crosspiece's end back in a final time.

But I didn't have a dowel plug. Or a drill. "Mostly it's the music business, promotion and lining up gigs," Ann told me. "Sit in with other groups for money when I can. Most of all try to get session work. That's what I want: a session career."

I rummaged in my bag, found the bottle of white glue I kept with me for situations like this. I had a little mending kit in there too, with buttons, needles, and baby spools of thread.

But it was the white glue I used most. "That's when studios hire you to play on someone else's recording," Ann explained. "As a backup musician. No luck there yet, but I keep pounding at it."

She smiled at her own joke as I nodded toward the elaborate drum kit. "That all yours?"

It was a lot of expensive stuff for a struggling musician. I couldn't help wondering how she'd afforded it, unless maybe her parents had bought it. Depending on where and how long they'd worked, a couple of retired government employees could be sitting fairly pretty in the financial resources department or teetering at the edge of penury.

"Uh-huh. It's mine, all right." Ann rolled her eyes. "Only thing I'm in real debt for. But you've got to have your kit if you want to work, so I bit the bullet."

Parents cosigned the loan, then, maybe. And even with room-mates, the part of Brooklyn she'd mentioned wasn't cheap. I filed the thoughts away for future consideration.

She'd finished her salad and most of the grapefruit soda. "And it *is* a lot of work," she declared. "But then when I'm with Jen, say on a vacation in Florida or here, I live the lush life, you know? So it's not so bad."

Sure, and so what if her version of luxury was picking up crumbs Jen dropped for her? It didn't sound sustainable for the long term but it made a nice change from sharing an apartment with a bunch of near-strangers, I supposed, even if her home was in the too-cool-for-school section of the city.

And she'd answered at least part of my question about money. "Jen pays your way?" I asked casually. "When you travel, or hang out with her here . . . ?"

Because I doubted a couple of sensible retired government em-ployees would pick up the tab for much of that, sitting pretty or not. Ann confirmed my idea.

"Sure, Jen's the money-honey one of us. Let's face it, she's rich and I'm poor," she added with a candor I found refreshing; in general I'd discovered that if you want people to lie to you, just ask them about their finances.

"If she wants me around, she doesn't have a whole lot of choice. She knows I sure don't have the cash. You know the old joke about how to get a drummer off your doorstep, don't you?"

I did, but before I could say so she supplied the old punch line. "Pay for the pizza."

She leaned curiously over the edge of the table. "What're you doing down there, anyway?"

By then I was kneeling on the floor; fortunately, the Bayside was so clean I could've eaten Ann's salad off it if I'd wanted to. "Fixing this broken chair. Hand me a couple of those toothpicks from the jar on the table, will you?"

I couldn't get the crosspiece out without disassembling the chair entirely, so instead I coated the end of one of the wooden toothpicks she handed me with glue, then shoved it into the gap that made the crosspiece so loose.

"Cool," Ann commented. I shoved another one in, then several more, forcing the final few tightly into the gap with the blade of my Swiss Army knife. Now when I tried wiggling the crosspiece it didn't move at all.

"There," I said, setting the old chair aside in favor of one that hadn't recently been repaired by an amateur using white glue and toothpicks. It would be fine when it had dried, though; from behind the counter the Bayside's owner telegraphed thanks and finger-signed the letters IOU.

Good enough; a waitress went by with brownies on a tray, so I snagged her and got one. "What was the deal between Jen and Cory, anyway?" I asked Ann.

Her answering look was pert. "I told you, he thought she was hot. Well, lots of guys do, of course. But he was . . ."

She fluttered her fingers in the air to mime how infatuated Cory was. "And she liked that, she liked it that he'd drop anything to come when she called and do anything she said. As for what they did when he did show up—she's a girl, he was a guy. What do you think the deal was?"

The familiar growl of a sports car interrupted as through the Bayside's wide front window we watched Jen speed by in a silver Alfa Romeo convertible. Nice wheels; with her face turned up to the sun and a pair of Ray-Bans on, she looked carefree and rich as sin, a ruby red scarf streaming out behind her.

"I keep telling her she'll pull an Isadora Duncan with that scarf one of these days," Ann remarked, frowning.

The dancer and free spirit from the twenties who'd died suddenly when her own trademark trailing scarf got wrapped around a wheel of her car . . . the spiky-haired, multiply pierced percussionist sitting across from me was turning out to be a smart cookie.

Meanwhile, though, the scarf-around-the-neck mental picture was a little too close to the recent scene at Henderson's barn for my comfort. I shivered; Ann caught me at it and understood.

"Yeah, it was awful about Cory, wasn't it?" she asked quietly. "But it honestly wasn't Jen's fault. She just wants to have fun. On her way to college, why would she be in the market for a big, heavy-duty relationship?"

"Which was what Cory wanted?" The car's guttural growl faded into the distance. Around us the hum of conversation blended with the varying rings of cell phones—pop, hip-hop, the occasional syrupy dirge of Pachelbel's Canon in D.

"I guess," Ann replied. "It's probably the reason why she couldn't get rid of him even after she testified against him in court. Most guys with any brains would get discouraged by that, wouldn't you think?"

"Wasn't she out of his league anyway, though? A carpenter's helper and the rich girl from the big house on the hill . . ."

I let my voice draw the conclusion Cory Trow would have hated above all else: *not good enough.*

Ann agreed reluctantly. "You want my opinion, he wasn't even okay for laughs. He was the type who's always out for what he can get. But that's another thing about Jen, that's not the way she picks her friends. I mean whether they have money."

Why would she, since she obviously had enough to go around? And she enjoyed the contrast, maybe, especially with herself at the rich end of it. "Admirable," I said drily.

Ann bridled at the implied criticism. "Hey, it's not like Jen chased Cory, you know. Not that she never did that, if she got interested in a guy." So I'd heard. "But he was the one who started pestering her back when he was working there," Ann finished.

Flowers don't chase bees, either. But the bees can't help homing in, especially if the flowers make a point of waving themselves under the bees' noses.

"The attention was flattering at first, right?" I asked. "But Cory didn't understand that it was just all fun and games with her. To him maybe it was something more. So when she got bored and was ready to move on, he wouldn't let go?"

"Something like that," Ann conceded. "I mean it's not as if she's perfect or anything. If a tree falls in the woods and Jen's not there to hear it, it definitely doesn't make a sound as far as she's concerned."

That matched my own first impression of her: self-absorbed to the max. Jen Henderson wouldn't have just dropped Cory Trow; she'd have forgotten all about him two minutes later. If she'd really dropped him, that is, not just told everyone she had.

Ann seemed about to go on but instead a listening expression came onto her face. "What's the matter?" I asked, but she waved me silent.

Then I heard it, too, that unmistakable low growl. The sports car was coming back. For the first time Ann looked nervous; to cover it she reached out and took a chunk of my brownie, popped it into her mouth.

"And then it turns out that he's married with a kid. Can you be-lieve it? Maybe from an older guy you'd expect that, but what a jerk," she said, swallowing.

"When did Jen find out?" The rest of the brownie lay on the plate between us; I broke it and handed Ann half.

"Not until yesterday," she replied, cutting this piece with a fork and eating it carefully, in tiny sections.

I demolished mine in two bites as the car flew past again outside. Jen was buzzing us, I realized; angry that Ann hadn't answered her cell phone call and knowing she was in here from the bike parked outside.

Ann's cell rang again; she shut it off without looking at it. "The story started going around after we found out he was dead. Although nobody's seen her. The wife, I mean, or this alleged baby, so I can't say I'm sure I believe it."

"What's Jennifer's father do?" I asked casually. I wanted to ask her about the alarm systems at Henderson's place, as well, along with a few other things.

But at my question, Ann's hand jerked abruptly, knocking over the salt shaker. She pinched up some of the spilled crystals and tossed them over her shoulder.

"Old habit," she said with a half-laugh of embarrassment, seeing me notice the superstitious gesture. Suddenly a couple of other things swam into focus: the tiny gold pendant on a gold chain around her neck was a four-leaf clover. And the fuzzy object dangling from a key chain on her cell phone case was a rabbit's foot.

"Jen's father is retired. But he used to be in management and distribution," she said.

Lying, however, is like glazing a windowpane or hammering a nail in straight. Or playing the drums; to be any good at it, it helps to stay in practice.

Walter Henderson was a manager, all right; a hands-on manager of murder. After that, he distributed the body parts. And however she tried to cover her awareness of this, I felt certain that Ann Radham knew it.

"I stay clear of him," Ann told me. "He's got a temper. And it's not like I have anything in common with him, so . . ."

To have much in common with Walter Henderson, you'd have to be the BTK Killer. "Anyway," Ann repeated, "Jen's loyal, generous to her friends, likes to have fun . . ."

Probably loves puppies and kittens, I thought sourly, and helps old ladies across the street. All this defensiveness on Jen's behalf was starting to grate on me.

Unless she needed defending *about* something. And for that, Ann Radham seemed remarkably well prepared and equipped. Suddenly I didn't feel like wearing the kid gloves anymore.

"Where was Jen that night?" I asked. "The night Cory Trow died, what was she doing?"

This time around, the sports car skidded to a stop outside. "Home in bed," Ann answered promptly. "There'd been a softball game that afternoon, local team and Jen pitched, so she was tired. I was here, I played a couple of sets."

"So she wouldn't have called Cory? Maybe invite him over the way she used to? Because maybe she hadn't really broken up with him, only said she had on account of her dad's temper?"

"And then do something to him? Like what?" And before I could reply, "Come on, the guy *hung* himself," Ann declared with scornful impatience. "And he was hooked on her, sure, but not so hooked that he'd just do it if she told him to put a rope around his neck."

"That's not what I was wondering, actually. Maybe more like her father happened to run into him out there. Accidentally. Or accidentally on purpose."

Henderson had ordered his daughter to testify against the boy. He might also have told her to get the kid over there, say for instance if he'd found out somehow that Cory didn't plan on showing up for his sentencing hearing.

And Jen might've obeyed. A dark look of caution flashed behind the horn-rims before Ann could conceal it. "I don't think so," she denied flatly just as Jennifer swept in, her blue eyes narrowing as she spotted me and Ann together. Angrily, the tall blonde girl stalked toward us.

"Jen," Ann began, her hands up in a placating gesture.

But Jen wasn't listening. "What the hell are you doing? You think this is a joke? Like maybe I need any more rumors going around about . . ."

Time to step in. "She's not telling rumors. I wanted to know more about Cory Trow, that's all."

Jennifer ignored me. "I thought you were my friend," she told Ann, her voice rising. "So I include you in everything I do, I pay your way everywhere, this is how you pay me back? Gossiping about me with nosy strangers?"

Her tone attracted glances from the laptop-using patrons at other tables, discomforted at the sight of human conflict not yet sanitized by translation into pixels. This, their expressions said uneasily, was Not Nice.

"What're you all looking at?" Jen snapped in a voice like a whip-crack. Faces turned hastily back to screens except for one weird little guy in the corner, nursing a coffee.

He was short and bald with a strange mustache, the long, wiry kind with waxed curls on the ends, and he ducked his shiny head when he saw me noticing him. Jen went on berating Ann, not quite stomping her widdle footsie to punctuate her tirade.

"If I'd known you were going to cause this much trouble, I'd never have . . ." A red flush crept up Ann's neck. Walter Henderson wasn't the only one with a temper, it seemed. Jen had inherited it and was taking it out on Ann big-time, for what seemed to me a minor offense.

But the spiky-haired girl kept her cool better than I could have, displaying calm assertiveness. I would've probably had a fist raised by now.

"Come on," she told the young woman towering furiously over her. "You need to get out of here, you're making a scene."

Angry resentment still flamed in Jennifer's eyes but she backed off as if even through her rage she knew Ann was right. The two of them went out together without another glance at me, and the car sped off.

When I looked again the weird guy had departed, too. His cup was still steaming on the table where he'd been sitting. I thought his avid interest had seemed somehow more than idle curiosity; paying the check, I hurried out but he wasn't on Dyer Street, or in the park behind the library.

I crossed to look behind the gazebo where in summer there were band concerts, but he wasn't there either. Someone else staggered across the library lawn at me, though.

"Mom!" Sam called.

At the sight of him my heart sank. He wore the same gray sweatshirt he'd had on two nights ago, over a turtleneck that had originally been white, and wrinkled corduroy pants. Untied sneakers were on his feet, laces flopping.

"Mom!" he bellowed delightedly. "I found you!"

He hadn't been asleep. He'd been drinking all this time, I realized; in there alone with the shades pulled and a glass in his hand, applying the stuff like salve.

"Mom!" Plunging toward me, he lost his precarious balance and steadied himself with a hand clapped too hard on my shoulder. It hurt; I backed away reflexively.

But it wasn't what hurt most. "Oops. 'Scuse me. I gotta talk to you."

Oh, good Christ. "Sam." I tried steering him but he wouldn't let me, veering away from me like a little kid who doesn't want to be captured and is trying to make a game of it.

"I remembered," he said proudly, "what I wanted to tell you."

He smelled like a distillery. Anyone else would've been comatose. "What is it, Sam?"

I wanted to weep. But I managed a smile; it was my best hope of getting Sam out of the public eye without any more of a scene than we were already putting on. At least, I thought with a burst of resentment at him, Jen Henderson hadn't been drunk.

His expression grew sly. "I know something you don't know," he chanted.

"What?" I asked for the final time, and by my tone I made sure Sam knew that it was final.

"The girl," he said, owlishly resentful all at once.

"What girl?" By now I'd abandoned all thought of warning him to be careful in the car, of telling him that somebody had tried running me down and that his own "accident" might not really have been one, either.

Because he wouldn't have remembered, and anyway he wouldn't be driving until further notice. The moment I could, I was going to his house for the car keys he still had, and taking them.

The car too, just in case he had a spare set. From now on, he could walk if he wanted to go somewhere.

"The girl, the one that dead kid's s'posed to be married to," he slurred. "Name's Trish."

His giggle ended in a hiccup. "Trish, wish, fish."

"What about her?" It didn't surprise me that he might know something about Cory; you hear a lot of things when you hang out in bars for hours. Sam was just barely of legal drinking age now, and he made the most of it.

"Gone," he pronounced morosely, swaying. His eyelids drooped and he struggled to control them. "Gone, gone, gone, gone . . ."

"Sam, what do you mean?" Just then Ellie appeared, coming down Key Street toward us with Leonora riding piggyback.

"Hi!" Leonora shouted as Sam's knees buckled. Luckily, Ellie had seen Sam this way before.

"I'll call George," she said, and took Lee into the Bayside to do so, then returned to sit on the lawn with me.

"Jake, I've just heard something awful."

Me too: Sam's drink-sodden voice. "In the Bayside?" By now George would be on his way.

"No, just before I came down here. I was on my way to try and find you. Bella heard it a little while ago from one of her friends over in St. Stephen. The friend called Bella, and she called me, and . . ."

That got my attention. St. Stephen, the Canadian town where Cory Trow's rumored wife and baby were supposed to be living . . .

Sprawled at our feet, Sam snored. "There's been a bad fire," Ellie said. "In St. Stephen. A house fire, the entire place went up."

"Night-night," Lee cooed to Sam as I stared at Ellie, trying to figure out what she'd told me might mean.

But knowing, really:

Gone, gone, gone.

To: hlrb@mainetel.net <Horace Robotham>
From: ddimaio@miskatonic.edu <Dave DiMaio>
Subj: Eastport book analysis results

Horace

   I'm attaching a file of the final results on the ink, paper, glue, binding,
etc. Also a nice computerized comparison
analysis of the handwriting's likely his-
torical period. Early 19th century, without much doubt.
   Note the mass spectrometer results on
the ink. Ever seen a better profile of
hemoglobin breakdown by-products?

Dave

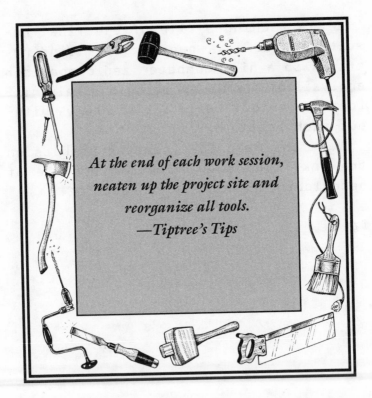

Chapter 7

At the end of each work session,
neaten up the project site and
reorganize all tools.
—Tiptree's Tips

Goose chase," Ellie muttered under her breath at the border crossing between Calais, Maine, and New Brunswick, Canada.
Fortunately, I was driving this time, so the uniformed guard in the
booth didn't hear her.

"Shopping," I told him, this being the correct description of your
errand at any border not decorated with rolls of barbed wire and su-
pervised by men carrying machine guns.

This one consisted of the tollbooth-style enclosures that the crossing guards sat in, a two-story brick administration building, and a truckers' byway with its own buildings and area for cargo inspection.

"Ellie, if that girl's hurt or killed, it was no accident," I said as the guard scrutinized all our identifications, even the baby's, and ran our vehicle's license plate.

"I mean does somebody have to draw us a picture about that, or what?" I added.

The guard scowled down at his computerized database. Regular commuters across the border lived in terror of the day one digit would be accidentally transposed, and they would be mistaken for terrorists. I waited with interest to see if I was on any lists, and whether or not Wade's truck was.

I'd snagged the keys and the Fiat from Sam, but carrying Leonora around in the little vehicle was inconvenient; she'd outgrown the car seat I'd had installed in it soon after she was born. But there was plenty of room in the oversized cab of Wade's pickup.

"Maybe so, but I doubt we can learn much from the burned-out scene of the crime," Ellie retorted. "I'm as anxious about this girl as you are, but we'd be better off—"

"Snooping in our own territory. You always say that." And usually she was right. Ellie's familiarity with Eastport and its citizens was our ace in the hole.

"But I can't help it," I added. "I have to *see*."

Besides, I needed to get out of Eastport. George had come and loaded Sam into his own truck and gotten him home. But in my current mood I was in serious danger of grabbing that boy and shaking him until his teeth rattled out of his head like a set of cheap dentures.

"Fine, right, have it your way," Ellie gave in, unfooled as to my real motive. At last the guard waved us on through into St. Stephen, a small city just over the St. Croix River from Calais.

Taking the turn out of the border facilities past the duty-free shop, I felt as usual that if not for the formalities of the crossing we might as well still have been in Calais. The pair of cities had always been linked by blood and convenience; they cooperated on fire protection, their citizens had been marrying one another for decades, and in 1812, St.

Stephen donated enough gunpowder for Calais to celebrate the Fourth of July, although their parent countries were already at war with one another.

A few things, however, were different. On Market Street we passed a currency-exchange office, but since we lived so close to the Maritime Provinces we had loonies and toonies in our purses as usual. In place of paper, the Canadians had dollar and two-dollar coins, the first nicknamed for the loon on the back.

Also, and this I could never quite get over, the Canadians had a Queen. Looking around, I always thought about how different it must feel, bearing allegiance to royalty even if so much more distantly than in the past. Canada was now of course a fully independent nation, no longer a British colony.

But here in St. Stephen they had something that interested me even more: the Ganong chocolate factory, whose product Ellie insisted we ought to trade a few loonies and toonies to acquire. So we entered the factory shop where the five-cent chocolate bar and the red heart-shaped candy box were first invented, and went in.

"I keep feeling that I've forgotten something important," I said. "Something I was supposed to do, or get ready for . . ."

The smell of chocolate filled my head, a sweet intoxicating aroma that drew me along helplessly. "You'll think of it," Ellie reassured me. And then, "Jake, are we dead? Because I think I'm in . . ."

Heaven. Fifteen minutes later, equipped with a cellophane bag of what Ganong called chicken bones—cinnamon-flavored hard candy over a soft chocolate center, loved by Wade—and a paper bag of milk chocolate chunks for us to eat now, we followed directions given us by the candy-counter lady to the street west of the business district where the fire had happened.

"Any luck with Ann Radham?" Ellie asked.

"Nope." I peered at the street signs. "She was just starting to open up with me when Jen showed up. That was the end of that."

And upon reflection now, what little I had learned from the girl didn't seem very useful.

The wide, well-kept avenues of St. Stephen devolved to smaller offshoots and at last to a neglected-looking row of wood-framed houses in various stages of decay.

"Here we are." I waved at the street full of beat-up parked cars, rickety front porches, and paint-peeling buildings. Some of the roofs had blue tarps nailed over them and others should have. At the thought, something pinged in my memory: that's what I'd forgotten, the tarps. But there was something else, too . . .

"Oh, my God," Ellie said, staring as I pulled the car to the curb. A large multifamily structure had stood recently among the poor but studiously neat single-family dwellings. Nothing else could've made the blackened rubble-heap mounded there now.

A twisted metal fire escape lay atop charred wood, smashed glass, and soaked lumps of burned furniture, while a fellow in a red windbreaker and jeans stood photographing the mess.

We got out. Crime-scene tape surrounded the chaos. "Excuse me . . . ," Ellie began to the picture-taking fellow.

He turned impatiently. By the amount of gear in his shoulder bag, I could tell he was no looky-loo. "What?" he snapped.

A name tag on his shirt read "Maritimes Sentinel." I stepped up beside Ellie. "I just heard about the fire. A friend of mine lived here," I lied. "Do you know if anyone was—"

"No idea, they just send me out for the pictures." He began snapping more of them.

"Well, do you know . . . ?" I tried again as Ellie wandered off.

He lowered the camera. "Lady, they could all have gotten barbecued in there and I wouldn't know a thing about it."

Or care, apparently. Something else about what he'd said also resonated with me but I couldn't put my finger on it. "Hey, Jake," Ellie called. "Over here."

Across the street in a small neglected park a half dozen women and a bunch of children had gathered around broken benches and a clutter of playground equipment. The moms slumped on the benches chatting while the kids ran around yelling.

The moms all looked weary, irritated, and not up for a pair of nosy strangers; I sympathized. Back in my own young-mother days there were plenty of times when my own life seemed the color and consistency of strained peas, too.

Ellie had the credential that counted, here: a small child of her own. She set Lee down among the toddlers and strolled over to the benches while I scanned the burned building some more. But nothing useful caught my eye. The stench was a combination of doused campfire and rotting refrigerator contents; the chocolate in my stomach turned over.

Soon Ellie returned, leading Lee in short, toddlerish steps. "Bye!" Lee shouted, turning to wave. "Bye-bye!"

"So what's the news?" I asked when we'd all gotten into the truck again.

Lee didn't like her safety seat and said so in klaxon howls like the ones you might hear on a torpedoed submarine just before all the water starts gushing in.

"She lived there," Ellie shouted. "Trish Bogan, those girls said her name was. They live in some of the houses around here."

"They knew she was married to Cory?" I started the truck, hoping the engine vibration might calm Leonora.

It didn't. That was the other thing I remembered about my young-mother years: the noise, as if someone were always beating a gong right next to my head.

"They knew," Ellie hollered. "Said she kept her name."

Not that I wouldn't have given my right arm to go back, do it all over. Better, maybe. Once George took him home, Sam had passed out again on his couch.

Ellie rummaged through her bag. "They recognized Cory from my description," she added at the top of her lungs. "Said he'd come around a little more often since the baby."

"So what's happened to her?" We headed back downtown. "Was she. . . . ?" Bad pictures danced in my head: flames, glass shattering.

"No, she's okay. The moms said she moved out yesterday all of a sudden, in a big hurry from what they saw. Didn't take any furniture or housewares, nothing like that. Just packed up her clothes and the baby's stuff and . . . *here* it is," Ellie breathed in relief as from her bag she produced a small plastic bottle with an eyedropper screwed into the top of it. "Told one of the girls she was going back to St. John, where she's from. Seems she had jewelry she could pawn, so she planned to do that for money to live on."

"What're you doing with that bottle?" I asked. We were both still shouting.

"Magic. Or something. All I know is . . ." Ellie leaned into the back-seat. "Presto, chango," she uttered, waving the bottle.

Lee's howling mouth clapped shut; her plump hands reached out eagerly. "Wow," I said into the sudden silence. "How does that work?"

"I have no idea," said Ellie. "And I'm afraid if I try to find out, it might *stop* working. So . . ."

"Bah," Lee whispered confidingly to the eyedropper bottle. "Bah-bah."

"Yeah," I said. "Don't mess with success." The light changed and I made the turn onto Market Street, headed back to the border. "Now, as for Trish . . . Bogan's her maiden name, is it? And did her friends mention how to find her in St. John?"

Unlike St. Stephen, so small that you could locate somebody just by asking around if you kept at it long enough, St. John was a biggish city.

One she could hide in if she wanted to. "And . . . did any of them say *why* she was moving?"

"They said she was scared but she wouldn't say of what, only that she and the baby weren't safe here."

"I guess not," I said. But how had Trish known? A car pulled out from the curb behind us, one of those anonymous small white rentals you can get at most any airport and lots of other places, too. It bore a Maine license plate but I couldn't quite see the driver.

"I asked if Trish ever left the baby with any of them," Ellie said. "Or with anyone else."

I took my eyes off the car in the rearview long enough to grin at her. "You genius. Like maybe the night Cory died?"

Because I was sure now that if he'd been murdered, Henderson had done it. Call me crazy, but the combination of a dead guy and a known killer with a grudge against the victim was just too much of a coincidence for my taste.

But that didn't mean I'd ignore other theories. To nail Walt Henderson the way I needed to do it, they all had to be ruled out.

"Yup," said Ellie. "But Trish was home that night, they said. Most other nights, too."

The white car stayed behind us. "It was their one negative comment," Ellie went on. "That she was picky about taking care of the baby. They said she made them feel she didn't think they were good enough."

It was past midafternoon and the sun's glare kept me from seeing into our tail-car's passenger compartment. I couldn't tell if it was the one that had nearly run me over the night before, either. I put my signal on, swung a fast U-turn in the middle of St. Stephen's downtown traffic; no cop around, luckily.

Or unluckily, depending on how this turned out. "There was one other thing," Ellie said, taking a cue from my body language and glancing in the mirror herself. "They said the police were there for a long time at the fire. Everybody got out safe," she added, "but it was close."

"And?" Once we left the downtown area the city thinned to a couple of shopping malls, fast-food joints, some car dealerships, and a garden center. After that it was an hour and a half or so through the hinterlands until the city of St. John.

Too far to go today. "*And*," Ellie replied, "the women said the fire in Trish's building was definitely arson."

I frowned, peeking at the rearview again. "Oh, come on. How would they know? It would take days for an investigation, and . . ."

Ellie shook her head as I put on my signal, waited for a chance in the oncoming traffic, and turned left into the parking lot of a veterinarian's office. A lady with a Great Dane in the passenger seat of her VW bug gave me a dirty look, then pulled out.

"That's what I thought. But one of those moms lives right next door to the burned building," Ellie replied. "She heard all the sirens and went outside to see what was going on."

Leonora slept. Ellie reached back for the eyedropper bottle just as the car that had been behind us shot by, too fast for me to glimpse the driver.

"*And* her husband's a Boy Scout troop leader," Ellie said. "And you know how when they go on camping trips, they're supposed to start the fire by rubbing two sticks together?"

I highly doubted that this particular blaze had been started by rubbing two sticks together. "Ellie, just where are you going with this?"

"But it's not easy," she went on. "Half the time the scouts can't do it. So troop leaders always bring along these tablets."

"To write on? But why would . . ." Then the light dawned. "Oh. You mean trioxane tablets."

Used for starting campfires quickly, the tablets were small, easily obtainable—from hunting-supply catalogs, for instance—and they burned hot. I knew about them because in the old days Jemmy's pals used them on nightclubs they'd muscled in on, after they'd ruined them by laundering money through them and running through the original owner's line of credit.

Then when the clubs were so bad off that they couldn't even run hookers out of them anymore, they burned them. "Some of the tablets were lying around on the ground," Ellie confirmed. "The girl I talked to recognized them."

I turned back, toward St. Stephen and the border crossing. "So maybe Trish was right to hightail it to St. John when she did."

The white car that had been tailing us pulled over onto the high-way's shoulder, waited for its chance to merge, then swerved in a fish-tailing U-turn of its own.

Still following. Lee's eyes snapped open again. I guessed she'd no-ticed the eyedropper bottle was gone.

"Give it back," I told Ellie, returning my attention to the road. "Give it back to her *now*."

"Wah," Lee uttered experimentally, her breath beginning to come in gasps. "Wah!"

What happened next drove just about everything out of my head, other than the strong desire to encase it in styrofoam or maybe even concrete to protect the fragile structures inside.

"Wah!" Leonora cried. "Wah! WAH!" The noise was stunning, an onslaught of outraged, not-to-be-comforted distress. Through the barrage it was all I could do to keep my concentration focused enough to drive without crashing into something.

Because this time the magic eyedropper bottle didn't work and neither did anything else. Wrapping what was left of my mind around the idea of just getting home fast, I gripped the steering wheel and let the sound wash over me. It was a tactic I'd learned long ago while driving Sam places in downtown Manhattan traffic; he'd hated his car seat, too.

So it wasn't until we got on Route 1 headed south past the turnoff to the cottage that it hit me:

Barbecue. Wade's barbecue at the lake, set for today.

That's what I'd forgotten.

• • •

Being stalked is possibly my least favorite way of getting attention, and it didn't help my mood any that when Ellie and I finally got to the lake, we found my husband, Wade, her husband, George, and my old pal Jemmy all sitting around the table inside the cottage plotting murder.

Sam was outside, looking like death warmed over. "Sorry," my sobered-up son moaned miserably as I approached.

"No kidding," I said, stepping around where he sat on the cottage steps with his face in his hands.

If my tone was crisp it was only because I was so angry with him I could've spit. Also my nerves were still ragged from having been tailed by a strange car.

Come to think of it, the rest of the situation was pretty nerveracking as well: a dead kid, a burned building, and a girl and her baby missing. Oh, and have I mentioned my friend Jemmy Wechsler and a notorious hit man, locked in mortal combat?

At least the car hadn't followed us across the border, or anyway I hoped it hadn't.

Sam was dripping wet. That plus his expression and a fresh pattern of damp footprints told me that someone—probably Wade—had wrestled him down to the edge of the water and pushed him in.

Too bad; right then I'd had poor-Sam-and-his-drinking-problem up to the eyeballs. "Go get some dry clothes on," I told him, "or we'll be nursing you for pneumonia, too."

"What can I say?" Ellie apologized, coming up behind me and looking just as shell-shocked as I felt. "The eyedropper bottle trick doesn't always work."

"Don't worry about it," I told her, thinking that if all my own kid did was scream, I'd be a happy camper. Carrying Lee, who'd fallen silent as she was lifted from the truck, she went inside and I followed.

". . . shotgun," Jemmy was saying. "I could do it with a . . ."

Noting my expression, Wade frowned questioningly; I nodded at him, signaling *I'm all right.* Next Sam came in, regarded us all in hungover silence, and climbed to the loft for dry apparel.

"Too messy," George Valentine objected to Jemmy. "And too obvious. You need something more accidental looking. A drowning, maybe."

They were talking about Walt Henderson. Killing him, I mean. Or at any rate they were humoring Jemmy about it. Wade rolled his eyes at me so I'd know he and George weren't really serious.

But I thought Jemmy was. "Hmm," he said of George's drowning suggestion. "Yeah."

He'd traded his city garb of shirt and gray slacks for a sweatshirt, jeans, and sneakers, and looked fairly convincing in them. Once his hundred-dollar haircut grew out, he'd be all set.

"He could fall off a boat, couldn't he? Into that cold water in the bay," Jemmy went on.

"Which means all you need is a boat, a way to get him on it, a way to get him off it, and a way to get back with him *not* on it anymore without the whole town noticing," I said, not bothering to conceal my sarcasm.

The groceries for the barbecue were already spread out on the cabin's galley counter. Grilled steaks, baked potatoes, and salad, plus a store-bought chocolate cake, I saw with relief; in my absence someone else had taken care of it all.

Wade, again, I guessed. "Hey," Jemmy replied, snapping his fingers. "Easy-peasy."

"Yeah, well, don't be too sure. Eastporters are funny that way, they notice murder," I said.

"Especially some of them," my father commented from his chair in the corner. Wearing clean overalls, a red flannel shirt, and a vest with slots for shotgun shells sewn into the front of it, he fit right into the cabin's rustic decor.

When Sam came down we were all drinking sodas. He looked around, shook his head in heavily put-upon dismay, and stuck his hand out for some car keys; any car keys. "I've told you guys before, you can drink in front of me," he said.

Had to, actually. He was rigid about our feeling free to enjoy a cocktail whether he had one or not. The trouble was, sooner or later he always did.

"Come on," he added. "If you're going to treat me like some poor boozer who has to have his glass just 'cause you are . . ."

Then I'm leaving, he meant to finish. But Wade didn't let him. And he didn't offer keys. "Sit down and shut up," Wade told Sam conversationally, smiling.

But under the smile was a sharp glint of something we didn't often see from Wade, whose capacity for sympathy had finally been exceeded just as mine had, I gathered. Sam was so astonished, he dropped like a marionette with its strings cut, his butt hitting the chair George shoved behind him with a soft, vulnerable-sounding thump.

Then Bella came in carrying a scrub brush and what remained of a steaming kettle of water. "Them fish-cleaning tools somebody left in the shed was mighty powerful in the stink department," she announced, leaving no doubt as to what she had been up to.

Wade must've brought her along, too, and I shot him another look of gratitude; I may joke about her but the truth is that everything always looked better, smelled better, and even tasted better when Bella was around.

Our steaks, for instance; she'd scoured the grill clean of burnt drippings and afterwards insisted on doing the dishes so the others could socialize–my father, I noticed, jumped right in to help her–and so Jemmy and I could go out in the kayaks.

Floating on the silent lake with a lavender sky fading over our heads, Jemmy spoke. "Kid's got a problem."

But Sam wasn't what I needed to discuss with him. "Listen, Jemmy, I can't have you out here planning . . ."

Murder. "If I don't, he's going to," he said bluntly, leaning back in the kayak with the paddle on his knees.

I ignored the remark. "It's not that I don't care about you. But I'm not going to be an accessory before the fact. I'm sorry, but I'm just not."

He considered this briefly. "Who do you think was following you?" he asked.

Paddling out, I'd told Jemmy about the car in St. Stephen, Sam's accident, and about my near-miss episode the night before on Sullivan Street. "I don't know."

I dipped the kayak paddle, watched slow blue waves ripple from it. A hundred yards off floated the buoy Ellie and I dropped to mark the sunken dock block; over dinner we'd regaled the company with the story and George had promised to crank the block in on a winch for us.

Minutes passed. "So did Dr. Destructo ever get rid of that piano?" Jemmy asked out of the blue.

Dr. Destructo had always been Jemmy's name for my ex-husband Victor. "No. It's still in his house. New people bought the place furnished."

When I met him Victor had been the kind of guy who thought he had great untapped musical talent, that if only he weren't a medical student he would have turned out to be Billy Joel.

The truth was, Victor had memorized three chords at age sixteen and never forgotten them. Surgery was his talent; that and the ability to charm women's socks off in minutes.

I let my hand drag in the cold water. "Near the end," I said, "he got fond of a drink we called Clammy Mary. One-fourth clam juice, one-fourth tomato juice, and the rest straight gin."

A breeze riffled my hair. The concoction had at last become the only thing Victor was able to keep down; nowadays I couldn't even look at a bottle of clam juice.

"Didn't matter what kind of gin," I went on. "But he liked rotgut best, I think. And he liked a slice of lime on the glass, thin enough to read a newspaper through."

A fish jumped nearby, landed with a splash. "Not that he was reading any newspapers by then. I miss him," I said.

More silence. Jemmy was as sensitive as a snake's flickering tongue when he wanted to be. Too bad the other associations the thought summoned about him were equally true.

He changed the subject again. "Jake, don't you get it? Walt Henderson came here just to keep an eye on *you*. He built that big house in Eastport in case I showed up."

So Jemmy had seen the house. I processed the thought without comment. "Now he's warning you off," he went on. "He didn't mean to hit you last night or to hurt Sam. He just wanted to make an impression."

Near the far shore a loon sat on the water, its thick neck curving snakelike above a blocky, black-and-white feathered body. Behind me my father said something I couldn't quite hear; Bella's laugh in reply was like a violin being scraped with a stick.

The loon took two long splashing steps before rising toward its nesting place on the next lake south. The evening star came out, suddenly bright. "And he knows I'm here," Jemmy said.

Lights went on in the cabin. Since he'd moved in, Jemmy had put the solar panels on the roof and gotten them connected to the storage batteries. By mounting a barrel on a rack under the eaves, he'd gotten running water to the sink in the kitchen, too, and to the basin in the loft so you could brush your teeth.

I hadn't thought he would do very well out here, but he'd surprised me. Then again, he'd always been adaptable, another of the secrets to his success.

And to his survival. "That guy's got nerve endings like a cruising shark," he went on. "He knew the minute I hit town. He can *smell* me." Yet he had hit town anyway instead of avoiding the place. And it wasn't like Jemmy to force an issue unless he was under a lot of pressure.

With only about half an hour of light left, I was ready to go in, but he paddled toward the birch-clad spit of land dividing our cove from the rest of the lake. Mist hovered on the water.

"How come he's lasted so long?" I asked. Unlike the rest of his ilk: dead or in jail, their kids not amounting to much.

"Henderson? Takes precautions, is why. Works alone. He never even hires guys directly, keeps 'em distant and cuts 'em loose as fast as he can."

So it was as I'd suspected. If I could get rid of Henderson the rest of this would end, too.

"Nobody's ever been able to get near him," Jemmy went on. "Wearing a wire, anything like that. There was some talk not too long ago about trying again, but . . ."

I looked over at him, interested; seeing this, he changed the subject abruptly. "How did *you* keep them from following you here, anyway?" he asked.

My old clients, he meant. Ahead a beaver swam anxiously back and forth, trying to block our way into the narrow flowage leading to a stretch of wetlands. A massive dam crossed the far end of the flowage, flanked by a beaver lodge.

Thick white birch saplings stripped of their bark formed the lodge's top, a mound about fifteen feet in diameter rising five feet off the water. "I never let any of them tell me anything they didn't want repeated," I said.

During the day a snake as thick as my forearm often lounged atop the lodge, but it had gone in. "Sure," Jemmy said skeptically.

The beaver rolled into a dive, his big flat tail making an angry *slap!*

"Gimme a break, Jake," Jemmy protested, "you knew it was all blood money, and they *knew* you knew it was . . ."

"Not all of it." The beaver resurfaced, sleek and dark, his eyes full of fury.

The truth was, I'd had documents; if anything happened to me they would've surfaced and the result would've been unpleasant for my clients. But the papers didn't exist anymore, the clients knew it–to avoid misunderstandings I'd destroyed them when I left Manhattan– and anyway it wasn't any of Jemmy's business.

"Whatever I did must've worked, though. Because they didn't follow me, did they?"

I pivoted the kayak, turning to watch the circling animal; I'd never heard of a beaver attacking anyone. I'd had one of them pop up a few feet from the side of my kayak, though, close enough for me to inspect its curved yellow incisors.

This beaver kept its distance. "Besides, that was then and this is now," I said.

Jemmy laughed, not pleasantly. "Okay, so we're not going to hash over old times."

"We already did. Unless you want to talk about you getting your start as a car thief. Stealing them to order off streets and out of garages, chopping them up for parts yourself to save on the middleman."

Jemmy liked to pretend he'd always worn good clothes and had clean fingernails. But I knew he had been a wizard with ignition wiring once upon a time, so good he didn't even have to break anything. If it turned out his buyer didn't need that particular car after all, Jemmy could put it back where its owner had left it with nobody the wiser.

"You have warrants out?" For his arrest, I meant, knowing he probably did.

"A few," he acknowledged as I sidled the kayak parallel to the beaver dam. It was about seventy-five feet long, twelve feet thick at its underwater base, made of mud, grass, and sticks. A little water trickled through but not much.

"How'd you hear about another try at getting next to Walter Henderson?"

"What is this, Twenty Questions?" Jemmy back-paddled away from me. "I hear things, that's all," he acknowledged finally.

"From who? Someone in the program?" Jemmy had always been on speaking terms with a variety of people in and out of the Witness Protection Program.

But this was different. His paddle trailed droplets in the dying light. "Maybe," he conceded.

My ears pricked up; this was the first time he'd ever talked to me about the program without mocking it. "Don't look shocked," he said.

"I'm not shocked." But there was only one reason for him to be in recent touch with any of those people. And they wouldn't protect him unless he testified.

Against Henderson; maybe even against me? And all the head games I'd played with myself back then—no blood money, indeed— wouldn't cut any ice with a federal prosecutor.

"Well," I said. "This is a development."

And yet another reason for Walt Henderson to want to kill Jemmy. Anxiously I scanned the shoreline where the new leaves had thickened the underbrush to a screen, especially at night.

"It's not a development unless it has to be, Jake, and I'm a long way from it. And don't look so nervous, Henderson won't show up while you're here."

We paddled back to the cove and approached the shore; with no dock the kayak dismount was tricky and I reached out to steady his boat for him. But he was, as I should also have remembered, as agile as an eel.

Slippery, ingenious. The thought wasn't as comforting as it might have been. "And tonight when we're gone?" I asked him as we climbed the path to the cottage. "What about Henderson then?"

It was already nearly pitch dark. Night fell fast here once the sun went down. "I'm a light sleeper," Jemmy said with a small laugh meant to reassure me.

It didn't.

●　　●　　●

A full day every week with his daughter Leonora was a privilege George Valentine guarded jealously, so the next morning Ellie and I set out, minus the baby, for St. John, New Brunswick.

Fog wrapped Eastport like cotton batting; the streets gleamed with moisture and the bright banners in front of the Water Street shops hung soddenly. The tugboats at the fish pier hunkered half-seen, their massive sterns turned to the dead-calm water and their lines creaking with the incoming tide.

As we pulled into the ferry-boarding area the *Island Hopper* materialized out of the mist. We drove down onto the beach as the vessel's metal ramp lowered, scraping the stones.

Two cars with New Brunswick license plates came off first, pausing for two U.S. border officers in yellow slickers before vanishing uphill into the fog as if through a curtain. We drove on board; minutes later, the ferry reversed away from the shore, diesel engines roaring.

"Spooky," Ellie commented as everything disappeared. On a morning like this, if not for the gentle bump of the water under the barge part of the ferry—the *Island Hopper* was powered by a rebuilt fishing boat fastened alongside—you could believe you'd been transported to some other world.

"So we get to St. John and we try to find Trish. That's the plan?" Ellie said doubtfully, peering into the mist.

Not even the lighthouse beacons penetrated this stuff, and the foghorn when it let out a long mournful bellow made me jump, sounding unnaturally close.

"That's it," I agreed grimly. Halfway between Eastport and Deer Island lay the Old Sow whirlpool, the largest in the Western Hemisphere and a notorious mariners' hazard. "Trow isn't a common last name. With any luck she'll have relatives in the phone book. One of them will tell us where she is."

"Hmm," Ellie commented. "Or they'll shut up like clams." The *Island Hopper* entered the whirlpool with a faint lurch.

There was an Old Sow Survivor's Club open to anyone who made the crossing, with a plaque suitable for hanging and framing. My breakfast did a buck-and-wing in my stomach, then settled; I was going to earn that plaque, I suspected.

"We'll just have to risk it," I said, rolling the car window all the way down and sticking my head out. Why being miserably damp and chilly helped seasickness I had no idea.

But it did. "Because you were right, the way to stop Walter Henderson from killing Jemmy or vice versa is to get Henderson put away." Also it would keep Jemmy from having to enter the Witness Protection Program, with all the inconvenient revelations *that* might entail.

"You still think Henderson killed Cory?" Ellie asked. Deer Island loomed suddenly out of the fog. The ferry made the turn into the landing and scraped ashore.

"Oh, of course he did it," I replied impatiently as we drove off. "He wanted Cory to leave Jen alone and Cory wouldn't. And Henderson's a man who's accustomed to getting what he wants, one way or another."

The next leg of our journey was a narrow, winding lane between stands of old tamarack, pristine freshwater ponds, and clusters of small wooden houses, most with boats in the yards and lobster traps piled alongside the gravel driveways.

"So there's your motive. As for method, if you hold a gun to a fellow's head, he'll probably cooperate pretty nicely in letting a rope be put around his neck," I added.

Compared to the tiny *Island Hopper,* the St. George ferry was a huge industrial-looking beast with high steel-mesh rails and a towering superstructure, loaded with cars and trucks. As we got under way the sun burned at last through the morning fog; Ellie and I squeezed between vehicles to reach the observation deck.

Cold salt breeze swept away the reek of diesel exhaust, the thrum of engines vibrating in the big steel plates under our feet. "But why would Cory agree to meet Henderson in the barn?" Ellie objected, leaning on the rail. "Seems to me he's about the last person Cory would want to run into."

"Maybe that's not who Cory thought he was meeting," I said. "Maybe he expected Jen. It would account for a lot if she lured Cory out there, maybe not even knowing what her dad had planned."

A wonderland appeared through the shining remnants of mist: low gray islands with tiny cabins clinging to rocky outcroppings, bald eagles sailing above. Porpoises arced in the waves, running alongside us; a humpback whale slapped flukes and flippers, then rolled massively and sank once more into the briny depths.

A low shore with wooden piers and a narrow road leading from it materialized on the horizon. "Anyway," I said as we returned to Wade's truck—after Sam's accident in the Fiat I didn't feel confident enough to take the car on a long journey—"Trish wouldn't be on the run unless she had a reason. And I want to know what it is."

Before we find out by accident and it bites us in the butt, I added mentally. We drove off the ferry past a low motel and a few small dwellings, following signs leading to the main highway. Here it ran through territory so remote and sparsely settled, it had only three lanes: two for travel, a center lane for passing and left turns.

That and the hills, like foothills of a mountain range, made the road feel as if it deserved its local nickname: Death Alley. But owing to my habit of letting even the slowest other vehicles pass, we survived with only a few close calls—motorists out here seemed to believe you really could outrun death if you drove fast enough—and three hours later reached St. John, New Brunswick.

A bridge led through a tollbooth and over the St. John River, a waterway whose massive flow ran upstream twice a day on account of high tides in the Bay of Fundy. Nova Scotia was a mere two hours east by ferry. Beyond that lay the vastness of the open Atlantic. "Now what?" Ellie asked.

In 1877 a fire in a hay barn had ended up consuming most of the city because in a cost-saving measure the fire-engine horses were out with a road-repair crew that day. Now brick commercial buildings lined the central streets; urban blight had taken a nibble here but not a big bite.

"Damn." I dug around in my satchel one-handed. "Forgot the phone book."

Ellie shook her head at me but came up with a backup plan. "Trish was going to pawn jewelry. So let's go to pawnshops, and while we're in one we'll ask to use theirs."

"Great. Trouble is, we'll need one to find the pawnshops."

A man went by pushing a shopping cart with what looked like all of his belongings in it. St. John had a fabulous harborside shopping district, I recalled, but this wasn't it.

An Indian takeout joint crouched between a discount store and an outlet for hair salon supplies. Stenciled signs advertised the businesses of tenants upstairs: AAA-1 Accounting, The Beauty Part Hair Weaving and Straightening, and Dr. Bontatibus.

His area of expertise was Painless Dentistry. "Jake?" Ellie said. "We don't need . . ."

At the moment, my own stupidity was giving me a toothache. How could I be so dumb as to forget the . . .

"What?" I snapped. But I followed Ellie's gaze, and sure enough there it was right in front of me: a pawnshop.

• • •

A bell over the door jingled merrily as we entered. Inside, the shop was jammed full of furniture, ice skates, silverware, paintings, and just about anything else a human being could sell for money—except guns. Canadians were funny about those, preferring their citizens not to be armed like the Seventh Cavalry Division.

The jewelry was under the counter in a glass case. Watches, eyeglasses, a clutter of old wedding rings and costume items spread out in tarnished splendor, none worth much.

"Help you?" the proprietor inquired, not quite rubbing his hands together at the sight of potential customers. He had on a fraying cardigan over a dress shirt whose collar had seen better days. Ellie was already in a far corner examining a box of books.

"Just a question," I began, and his smile dimmed. I had a feeling more stuff came in here than went out. But he was nice about it. "I wonder if . . ."

"*Psst!*" I glanced sideways. The sound came from somewhere near a tangle of musical instruments: banjos, guitars, fiddles, mandolins, each with at least one broken tuning peg and a snapped string. A tuba topped the shelf.

"*Psst!*" A guy peeked out from behind the display: maybe five feet tall, bald and delicately featured, with a long waxed mustache.

A *familiar* mustache. It was the guy who'd been staring at me in the Bayside when I'd met there with Ann Radham.

Ellie turned curiously from a bin full of women's gloves, their yellowish softened shapes creepily recalling the outlines of the original owners' hands. She'd already taken possession of the book box.

The guy jerked his head in summons: *Over here!* Today he wore a crisp white shirt with some kind of an official emblem on the pocket, navy uniform pants with matching jacket, and shiny black shoes. A red tie knotted with military precision held his collar tight.

"*Psst!*" he repeated urgently, waving his small, fussy-looking hands for additional emphasis.

"Excuse me, please," I said to the pawnshop man, who didn't look happy. Another minute, he likely thought, and he could have sold me one of those mandolins or maybe even the tuba.

Impatiently I approached the fellow. "Okay, what do you . . ."

Want, I would've said. *And who the hell are you and what've you got to do with . . . ?* But Ellie interrupted.

"Fascinating," she exclaimed, meaning his outfit and his perfect grooming, right down to his clear-polished nails. Except for the mustache his shave was so close it looked as if he'd gone over his skin with emery paper.

The shoes were patent leather. "Why were you in Eastport?" I demanded. "Were you following me in St. Stephen, too?"

His small pink mouth opened but no sound came out. "Jake, you're scaring him," Ellie admonished.

"That's not all I'll do if he doesn't speak up," I said as the feeling of nearly being run down by a speeding car came over me again. I seized his shoulder; as he jerked away, a sound came from one of his pockets.

It was the clink of jewelry. Good jewelry, maybe, the kind someone might pawn if she needed money.

"Come on," I told the little man brusquely, hustling him along. The bell over the shop's door jingled again as we went out.

"So what have we here?" I demanded as soon as we reached the sidewalk. Plunging a hand into his jacket pocket, I extracted a pair of bracelets, one set with red stones and the other with green. Last to emerge was a ring with a diamond as big as a Ritz cracker in it.

Well, maybe not that big. But back in my glory days of money handling in the city, I'd gotten familiar with the things rich people liked to transform into cash: coins, furs, diamonds, and gold bars, plus sealed packets of cocaine as fat and white as the ones you find in grocery-store boxes of powdered sugar.

Even so, I couldn't tell paste from the real thing without a jeweler's loupe. But I knew nobody put worthless stones into platinum Tiffany settings, and those I did recognize.

"They b-belong to Trish," the little guy managed. He'd gone completely white.

I let go of him. "What're you doing with them, then, and how do you know her?" I demanded. "And . . . did Cory know about them?"

As the guy reeled away from me it occurred to me again that maybe Trish Bogan didn't even know Cory was dead; she could've been running from *him*.

The mustached guy interrupted the near-fainting process to shoot me a look of scorn. "Cory," he uttered. "As if."

Scorn and something else. At my mention of Cory a surge of visceral hatred radiated from him, powerful as a slap. Ellie was still inside; through the store window I saw her buying the books.

Sighing at the very thought of putting even more old objects into my house—with baby gear practically falling out the windows, Ellie's certainly had no room for them—I decided that maybe Bella would like the volumes. Besides her incessant puzzle solving she read everything, so fast that Wade said it was a wonder wisps of smoke didn't rise from the pages.

Meanwhile out here on the street, pedestrians glanced at me and the quivering mustached guy, no doubt wondering whether to call a cop. "Come on," I told the fellow as Ellie emerged with the box in her arms. "You're coming with us."

I shoved him toward our car. "*And* you're taking us to talk to Trish."

"N-no!" He squirmed from my grasp. Frowning, a woman clad in business garb—suit, heels, briefcase—drew a cell phone from a bag. And at the moment we did *not* need the Canadian Mounties.

"I . . . I drove here. You can follow me," he said. He reached into his breast pocket—for an instant I thought *Gun!*—and drew out a small white card.

Puppets in Motion, Fred Mudge, Puppeteer, it read; address and phone below. "You're Fred Mudge?"

I looked from the card to his face, which had regained some of its color. He nodded energetically. "I'm a friend of Trish's. She sent me to pawn these things for her."

He reached out his small manicured hand for the jewelry. I dropped the items into my bag instead. "Uh-uh. Not so fast, bud. First you take us to Trish and we'll hear what she has to say."

Surprisingly, he accepted this. "Okay. That's my car." His wave indicated a midsize sedan, medium green.

Not a white rental. And what the heck; it sure seemed like he *wanted* us to find Trish. So we followed him to the industrial side of the harbor: tank farms, warehouses, and truck terminals.

"Are you sure we ought to be doing this?" Ellie asked as we drove. "I mean, without letting anyone else know where we are?"

Mudge signaled a turn well in advance so we could get into the proper lane behind him. Along the working harbor's edge were streets full of three-story brick row houses, now divided into three-family dwellings with iron-railed steps leading up from the basement apartments.

Moms in blue jeans and sweatshirts sat out on the stoops chatting and smoking cigarettes as they watched the kids playing on the sidewalks. Down the block a guy worked on an old car, its hood up, radio blaring. Two mutts sniffed a fire hydrant.

"I don't know," I said, pulling in behind Mudge to park in front of one of the buildings. He had driven very sedately, not at all like a wise guy. "Guess we're going to find out."

In front of one of the better-looking row house entries—no basement apartment, only one doorbell at the top of the steps—Fred Mudge waited, then led us inside.

Chapter 8

Looking for old house parts?
Check out nearby renovation jobs
for their possible discards.
—Tiptree's Tips

I sent Fred to pawn the jewelry," Trish Bogan confirmed when we'd entered the row house he led us to. "I thought he'd get a better deal."

She was maybe eighteen and from the curl of her eyelashes, the angle of cheekbone still visible in her heart-shaped face, and her full, bitten-looking red lips, you could tell that not too long ago this girl had been what Sam would've called a fox.

Now jouncing a baby on her plump shoulder she stood frumpily barefoot in the gleaming kitchen of Fred Mudge's place warming a bottle of formula on the gas stove.

"I didn't know what else to do," she added plaintively, brushing back a strand of brown hair. "I came here because I had nowhere else to go, and now Fred wants me to stay."

Her expression hardened. "But I still want my own place. And besides, he won't like having a kid around once the novelty wears off. He thinks he will, but Fred likes things kept neat."

Neat wasn't the word for it. Back in the city I'd seen fancy apartments; heck, I'd lived in one. But this place took the cake: high ceilings, plaster smooth as that baby's bottom, and paint so fresh it made me look around for an open bucket.

And all that was just the beginning in Mudge's unexpectedly plush digs. "The ring and bracelets belonged to your mother?" I asked Trish.

Mudge had stopped on the steps to tell us so before bringing us in here, as if now that we knew he hadn't stolen the jewelry we might decide Trish had. After all, unwed young mothers didn't often own the kind of bling that would have looked just right on Zsa Zsa Gabor.

Trish nodded agreement while in the next room Ellie kept Fred Mudge busy by letting him show her around some more. I'd already seen plenty; the oaken woodwork, maple floors, and cherry staircase banister all glowed with decades of polish, and the marble fireplace mantels shone mirror-bright.

"Yes," Trish said sadly. "The bracelets and ring are all I have of my mom's. But now I'm going to have to get rid of them."

Soft rugs in a variety of neutral shades complemented the furniture upholstered in nubbly wheat, each sitting area with a brass lamp, velvet or needlepoint throw pillows, and an ottoman covered in tapestry or leather.

Trish tested the bottle on her arm, then cradled the baby, who took it eagerly. "See, as soon as I found out Cory was dead I knew I had to get out of St. Stephen . . ."

Her voice broke, blue eyes filling with tears. So she had known. "Who told you?"

At least it hadn't had to be me. "Fred," she replied. "He'd go over there sometimes, to check up on what Cory was doing. Spy on him, really, so he could report all the bad stuff to me."

Sure, smear his rival; that made sense. Trish went on: "And the next day of course it was all over Eastport. That's how Fred heard about it."

She bit back a sob, then stubbornly regained her composure. "I tried to tell Cory that girl he was seeing would only get him in trouble. He just thought I was jealous."

"Were you? And how did you know about her, anyway? Did Fred tell you that, too?"

She shook her head. "Cory told me, after I smelled perfume on him. He would've gotten over her," she added.

Yeah, maybe. "And after he got convicted of stalking her?" I asked. "What was his attitude then?"

She sat at the tile-topped kitchen island, her listless wave inviting me to do the same. "Typical Cory. It just made him mad. Nobody was going to tell *him* what to do, you know?"

"Ever meet her?" And when she shook her head no: "Trish. Think hard, now. Was there anything Cory knew about Jen or about her father that either of them might've wanted kept secret?"

Because with the fire in St. Stephen, things had changed. Getting rid of Cory was one thing but going after Trish implied considerably more of a motive than just eliminating a daughter-pestering punk.

And if Jen's only link to Trish Bogan was via Cory *telling* Trish about her . . . "No," Trish answered sadly. "I didn't want to know about her."

The dozing baby woke with a sudden shriek; startled, Trish dropped her cup. It hit the expensively tiled counter and took a chip out of it. "Oh, God," she whispered, appalled.

From the next room Mudge's and Ellie's voices still mingled. Trish looked up, stricken. "When he sees that, he's going to . . ."

My eyebrows must've lifted. "Oh, no, wait a minute," she said hastily. "Fred's not . . . a problem. Not like that. He's a good guy. It's just that he cares so much about this place. He's so kind to me, but . . ."

In the dish drainer by the immaculate sink lay a grinder, the kind of low-tech, hand-cranked food processor you clamp to a counter. For making baby food, perhaps; pureed spinach or mushed-up chicken. I pulled the bottle of white glue from my bag.

"Gimme that," I said, indicating the device.

By the time Trish had settled the baby in a portable crib and returned with the grinder, I'd searched the floor and located the chip of tile her cup had removed.

The grinder's clamp consisted of two flat rubber-padded surfaces, plus a turn screw to hold them together. "Okay, now." From the other room, Ellie's and Mudge's voices approached, so I had to work fast.

"First you coat the hole and the chip with white glue." I demonstrated. "Next, you position the chip in the hole, precisely where it belongs, and I mean precisely."

That was the tricky part. "Now get me a wet paper towel." I wouldn't have a second shot at wiping off the glue squeeze-out, so I pushed the chip in with my finger, then wiped all around it without moving the chip.

I hoped. Inevitably there would still be more white glue to ooze out once the clamp was applied, and I sure didn't want the grinder to end up glued *to* the counter. "Waxed paper?" I asked.

That would keep the glue from sticking to the grinder, and the paper itself wouldn't adhere. Swiftly she retrieved some from a roller under the cabinets; I placed a patch of it over the repair and carefully clamped the grinder to the counter, directly on top of the paper.

"There," I said. "Leave it clamped for an hour, more if you can. Then *gently* scrub off any oozed glue with one of those soft sponges you use to clean Teflon pans. Have you got one of those?"

Trish nodded; of course she did. In this house Mudge likely had all the tools and solutions they use to sterilize operating rooms; distantly I wondered if he might be related to Bella.

"You have to understand about Fred," she said once the fix was complete. The baby was asleep again. "He's loved me since we were in high school together. I mean like crazy love."

I must have shown my surprise. "Fred's way younger than he looks," she explained. "We're only three years apart. But with him going bald so early, and that mustache . . ."

Right. It gave him a mature appearance. That, anyway, was a kind way of putting it. "How'd he get this place?" I asked.

She shrugged. "Inherited it. His mom and dad were in a car accident the year before mine died, left him on his own with the house and buckets of cash. So he can just do the puppet thing if he wants . . ."

That business card, I recalled: *Puppeteer.* And what was up with that? "But he thinks that's socially irresponsible," Trish went on, "so he got a job with Canada Transport."

Of course; that's where I'd seen the uniform, in the tollbooth as Ellie and I were driving from the main highway over the bridge into the city.

"He wants me to marry him, adopt the baby." She sounded like somebody who's just heard she's going to be sold into slavery.

"He really loves me," she repeated in tones of despair. "I mean don't get me wrong, I love Fred, too. I've known him forever, our parents were friends . . . he's good to me. Really good, and he always has been. It's just that . . ."

Her eyes implored me to understand why she couldn't make the safe choice: a secure home, money for the baby's needs, the kind of predictable future a mother needs.

"I don't love him the way he loves me," she finished. "And that's why I can't stay here with him. He wants to protect me but no matter what's happened, I have to have my own home, some kind of . . . I don't know. Am I making any sense at all?"

"Maybe," I said, unsure suddenly what I might have done in her place. The baby whimpered, half waking.

"Fred's hopeless with Raj," she added. "Can't figure out how to warm up a bottle to save his life, and as for diapers . . ."

She made a face, and we laughed comfortably together for an instant. "Raj?" I asked.

"Short for Rajah."

I reminded myself that she was young, and that when the kid grew up he'd be perfectly free to pretend his name was Roger if he wanted to.

"With Cory, it was the other way," Trish went on. "He never loved me at all. I met him at a dance in Calais, the baby was just an accident, and when he finally decided he wanted to marry me, it was only another scheme of his, that's all."

She smiled wanly. "See, he thought us Canadians have it so much easier. Medical, subsidized college, benefits for the baby. You know—social support stuff. He said being a Canadian citizen was like living on easy street."

If only it were true. But it sounded like Cory, all right. "Did you know he'd bought a life insurance policy?"

"No. You mean he . . . no. He never said anything about it. Are you sure?"

"Mm-hmm. So you don't know that you and the baby, along with his mother, are beneficiaries." That's what it said on the policy his mother had showed me.

"No, I . . ." She went on shaking her head. But not believably.

"Don't get your hopes up. Suicide voids the policy."

"Oh," she said, stricken. "Well. I guess it was too much to hope for. That there might be a . . ."

Silver lining. "What about Fred, do you think he might've known anything about it?"

More head shaking. "No. He'd have told me."

"Okay. Seriously, though, can you think of anything that Cory might've known or found out, that someone might want to shut him up about? Something about Jen, maybe?"

"I don't . . ."

"Something he said?" I prompted. "Something he might've told you?"

"No," she repeated. "He'd tell me how skinny Jen was, how fat I was getting. Why couldn't I fix my hair, stuff like that." She paused, remembering. "This was when I was so sick with being pregnant, I was puking just about nonstop."

Nice guy. "What else *did* he tell you about her?"

Trish sighed tiredly. "Oh, that she was so cool, and about her friends, especially this one girl. Said Jen bought stuff for this girl, always paid her way, and the girl was real jealous of him."

Ann Radham, I realized Cory must've meant: Jen Henderson's long-suffering musical pal.

"But that was just Cory, too," Trish went on. "Of course he would think that about her. Because it's the way *he* always felt," she added with unexpected insight.

Ellie's and Fred's voices moved toward the kitchen. Trish looked embarrassed. "Listen, I lied about the insurance policy before. I was in on it. He had a plan, how he was going to fake his death. Then I would get the money, and he'd come back, and . . ."

Her voice faltered, because surely she knew by now how that part of the plan would end: he'd take the money. End of story.

"It sounds so awful now. That's why I didn't want to tell you. But the thing is, Cory would never have killed himself," she insisted. "Why would he? The money was going to be his big score. It's why he kept coming around, to make sure I paid the premium. Fred," she added shamefacedly, "was giving me cash."

But I still thought the part about the suicide clause had come as a surprise; she'd looked so disappointed. "Did Fred know about the scheme?"

"Oh, no! He'd . . . he's very law-abiding." Shaking her head sadly, she continued, "Anyway, when I heard Cory was dead, I got scared, that's all. For me and Raj. I didn't know what might be going on . . ."

"And that's why you left St. Stephen? Because Cory was looking forward to the money from this scheme, so you didn't believe he'd kill himself?"

She nodded. "He'd been in a real good mood, actually. Even when Jen's father started the stalking case against him, Cory just said screw it. If he did go to jail there'd be a nice payoff from this other thing someday, he said. And then he even started insisting that he *wasn't* going to jail."

I asked her about the why of that, of course, but she didn't know, puzzlement filling her face again. Seeing it, sympathy for her over-came me suddenly; maybe the girl was no Rhodes Scholar, but . . .

"Trish, I'm sorry all this has happened to you."

"Thanks. But I kind of bought that trip, didn't I? Little late to be figuring it out," she added in a wry tone that gave me hope for her. "Anyway, like I said, I didn't know what was going on. So I ran."

By now Ellie and Fred Mudge were almost in the doorway. "I told Fred if I did stay here, though, I had to have my own money. He could sell the bracelets and ring for me or I'd do it myself."

She looked at me, suddenly realizing something else. "Um, if you don't believe me I can show you all the papers that came with them. From the lawyer and so on, when I inherited them."

"No," I told Trish gently. "I appreciate it, but it won't be neces-sary." The offer was plenty. "So," I shifted gears, as Mudge and Ellie came in, "how was the house tour?"

Meanwhile I found Mudge's card, brought it out and wrote my own phone number on the back of it, and slipped it to Trish.

Just in case. Ellie already had her own copy of his business card in her hand. "Fabulous," she replied. "You should see it. Especially his collection of puppets."

Mudge corrected her fussily. "Marionettes. Only the business card says puppets, because people don't understand."

"Right," she amended. "Okay if I show Jake?"

He hadn't seemed to notice the food grinder still clamped to the tile repair. "Sure," he said, his attention returned to the the young woman he loved.

And who didn't love him. We left them there, Ellie guiding me through the living room and down a hall past a sparkling bath, finally to a closed door. "Prepare yourself," she said.

But I couldn't have. Behind the door was a roomful of little people with faces like shriveled apples, their tiny fingers possessing veins, nails, even creases at the knuckle joints and in the scarily lifelike palms of their cloth hands.

Ranged out on shelves, windowsills, and chairs, each wore a differ-ent costume: a minister's suit, Bo Peep's blue dress, the embroidered cropped jacket and baggy trousers of an Alpine villager in traditional costume.

"Goodness," I said inadequately, half expecting them all to start preaching, sheepherding, and yodeling at me.

"But that's not all," Ellie said. "I wasn't supposed to see this, but when he left ahead of me, I peeked."

She opened a closet door. Inside, more puppets sat on shelves, with strings and sticks tucked neatly behind them, legs dangling. There were a dozen of them and at the sight of them my heart nearly stopped.

Soft brown hair, curled lashes, pert nose . . . the mouths were red and bitten looking, recognizably full-lipped. Each costume—evening gown, swimsuit, a sweater-and-skirt set that contrasted sharply with the next one's hot pants, midriff bandeau, and boots—was perfectly sewn. My own clothes should've fit so well.

The bride's dress, a confection of white lace that must've cost a fortune to create, was the loveliest. "He makes these," Ellie told me. "Bodies, outfits . . ."

And faces, each doll carefully stored where it could come to no harm. I shut the door on the motionless bodies and closed eyes, returning them to the silence of their closet.

"Oh," I breathed, still seeing them in my head. Alone in the dark . . .

"Yes," Ellie agreed, not needing to say more. Because the faces on the hidden-away marionettes all belonged to Trish Bogan, and from them it was clear Fred Mudge didn't just love the girl.

He was obsessed with her.

• • •

Outside, I put my arms on the steering wheel and my face on my arms. "Oh, man," I exhaled. "If I were Walter Henderson's defense attorney, Fred Mudge would be my new best friend."

"But, Jake," Ellie objected, "do you really think Fred's got the physical ability to do something violent to Cory Trow?"

"Doesn't matter. He's weird, he's in love, and he was in Eastport around the time when Cory died. It might not be enough to convict *him,* but it's plenty of reasonable doubt for someone else. Any jury in the world would think that where there's a will, maybe there's a way."

I sat up. "He could even have torched Trish's building, to make it look like somebody else was after her. Knowing himself that she was out already."

Ellie frowned. "I don't know about that. Weird, yes, but he doesn't seem like the type who would risk a lot of other people's lives, just to . . ."

Wordlessly, I passed the morning's *Maritime Sentinel* to her; I'd been reading it while Ellie lingered inside oohing and aahing over the infant Raj.

He was indeed an adorable little peanut, just as she said. But the baby bore too much resemblance to his father for me to take any pleasure in inspecting him: blue eyes, pale curly hair. In the paper was an article about the fire in St. Stephen, complete with pictures the surly photographer had been taking the day before.

"Trish's building was slated for demolition," I said. "There were no near-escapes after all. The other tenants moved out even before she did." I started the truck.

"Henderson's still our guy, don't get me wrong. He had the best reason, he's a career killer, and it happened at his place. It's just that he's so good at it, it's hard to nail him down." We pulled away from the curb. "And I'll tell you something else. If he went after Trish he had a reason for *that.* I just wish I could figure out what."

Mudge had given us directions back to the main highway. I took the turn he'd advised, onto Truro Street toward downtown. "I'm hungry," Ellie said.

Me too, so after some discussion we decided to go to the trendy Harborside District for a meal that would inevitably, I supposed, include arugula. Probably it would also feature that other chic but inedible impediment to happy lunching, the sun-dried tomato.

But Ellie and I were equally opposed to fast-food burgers and we didn't know St. John well enough to have any regular restaurants at our mental fingertips. So we abandoned Mudge's instructions temporarily, threading our way through downtown streets.

"Stop!" Luckily we were at an intersection and the light was red.

The last time Ellie had uttered that syllable so forcefully, I'd been about to back off the end of a pier.

"What?" No lunch places were in evidence, only an Army-Navy store, a stationery supplier's, and other vehicles.

Lots of them. "Back there," Ellie said. "On a cross street. I think I saw— Go around the block, will you?"

I obeyed even though we were in the wrong lane for the left turn. But New Brunswick drivers in cities weren't anywhere near as bloodthirstily goal-oriented as the ones I'd encountered out on the highway. Thus only a few earsplitting honks and vividly interesting hand gestures later, we were on the desired side street.

Moments after that we pulled up in front of a small diner whose tattered awning read *Le Mont Bleu*. A *French* diner; despite grimy windows and a gray, cruddy-looking exterior, my heart lifted hopefully; that meant they might have . . .

"Poutine," Ellie and I pronounced together when we got into a booth. The waitress, wearing a shiny black uniform dress with a white gauzy apron and black shoes, smiled approvingly, exposing nicotine-stained teeth.

"Et vin?" she asked, her pen poised.

Oh, indeed. Two jelly glasses of red house wine appeared; an unpretentious little vintage poured from an unlabeled gallon jug.

I took a swallow. You could've tanned leather with the stuff. "Nice place," I managed, blinking tears away as I glanced around.

It was a long narrow room with suspended schoolhouse lamps, an octagonal-tiled floor, and mirrors behind the counter opposite the row of booths. Men in rough work clothes sat at the counter eating lunches of sausage and potato and drinking their *vin*, dragging on Gauloise cigarettes between mouthfuls and conversing in a patois that I supposed was related to French.

Our plates of *poutine* arrived, smoking hot. *"Bon appétit,"* said the waitress, but *bon* wasn't the word for it; *angélique,* maybe. Because *poutine* can consist of frozen french fries, canned gravy, and Cheez Whiz, slopped together and nuked in a microwave until the mess bubbles unappealingly.

Or it can be this: fresh homemade fries peeping crisply from beneath a generous topping of crumbled cheese curds, the gravy ladled over it a rich, medium-brown liqueur of piquant beefiness, the whole dish sizzling and served on a plate too hot to touch. With it came lettuce and tomato, choice of dressing. No arugula.

"Wow," I managed around a mouthful; with enough *poutine,* I am certain that you could achieve world peace.

We devoted ourselves to our food until every scrap had gone. "Why do you think Mudge led us to Trish at all?" Ellie wondered aloud after our coffee arrived.

One glass of the jug wine had been plenty. I unwrapped and ate a sugar cube from the bowl of them. "Maybe he thought one of us had already recognized him. I'd seen him in Eastport."

"So he probably figured he'd look guilty of something if he ran," Ellie agreed.

The waitress poured us both more coffee: real cream, a hint of chicory. "Still, it seems to me he'd only think that if he *was* guilty of something," Ellie added.

I ate another sugar cube. After that lunch, I'd have smoked one of the Gauloises, too, if I could've done it without choking.

"Maybe not. It could be he's just a furtive little guy." I dug out my stash of Canadian bills for the lunch check.

Paying was a double pleasure, first because even with a generous tip the amount our good lunch cost was so tiny, and second because no matter how much of it I am spending, I do so enjoy money with the faces of women printed on it; there were benefits to having a Queen, I decided, even a distant one.

Outside, we waddled to the car. *Poutine* is delicious but it isn't inclined to make a person feel lively; more like ready for a nap. "What'd he talk about with you?" I asked Ellie.

We pulled out into the city traffic. "Well, like I said, he makes all his puppets. The costumes, too. That whole first floor of his house, the part that would be a basement apartment? That's his workshop. Although I didn't see it."

Signs pointed out the route back to the highway. "He puts on elaborate puppet shows all over New Brunswick and Nova Scotia," Ellie went on. "For charity. I gather he doesn't need the money."

"And other than the puppet stuff he does . . . ?"

"Highway toll-taker," she confirmed Trish's report. "Although he canceled some shows and took a leave of absence from Canada Transport when Trish showed up. So he could spend time with her, he said."

I could imagine how well Trish liked that. "He told me a few horror stories about the way Cory treated Trish," she added. "How he brought another girl to her apartment once when she was out at an obstetrician appointment, if you can believe it."

I could imagine that, too, and I must have frowned just as Ellie glanced over at me. "Oh, sorry," she said; she'd known my ex-husband well.

Once when I was pregnant I went out to keep a doctor's appointment but she—my own obstetrician—didn't show up. And later I learned that's who Victor was with back at our apartment, only I didn't find out until after she delivered Sam, which to this day puts a whole new gloss on my memories of the event.

"Never mind," I assured Ellie. By now we were approaching the final highway overpass before our on-ramp approach to the harbor bridge. "I don't . . ."

Something moved fast on the overpass just as we were about to drive under it.

"Jake!" Ellie cried in the fraction of an instant before the windshield exploded.

• • •

"Tossing a brick at a car is a punk's trick," Jemmy Wechsler said when we'd finished telling him the story a few hours later.

By some miracle, no one was badly injured when the windshield exploded; somehow I pulled over without hitting any other cars or being hit by them. Ellie came out of it the worst, with a flying-glass cut over her eyebrow that I thought deserved stitches, but the emergency room doctor who saw her in St. John hadn't agreed.

Then by the time we left the clinic it was too late to catch the last ferry of the evening, so we drove all the way around on the mainland back to the States and while we did, the cut started bleeding again. Thus we'd come here to the lake, where I had—courtesy of my late husband's medical bag—a really good first-aid kit. "Ouch!" Ellie said.

"Sorry." I pressed the wound's edges together, then taped it shut with Steri-Strips from the medical bag.

"What'd the cops say?" Jemmy asked, examining Fred Mudge's business card.

In our absence, he'd been busy as usual, splitting and stacking wood for the stove, painting the cabin's concrete-block interior chimney a warm chocolate brown, and setting up a propane heater so the kitchen sink now boasted *hot* running water.

Like I said: adaptable. In fact, after only a few days of Jemmy's attentions the whole place looked like a feature out of *Ladies' Home Journal* by way of *Outdoor Life*.

Also, something was cooking; chicken, maybe. I sniffed the fragrance hungrily. "The cops said what *we* say," Ellie told him. "That somebody dropped a brick off that overpass and hit us."

Jemmy raised an eyebrow at me. "So let's get this straight. This Mudge guy shows up at the same pawnshop you're at, and later you get ambushed while following directions *he* gave you?"

"Yeah," I said tiredly. "But it's the only good way to drive in or out of St. John if you're going where we were. Because you have to get on the bridge unless you want to take side streets, which we don't know how to do. So anybody who knew we were there in the first place might figure we'd show up near that overpass on our way home."

He looked skeptical but went on. "Okay, so who did know?"

"Nobody. And there was no one on the ferry with us when we left Eastport."

He made a face. "So if someone was following you in Eastport and saw you get on the ferry . . ."

I caught his drift. "The same person who followed us in St. Stephen."

"Sure. It was foggy, right? So in Eastport you might not've noticed. Somebody knows that Trish lived in St. Stephen, guesses you're on her trail and maybe also knows she went to St. John . . ."

"How would anyone know that?" Ellie objected.

Jemmy turned mildly, pushed the *Maritime Sentinel* at her. "The fourth paragraph," he said.

I hadn't gotten that far in the article, which turned out to name Trish Bogan as the last occupant of the burned St. Stephen house and her destination as St. John.

"Guess we weren't the first people those girls in the park talked to," Ellie commented sourly. "So if you knew or guessed we were on our way to St. John, you could hop in a car, drive around to it the long way on the mainland, and get there ahead of—"

"Wait a minute, wouldn't that take too long?" I interrupted.

"Not the way you drive." Which was a good point and made the whole thing sound possible, that someone had picked up our trail after we got off the St. George ferry. With that accomplished, it *would* be possible to follow us in St. John.

"But the other thing is, you can't just stand around on a major highway overpass with a brick in your hand," Jemmy pointed out reasonably. "Police officers tend to notice people who do." Meaning the timing was still tricky. "Same with a car," he said. "You could sit there with your flashers on, but . . ."

"I know, I know. Not for long. So what this shakes out to is that someone did know or suspect where we were going, and intercepted us at some point."

Jemmy nodded. "Looks that way. Stayed right on you, too, once you got spotted. Close enough to hustle out ahead of you at the right moment, be ready for the brick drop."

"There are an awful lot of possible ways for that not to pan out," I objected. "Lose us along the way somewhere or we take another route out of the city *after* whoever it was hurried ahead. We might've been planning to stay the night, even."

"Hey, it's not like the world would've ended if the plan didn't work," Jemmy pointed out. "Thing is, somebody tried it and it *did* work. On account of all the many things that could've gone wrong, didn't."

Ellie sighed. "He's right, you know." Then she looked around curiously. "What smells so good?"

Jemmy opened the iron kettle simmering on the woodstove; the aroma of stewed chicken I'd noticed earlier turned into a full-blown sensory event.

"Mmm," she said appreciatively. "I know I'm supposed to be the wounded patient and all," she added, "but I'm starving."

Likewise; the wonderful *poutine* we'd enjoyed seemed long ago and far away, and the jug wine even more so. Jemmy appeared delighted to remedy both deficiencies.

"Mudge said Cory Trow was wild about Jen Henderson," Ellie remarked as he ladled the stew out. Each big bowl held a biscuit, assorted vegetables, and the broth, rich with chicken and wild rice.

"Perfect," Ellie breathed, sipping it gratefully while Jemmy drank wine and I attacked my own bowl.

"Fred Mudge says," she went on after devouring a biscuit, "that Jen was the real problem. He said that even after her dad got that stalking case going, Jen used to call Cory on her cell phone from wherever she was. Invite him over and so on, right up until the verdict got rendered."

"Huh. How come you didn't tell me that?" I asked. The stew was fantastic; Jemmy beamed proudly.

"I was about to but then the brick hit the windshield," she explained. "Anyway, Mudge said Jen told Cory Trow that if he was a *real* man, he wouldn't be scared of her father."

Jemmy let out an amused snort. "More like if he was a *dead* man. Anyone with a brain knows to be afraid of Walter Henderson."

Including, I gathered, Jemmy himself. "Everything been quiet around here?" I asked him as we were getting ready to go.

We stood outside in the clearing. Behind us the solar lights he'd rigged up so handily suffused the cottage's interior with a cozy glow.

An owl hooted. "Yeah. So far," he answered, slapping a mosquito. "I've put up a bunch of check wires."

Threads, he meant, tied between the trees at cabin-approach spots. The strategy was low-tech but reliably informative; Wade used it when he went hunting, sometimes. If you went out the next day and any of the threads had been broken, something—or someone—had passed.

"I'm figuring now on using a scope," he added. "Maybe do it from out on the bay. If I sit out there in the dark in a dinghy, sooner or later he'll show up in a window. Don't you think?"

"Jemmy," I began exasperatedly; he was talking about a rifle with a telescopic sight, for heaven's sake. As far as I knew, he'd never even handled one.

Which wouldn't prevent him from trying. "On the other hand," Jemmy said, "I might come up with another way. I haven't really decided."

"Decide not to. I mean it, Jemmy, I told you once I don't want to be involved in . . ."

But I was. I already was. Jemmy smiled in the near darkness at me but didn't reply.

"I'm ready," said Ellie, coming out of the cabin to join us.

Driving away from the cottage, I slowed for a pothole on the dirt road and glanced in the truck's rearview mirror. Jemmy stood watching us go, his shape glowing red in the illumination of our brake lights.

I took my foot off the pedal and he vanished.

●   ●   ●

When I got home there was a note on the table and a message on the phone machine. The note was from Wade, saying he'd been called out to work on a freighter that was having trouble with its navigation equipment; he'd be back in a day or so.

Okay by me. Thanks to a hasty wash at the cabin, I looked halfway decent, but my husband tended to get bent out of shape at things like having a brick dropped on his truck. At least the towing service in St. John had brought it to a garage that offered emergency glass service. By the time we got there to pick it up, the windshield had already been replaced.

Small comfort; still, it was all I could muster as I stared at the ominously blinking light on the answering machine. Finally I pushed the button; if Sam was in some kind of trouble, I had to know.

And when I heard Bob Arnold's voice, I thought that must be it: jail, hospital. Or worse. But it wasn't.

"Autopsy results on Cory Trow just came back," Bob's voice said. "Little marijuana, some alcohol in the boy's blood."

Not Sam. "Cause of death was a broken neck. Instantaneous," Bob added. "One other thing . . . little mark in the middle of his back between the shoulder blades. Bruise, is all. I thought you'd want to know, Jake."

That the medical examiner had found no evidence for anything but death by Cory's own hand, Bob meant. The recording ended as I let my breath out, still relieved that it wasn't bad news about Sam.

Some other mother's son. This time, at any rate. And not a pleasant end for Cory Trow, maybe, but at least a quick one; my imagination let go at last of the slow-motion movies it had been showing me, of the agonies of gradual strangulation.

The dogs padded in, breaking my reverie. With Wade out on the water and Bella Diamond and my father already gone home, I was the only one around who might give them treats. "Come on," I said, glad for their company.

In the kitchen I found a box of tuna crisps that Cat Dancing liked, too, and distributed them liberally. But once that was done I was at loose ends again, alone in the silent house. Adding up the money spent so far by my dad on the roof job and writing a check to him for it didn't take long. Picking myself up off the floor at the cost of roof work at all, even at the low prices he charged me, was more challenging.

But even after all that I still faced a long evening. *Oh, grow up,* I scolded myself firmly, looking around for a project and spying the box of old books Ellie had bought in St. John.

I'd brought it in without thinking much of it. Now it sat on the hall floor, so I opened it, planning to keep some books, throw some away, and get rid of the box.

A whiff of mildew rose from the paperbacks it turned out to contain, the shabby covers bearing familiar old names: Christie, Sayers, Ngaio Marsh. I was pretty sure they were all worthless: tattered pages, water stains, some covers even missing entirely. Yet despite my intentions, when it came right down to it I felt unable to throw any of them out, as if in some way I couldn't put words to, I was their last chance.

Thus in the end I simply carried the box to the dining room and left it there. Bella could get something she liked out of it, probably, or she would be able to deal with its contents as hard-heartedly as I had not.

After that I took the dogs out, brought them in and got them settled for the night, and went to bed myself. But that didn't work very well either; the bed was empty without Wade and I knew I would tell him about the brick through the truck's windshield the minute he got home.

So around two in the morning I found myself climbing the stairs to the third floor of my ramshackle old dwelling, carrying a cup of coffee and trying to step carefully so the treads wouldn't creak, even though I was the only one around who could hear them.

•   •   •

Stripped of its wallpaper, an old plaster room that has never been painted is gray, tan, and cream, the colors of an exposed skeleton. Switching on the bare hanging bulb, I opened the bucket of premixed patching compound and got out the putty knife that I always left up there for nights like this.

The wallpaper's layers had already come off, separating between my fingers to reveal succeeding homeowners' decorating tastes. While removing it I'd thought about how happy somebody had been, seeing it up there new and fresh; it had seemed only right to admire it a final time before disposing of it.

Although I confess I'd left a triangle of the oldest stuff in a half-hidden corner, where a lavender lady still twirled a frilly parasol in a lavender garden scene. Now I dipped out some plaster patch with the putty knife, smoothed it into a gash in the old wall, and scraped it smooth.

Dip, smooth, scrape; I kept on until I got into a rhythm, the soft material sliding into the ragged holes and the excess coming off cleanly and satisfyingly. It was tranquilizing to work in silence this way, almost hypnotic. The lavender lady looked as if she had been expensive, that being another thing about old wallpaper layers; like the rings in tree trunks, they mark growth periods, because people only redecorate when they have money.

After a while of dipping and scraping I almost forgot where I was. But eventually my present difficulties crept back into my thoughts: the awareness, for instance, that if I didn't find a way to solve Jemmy's problem, it would become my own.

That in fact it already had done so. If Jemmy couldn't get rid of Walt Henderson and the threat he posed, he had decided to become a federal witness. He'd practically said as much; that if he had to he would enter what in the past he'd always scorned by calling it "Witless Protection," try to salvage what he could of a life.

But going in meant testifying, not only about yourself but against other people. Such as, for instance, me. I'd taught quite a few career criminals how to invest their money legally. But the way they'd gotten it wasn't legal, not even a little bit.

And I'd known it. What a federal prosecutor might make of that I didn't know in detail, but I was certain that it wouldn't be good; in short, the past was in serious danger of swinging around and biting me in the tail big-time.

And the only way to stop it was to get Walter Henderson out of the equation, preferably by involving him so deeply in his own legal troubles that he wouldn't be able to threaten Jemmy anymore.

Now, though, however much I was convinced of Henderson's guilt in Cory Trow's death, I knew that to anyone else his motive would seem no stronger than that of Cory's rival for Trish Bogan's affections, the puppeteer Fred Mudge. And once Henderson's legal beagles got done demonstrating *that,* he would be exonerated and freed as fast as a jury of his peers could pronounce the phrase "reasonable doubt."

As a result, I thought unhappily, the two situations—Cory Trow's death *and* the Jemmy/Walt Henderson problem—were rapidly turning into what Sam would've called a fuster-cluck.

"Jake."

I gasped, nearly dropping the putty knife. The third-floor room with its falling plaster, bare overhead bulb, and unfinished plank floor was empty except for me. *"Jake . . ."*

Like a syllable spoken through water. It was a real sound, not merely in my head; audible in the sense that I felt certain I'd heard it with my physical ears.

Whether or not it was physically spoken was another matter. An image of Victor as he had been in life popped into my mind: dark curly hair, long jaw, clever fingers, and intelligent eyes.

Outside, dawn brightened, turning the bay to pewter. Birds began twittering, racketing around in the gutters where they built nests every spring no matter how we tried stopping them. Our most recent effort was a life-sized plaster owl Sam had named Raoul; the birds had pecked it to bits.

I waited a little longer, heart thudding, but when nothing else happened I closed the plaster bucket. Then, carrying my coffee cup and the putty knife to clean at the kitchen sink, I went downstairs to begin my day.

Or started to. Because on the stairway it suddenly occurred to me—

This, you see, is yet another benefit of emptying your mind via doing your own home repairs, for Nature abhors a vacuum and as a result something useful or at least clarifying may pop in.

—that maybe they weren't.

Two different situations, I mean.

Maybe there was only one.

```
To: hlrb@mainetel.net <Horace Robotham>
From: ddimaio@miskatonic.edu <David DiMaio>
Subj: Eastport book again

Horace


   In my excitement over the lab results,
I neglected to reply to your point re what
```

we ought to tell the book's owner. Though
I think "finder" might be a better term
since I believe it's safe to say original ownership probably has not been re-
linquished...

Anyway of course you're right. Tangled
webs and so on. Besides, her own name's
in the damned thing and considering the
context how else could we explain that?

Winding down the spring term's obliga-
tions here, so will be able to devote
more time to this whole matter soon. Kids
today! Though it seems just moments ago
that our own professors were saying the
same about us, no doubt as despairingly.

Best!

Dave

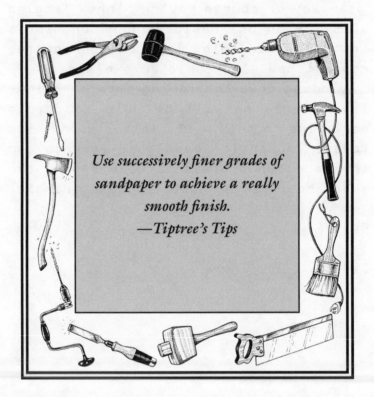

Chapter 9

*Use successively finer grades of
sandpaper to achieve a really
smooth finish.*
—Tiptree's Tips

What if Cory Trow knew what Henderson was up to?"
I asked Ellie when she arrived at my house later that morning.
"Maybe not specifically about Jemmy," I added, "but enough about
Henderson's past so people would look at him funny if Jemmy
showed up dead. That is, people other than me."

Considering this, she wrinkled her forehead and winced at the result. The edges of the cut had stayed together all right, but they

looked red. "I like it," she said of my idea as I handed her a tube of bacitracin.

"Here, smear this on," I told her over the snarl of a power saw. My father was on the roof again, cutting out the rotted part of the old sheathing.

"I like it because it's an actual practical motive," Ellie continued, gingerly applying ointment. "And to me that's been a problem all along."

To me, also. Because Henderson was a professional killer. And no matter how I tried, I couldn't quite accept the idea that he'd killed Cory for personal reasons, any more than a dentist would perform root canals for fun.

Ellie took a blueberry scone from the bag she'd brought over and sliced it in half. "Because Henderson wants to kill Jemmy." She popped the two halves into the toaster. "That, according to Jemmy, is Henderson's whole reason for being here."

"Yup." The aroma of toasting scone floated through the kitchen. "He's spent a lot of time, money, energy . . . all so he can do a job no one else has been able to do."

The scone halves popped up. She buttered them and handed one to me. "So what if Cory found out what Henderson really is?"

I bit in, the wild blueberries exploding on contact with my teeth. "Precisely," I mumbled. I want hot buttered scones served at my funeral, and I want some put in my mouth, too, just in case they really are good enough to raise the dead.

"Jen could've told him," I reasoned. "And then . . ."

Ellie nodded wisely. "Then came the stalking accusation, and the guilty verdict, and she might've said, 'Daddy, maybe it's not a such good idea to make Cory mad. Because I know I shouldn't have, but I told him you're a . . .' "

"She wouldn't want to confess her indiscretion to her father right away. She'd put it off for a while, hoping she wouldn't have to." But once it started looking as if Cory really might see the inside of the slammer . . . "Then Cory might say, 'You'd better do something about this, or I'm going to tell something about *you*," I theorized. "And Henderson would."

The power saw my father was using on the roof took on a high, unpleasant whine, as if it were biting into something more substantial than sheathing material.

Another roof beam, for instance. "Okay, let's ask Jen about it," Ellie said, and I agreed if only to escape the house, which seemed to be getting demolished.

"Where's Lee?" I asked when we were in Ellie's car. Up and down Key Street springtime chores were bursting out as exuberantly as the buds on the lilac bushes, with flower beds being neatened and windows being washed and small damp leaf piles smoldering sweetly at the edges of the driveways.

Ellie buckled her seat belt. "George signed her up for baby swimming lessons at the pool in Calais. He says it's a safety thing, living by water the way we do. He's there with her now."

The mental picture of George in a pool full of moms and babies made me giggle; Ellie too, and I'm afraid we made some good-natured fun of George over it. But our laughter stopped when we reached the iron gates guarding the entry to the Henderson compound.

Suddenly our errand was real again, our enthusiasm for sleuthing fizzling palpably. "What if *he* answers the buzzer?" Ellie asked.

The wall still bristled with tall spikes. I estimated you could hang a dozen door-to-door salesmen, political activists, and/or religious proselytizers up there without even crowding them.

Or two snoops. "He won't," I said more confidently than I felt. "Look at this place—" I swung my arm wide at the enormous parcel of shorefront real estate. "He's got people to answer gates for him," I said. "And anyway for all we know he isn't even home."

I got out, pressed the buzzer on the box by the gate, and spoke into the microphone. A woman—probably the housekeeper—answered and after a pause the gates unlocked with a loud click.

"What'd you say?" Ellie asked breathlessly as we drove in. Going up the paved drive was easier than bushwhacking around the back way along the cliffs. Near the house the fenced pastures gave way to manicured lawn studded with topiary shrubbery.

"The truth." A small flock of sheep cropped a hilly pasture; I recognized the breed. They were South African Dorpers: long nosed, sweet faced, and so expensive you might as well just buy a dozen gold-plated lawn mowers. "I said we were here to ask Jen what she'd told Cory Trow about her dad."

As we entered the circle drive leading to the house, the pavement gave way to the white pea gravel I'd noticed before. "Because 'speak truth to power' is still good advice," I added.

We stopped; no sign of giant, slavering monsters . . . er, I mean dogs. "Although when the power carries a gun, maybe not so much," Ellie pointed out. "Here goes nothing."

"Last one in is a rotten egg," I agreed, and we dashed for the porch across the wide expanse of gravel just as the enormous animals launched themselves from beneath nearby hedges.

"Run!" Ellie yelled, which was not the advice I needed just at the moment. *Fly!* would've been better, along with precise, immediately comprehensible instructions on how to do it.

Liftoff in particular was the maneuver I wanted; I could feel the dog's kibble-scented breath on my neck. And then . . .

Wait a minute. I stopped, turning to face the dog. My heart was still pounding so hard that I could feel my tonsils pulsing at the back of my throat. But even in the face of that big toothy kisser right in front of me, it didn't add up: attack dogs *plus* a flock of purebred, fabulously expensive sheep?

Nuh-uh. "You don't bite, do you?" I asked the dog. "I mean, not unless somebody tells you to."

The dog's eyes, at first as cold and unfeeling as a pair of ball bearings, softened at my tone. Its tail twitched uncertainly and began wagging.

"Ellie," I said, but she'd stopped, too, staring as her own doggy pursuer skidded to a halt. Then, seeing we weren't going to provide them with further sport, both dogs sauntered back to the hedges and lay down again just as Jen Henderson came out onto the porch.

Honey-gold hair and long legs in white shorts, a T-shirt on a body that got a regular diet of serious athletic workouts . . . but from the look on her face I thought we'd have been better off running from the dogs.

"Get in here," she ordered, gesturing sharply at us as Ann Radham appeared beside her. Ann's horn-rims shone in the sunlight and her grin was chipper as usual. But it faded when she recognized me.

"Move their car," Jen ordered, "around back."

I tossed the keys at Ann, who ambled amiably to the vehicle. Today her earrings were little gold four-leaf clovers and the red filigree pendant at her throat was a Chinese good-luck charm.

Jen's angry tone drew my attention back. "My dad will be home any minute and he won't be happy to see you here," she said, beckoning us toward the porch.

Then why, I wondered, *are you letting us in?* But the answer to that was clear once we got up the carpeted staircase to her room. "What do you two want?" she demanded.

Which let me know *she* wanted to know what we were up to. "Did you tell Cory Trow what your dad does for a living?" I asked. "And later did you tell your father that you had?"

Her face flattened. "What are you talking about?" Her room's walls held posters of rock bands, snapshots of people at parties, torn concert tickets—all the small trophies of a happy teenage life, plus some large ones. Three gold-plated softballs mounted on teak bases sported inscribed plaques that read *All-State Champions.*

So she really was a softball phenom. "Come on, Jen. It's an easy question. Did you tell him your father's a hit man? That he kills people for money?"

Tears sprang to her amazing sapphire-colored eyes. "How dare you say a thing like that?" she demanded quaveringly.

Ann's voice came from the hall. "Hey, Jen, you okay?" Her purple-streaked head poked in through the half-open door.

"Fine," Jen snapped. Her mirrored dresser was cluttered with gadgets, including a BlackBerry and two cell phones, one of them the pink model whose directory had caused a famous "It girl"—her name rhymed conveniently with *heiress*—a lot of trouble.

Ann hesitated, not liking it that we were there hassling her friend. "Why don't you all come with me?" she tried. "I'm playing at the Bayside tonight, I need to go down there and—"

"Go on, then," Jen ordered impatiently. "They're not staying long."

Ann nodded doubtfully. "Here," she said, thrusting a handwritten poster at me. "For the gig tonight."

Always the promoter; I supposed the performers got a percentage of the fee charged at the door. I folded the poster without reading it and stuck it into my pocket. A moment later came the sound of the front door closing downstairs.

"My father is retired," Jen Henderson said tightly. "What he did for work is none of your business, but it's not true what you just said. And anyway . . ."

Ellie stood by the windows overlooking the long backyard. Through them the barn where we'd found Cory's body was visible, a sight that still gave me an internal chill.

I repressed it, concentrating on Jen. " . . . anyway I wouldn't have told Cory anything like that even if it was true. It'd be none of his business, either."

One of the dresser drawers was open an inch. Inside it a jumble of jewel-toned colors caught my eye. Without asking Jen's permission I walked over and yanked the drawer open the rest of the way.

It was full of silk scarves, the faint scent of her exotic perfume wafting from them. "What the hell are you doing?" she protested. "You can't just—"

"Hey, you know what? A kid got hung in your barn the other night. A kid you were playing around with like he was another one of your rich-girl toys."

Her face flushed. "Hey, *you* know what?" she shot back. "It wasn't my fault. I mean I'm sorry. It's a shame what happened to Cory. What he did. But I *told* him he'd better not—"

She stopped abruptly, biting her lip.

"Told him what, Jen? That if he didn't scram, your father would take care of him?"

"He already had," she grated out angrily. "That's how my dad *took care* of things, not the way *you* think. We made a complaint, he got charged and convicted, and he was probably going to jail."

"Right," I said. "Likely he was, especially after he didn't show up for his sentencing hearing. And from there, he couldn't keep coming around trying to get back in your good graces."

I couldn't stop looking at the scarves. Jen stalked past me and slammed the dresser drawer shut. "So what?" she demanded.

"So I guess his heart was broken," I answered with all the sarcasm the ridiculous statement deserved. "I guess Cory Trow, a scheming little delinquent so mean his own mother gave up on him, decided to end it all. Over you."

I paused to let the foolishness of that notion sink in. Jen was sharp enough to get it, too. "Maybe he just didn't want to go to jail," she offered weakly.

"Maybe. And maybe that's why he decided to use what you had told him." Ellie moved from the window, took a few quiet steps to the other side of the room.

"I *didn't*," Jen repeated insistently, but I interrupted her.

"Up in the barn loft . . . that's where you met, right? I mean that love nest in the hay wasn't from one of the landscapers meeting his favorite sheep up there or something?"

The crudeness was deliberate, meant to shake her further and distract her, if possible. It did; with her back half-turned she didn't notice Ellie's hand moving casually toward the drawer of her bedside table.

Opening it. "You're disgusting," Jen quavered. "Why would anyone want to kill Cory anyway?"

The last time I'd seen an expression like hers, it was on the face of a deer in the headlights one night when Ellie was driving us home.

"Sorry," I said as a tear slid down her cheek. "I guess girls like you don't enjoy thinking about murder. Living on the proceeds, though, that's another matter, isn't it?"

Yeah, like I should talk. But my own past wasn't the point. Ellie slid the drawer shut, having had a look inside. "Or maybe you murdered him," she suggested, out of the blue.

Jen was a big girl, tall and large-boned, and in good shape. Once she'd gotten him into the loft she could've overpowered Cory long enough to get a rope around his neck and shove him.

My money was still on her dad because this kind of murder–the kind planned in advance–took more than physical strength. Still, might as well follow up on Ellie's remark. "So where were you the night Cory died?" I asked.

She stiffened. "Asleep in bed," she replied promptly; just as Ann had said. "And I think you'd better go. My father will be home soon."

Right; we didn't want to run into him. And I thought we had all we were going to get out of Jen, for now. But at the door I turned.

"You did tell Cory, though, didn't you? About your dad, what he does for a living. It must've seemed like a good way to get rid of Cory, scare him off with what your dad might do to him if he didn't beat it."

Her lips tightened. "But facing jail," I persisted, "he decided to use what you told him. So you were forced to tell your dad that if Cory served any time on the stalking charge, he meant to spread some news."

Jen's eyes blazed but still she said nothing.

"And having that info get around would have screwed up something important for your father," I finished, "isn't that right?"

Wordlessly she shook her head, lunged forward. "Shut *up*!" She shoved me blindly. "Get *out* of here!"

The dogs stayed put; the gate at the end of the drive opened automatically to let us out. "Poor kid," Ellie murmured.

"I guess." Henderson could've used one of the scarves as part of a scheme to trick Cory into the loft somehow, I mused as we left the estate. And in the final struggle–although not much of a struggle, or there would have been more marks on Cory's body than a single small bruise–the victim grabbed a piece of it.

Unless it really was just a scrap of his mother's sewing project. "Ellie? The drawer you looked into . . . what was inside?"

She cleared her throat. "Um, well . . . let's see, now. How do I put this? She had some personal items."

I glanced at her, surprised. Ellie wasn't the shy type and there wasn't a lot in life that we couldn't talk about. Just for example, owing to a small scheduling problem, she'd had her baby in the middle of my kitchen floor.

We drove past open fields, boggy glens full of pussy willow, and the tumbled remnants of old house foundations, the latter like dire warnings of what could happen to mine if that roof didn't get fixed soon. "Well?" I demanded.

Her cheeks grew pink with embarrassment. "Oh, Jake. There was a pair of pink plastic handcuffs. Some bottles of stuff like hand cream, only it wasn't. And a . . . device. A sort of a battery-operated . . . device."

I personally wasn't a big fan of purchased sex toys, since in my opinion the human body already comes fairly well equipped with them. But as Wade would've said, whatever floats your boat.

"So Jen's a little kinky," I mused aloud.

Ellie giggled. "Cory must've thought he'd gone to heaven."

Yeah, even before he did. "No wonder he didn't want to give her up without a fight," I agreed. The silk scarves, I thought. Were they an element of the fun and games, too? Could that be why one of them had been used to help lure him to his death?

We turned past the ball field and the defunct railroad yard. What was left of the old roundhouse still showed through the newly green grass, although the rails and ties had long been torn up and discarded.

Three blocks later my house came into view, complete with an enormous blue plastic tarp spread over half the roof. My father had needed to buy it, I thought guiltily; his request had slipped my mind again. I didn't think the mountain of newly delivered lumber and roof sheathing was a good sign, either.

"Hey," said my father, striding out from behind the house. "There've been developments." What he'd torn out of the roof now lay on the lawn, and from the look of it there was enough scrap there to build another whole dwelling.

Or there would have been if it hadn't all been wormholed and rotten. Although . . . *were* they wormholes? I bent to peer at a chunk of old beam.

From the outside it appeared undamaged but what remained of its interior was a lacework of membranous wood, reducing the beam's strength to nearly nothing. Dry, powdery dust dribbled from within, but the beam itself was wet.

"Carpenter ants," I diagnosed sorrowfully. "And it looks like they've been here awhile."

"Yup." My dad looked sympathetic. "Leak around the chimney got the wood wet, and that's what those ants love. Looks as if half the beams are infested. Treat it all for insects, sister 'em up, we can probably save the rest."

Splice in new pieces, he meant, at a cost of approximately a gazillion dollars. And besides the materials, it would take real, professional carpenters and exterminators; this was no job for an old-house amateur, even one as good as my father.

I sighed. "I guess there's no other help for it, and it looks like you've got it under control."

If you could call all the brand-new roofing material plus the attentions of an ant killer who billed by the nanosecond "under control," that is. The phone rang inside and Ellie went in to answer.

"I'll just nail my checkbook to the kitchen counter where everyone can get at it conveniently," I told my father.

Ellie came back out looking troubled. "What now?" I asked. "Furnace exploded? Pipes backed up? Electrical wiring spitting sparks out onto the oh-so-flammable parlor carpets?"

Because when one big thing goes wrong in an old house, the other major systems all get the same idea, like grade-school kids acting out because one of their classmates did.

"That was Fred Mudge. He got your number off a card you gave Trish." I followed Ellie inside where I noted that no floors had collapsed and the panes weren't falling out of the windows.

"What's he want?" I opened the refrigerator. Cheese, baked

beans, half a loaf of Bella's spectacularly good brown bread, and a couple of bottles of root beer . . . at least we had lunch.

But in the next instant my appetite dwindled to nothing. "Trish and the baby are gone," reported Ellie. "Since last night, Fred Mudge says, and she didn't take anything with her, not even baby stuff."

When Sam was that little I'd practically needed pack animals to lug around his gear. "Did he call the police?"

"Yes. He says they came and got a report, but his impression was that they thought Trish probably left on her own."

"Darn." I hurried to the phone to call Fred back.

But he didn't answer.

•   •   •

"Ellie says Mudge** told her he still hadn't gotten around to pawning any of Trish's jewelry," I reported to Jemmy an hour later. "So she didn't have much money. And anyway I'm sure that she wouldn't go far without anything to take care of the baby with."

Of course Mudge hadn't pawned the valuables. That would've given Trish the means to leave him. The ring and bracelets were still there but she was gone, so what the heck had happened?

"You believed her?" Jemmy asked. That the items were real, he meant, that they belonged to her, and that she hadn't told anyone but Fred Mudge about them.

"Uh-huh." Once I got the news that she was missing, I'd put the dogs in the truck and gone up to the lake to run it by Jemmy, see if he could come up with any useful insights.

And to check on him yet again. I was increasingly uneasy that one of these times I'd find him dead, shot in the head with a weapon that no one would ever find.

Or something. "I saw the jewelry myself and I'm pretty sure it was real. And for a girl who's possibly not the sharpest hook in the tackle box, Trish is pretty smart about self-preservation," I told him.

In other words, I wasn't going for Jemmy's first theory about Trish Bogan's sudden absence: that maybe she'd gabbed unwisely about the baubles she'd inherited from her mom and somebody had snatched her, trying to get them.

We sat at the big table in the cabin, thin sunlight slanting onto the red-checked tablecloth. "And you figure *she* didn't kill this Cory, just to get him out of her life, to hell with the insurance money?"

Jemmy plucked one of the miniature muffins he'd baked from the cast-iron muffin tin I'd always believed was in the cottage merely for decoration, popped it into his mouth. He went on with his second theory.

"Now you and Ellie're poking around, making them feel uncomfortable, they're on the run? Maybe they're in on the whole thing together, her and this Mudge guy?"

The cabin smelled sweetly of the muffins, and of the soap and water he'd used to wipe down every surface. The floor shone, the firewood box was full, the carpet was swept, and he'd made fresh coffee in the blue enamelware percolator on the stove.

I drank some, shook my head. "Nope. First of all, Trish is the one missing, not Fred Mudge. He's probably just out looking for her." I reached for one of the muffins. "Also, she was falling-down in love with that little dope Cory Trow. Don't ask me why," I added, recalling the girl's face when she talked about him.

Jemmy just looked at me. "Oh, shut up," I snapped.

Because he was right, it was exactly like me and Victor; something about Cory just rang Trish's bells. And she wasn't experienced enough to know the tune they were playing: the shark music from *Jaws.*

"The suicide clause in the kid's life insurance policy did come as a surprise to her, I'm sure. But I doubt that means anything. If she'd wanted money she could get it out of Mudge."

I bit into the muffin, realized by its taste that it wasn't one and that I should've known. Jemmy would no more bake a muffin than he would whip up a loaf of healthy, grittily nutritious whole-grain bread.

It was a cupcake from the kind of mix that needs only an egg and a cup of water, thickly topped with chocolate frosting out of a can. I licked my fingers, took another.

"Yeah, I guess that makes sense," Jemmy agreed. "Why kill for money when you could just ask for it? And even if she did want to kill him, she'd have had to get to Eastport, get him out to the barn at Henderson's and up into the loft . . ."

"Yes. While carrying the baby around," I pointed out. "Or she'd have needed to let someone else take care of that child for a while, which as far as we know she never did, not even Fred."

He nodded thoughtfully again. "So if we're wondering about villains other than Henderson, maybe we can leave out Trish and the puppeteer?"

I finished the second cupcake. "Yes. And we're not wondering about them. We can leave them all out, Jemmy. Henderson did it."

"You sound pretty sure of that." He got up to stoke the fire in the woodstove.

"I am." I explained about Jennifer and what I thought might have happened. "She likes to drink, and she's got a stash her father doesn't know about. So she's up in the loft partying with Cory, she gets a little loose, and presto, she's blabbed the big family secret, no taking it back."

I thought a moment. "Or she tells Cory deliberately, as a way of getting rid of him. Either way, Cory tries using it against her to try to get leverage with her dad, and . . ."

"Jen makes an end run around Cory, tells dear old dad what's up. After that, Daddy steps in, settles the matter permanently," Jemmy finished, closing the woodstove door. He sat across from me again. "You're right, this'd be a bad time to have the spotlight of public interest focused on Walter Henderson and his doings."

Especially since in Eastport the spotlight was more like a laser beam. "But you said Mudge hated Cory. And maybe he's not much on brute strength, but from what you've told me about him he might be able to figure something out that would work as well as muscles. He's got it bad for the Trish girl, huh?"

"Enough so he'll take another fellow's child to raise if it means he can have her." I recalled the furtive-appearing little man with the weird mustache.

"But even if Henderson *weren't* the obvious culprit, there are still those dogs of his, and the alarms. I can't see Mudge doing anything effective against that kind of double jeopardy. On the other hand, if in a careless moment Jen did tell Cory about her dad's occupation, that answers why Trish is in trouble now. Because Cory might've told *her*."

"A loose end Henderson would want to tie up," Jemmy agreed. He was coming around to my way of thinking. "But now Jen wants to be sure she never has to testify to anything. So she says she was asleep." He got up, poured us more coffee.

"Let Jen worry awhile," he advised after a slow sip. "She might still get nervous enough to tell you the real story."

"Maybe. But I don't think so. She's tougher than I thought she'd be. You think I should warn Cory's buddies? He could've talked to them about Henderson, too."

He gave me a scathing look. "You warn flies before they get swatted?" He'd never had a soft spot for street punks.

Other than me. But then he relented. "Nah. Henderson can't just start mowing down the population. Cory *might* have told his pals, but Henderson's gotta stick to the ones other people could take seriously. What I'm wondering is why he didn't dispose of the body. You'd think with all his on-the-job experience . . ."

But I'd already figured that out. "First, he wants it to look like suicide. And second, he doesn't know how to dispose of bodies around here. It takes," I finished, "a degree of familiarity."

"With the territory, right." Jemmy nodded. "Better to have somebody else discover the body, too. Because . . ."

Because in real life he who found it is generally he who done it, to borrow a notion from Bella's box of used books.

"Good point," I agreed. "Anyway, I've got to go." And as an afterthought, "You've worked wonders here," I told Jemmy.

The stovepipe had been taken apart, polished, and put back together with new rivets. Minus their usual scrim of cobwebs, the windows glittered, and the broken-down settee in the corner had been replaced by a new daybed. Its crisp cover and pillows gave the whole place a clean, cheerfully cosmopolitan flair.

"Thanks." He waved at a desk he'd built out of some planks and cinder blocks he must've salvaged from behind the shed. "Got my little command central over there," he pointed out.

He'd set up a laptop computer and a lamp. There was even a wireless Internet connector complete with blinking lights. "How did you manage that?" I asked, surprised.

I'd never tried, just assumed we were out of range back here in the woods. "Figured I'd give it a go," he replied, waving at a new cell phone in a charging stand on a windowsill. "Turns out there's a new tower across the lake, wireless access as good as a phone line."

I'd never noticed the tower, either; it must've gone up over the winter. But it meant I could call Jemmy, a big improvement over driving all the way up here to check on him.

"Excellent," I said, writing his cell number on a napkin. Then another thought struck me. "How're you getting back and forth to town, anyway?"

"Necessity's a mother." He stuck his thumb in the air while taking a few steps in place to pantomime walking and hitching.

Which I thought sounded risky but he just waved me off when I tried to object to it. Together we went outside, where the dogs had finished investigating every deer-scat pile, rabbit warren, and porcupine trail on the path leading into the forest. Now they lounged under the hemlocks near the cottage.

"How's the kid?" Jemmy asked.

Sam, he meant. "About the same, I guess. All I really know is that I don't know what to do. He's headed down a hard road and I can't seem to stop him. We all want to help him but if we do something like not drinking around him, it just makes him angry."

Jemmy grimaced. "Well, sure it does. I mean come on, let's say you get diabetes so I start prickin' my finger six times a day, how'd that make *you* feel? Or hey, how about this, you need a transplant so I go get a new kidney put in, start actin' like now all your troubles are over. Would you like that?"

"No. Of course I wouldn't. I hadn't thought of it that way."

We stood there a minute in the spring sunshine, soaking it in. "You try that auxiliary group they got?" he asked. "Al-Anon? Bunch of whiners, I heard."

They weren't. But they'd been at it so much longer than I had, most of them, that it scared me to listen to them: what they'd been through, what I still had to look forward to.

"I knew a guy once," Jemmy said, "real rummy, you know the type. Sorry," he added at my expression. "Anyway, he quit drinking, just one day up and checked himself into a place. And you want to know what he said afterwards?"

"Yes." Despite the sting of the word "rummy," I still wanted to hear. Such stories to me were like grainy old news film of men walking on the moon: people had done it.

People could. "He said it was like giving up," Jemmy went on. "Like just puttin' up the white flag and takin' whatever came next 'cause at least you don't have to do *that* anymore. What you been doing."

His voice took on an echo of the rhythms I remembered from the street and made me feel briefly homesick for those times, the good old days before everything happened. But that thought led me back to his current predicament.

"So everything's still okay here?" Seeing me begin heading for the truck, Monday the Labrador scrambled to her feet.

"So far," said Jemmy. Prill the red Doberman stayed where she was in a nest of evergreen boughs. A blue jay let out its harsh call from somewhere in the woods.

"Maybe Henderson's lying low," he added. "Letting the Cory Trow thing settle awhile, you know?"

Maybe. Or maybe not. Jemmy went on, "Anyway, thanks again for letting me stay here. I know it's kind of awkward for you and I'm sorry about that."

Discovering his corpse would be awkward, too. "If you're really sorry you can prove it by lying low for a while yourself." I came to a decision, took a deep breath. "Just . . . somewhere else. Take off and let me try to do something about Henderson for you. Maybe I can still . . ."

Get Walter Henderson sent to jail, I meant to finish. Nail him with an accusation I wouldn't have to back up with a history lesson, one that reflected just as badly on me as it did on him.

Put him where he can't hurt you, I added to Jemmy mentally. *Fix this for both of us.*

Because some secrets are better kept. I turned from watching the jay's flight. "I'm just trying to help . . . Jemmy?"

Trees, water, sky. The jay cried distantly again. I rushed inside but of course he wasn't there, then back to where the path led into the trees, calling for him.

No answer. In the silence I turned helplessly, knowing now that his peril had been even more real than I'd understood.

And more imminent. "Jemmy!" I cried a final time. But there was no answer, only the stealthy crack of a stick behind me on the path.

I whirled, instinctively putting my hands up, but whoever it was stayed nimbly at my back, unseen. Next came a crashing pain, the thud of impact, and a white, bright light in my head . . .

The light faded to gray, then black.

```
From: hlrb@mainetel.net<Horace Robotham>
To: ddimaio@miskatonic.edu<David DiMaio>
Subj: Best policy


Dave,


    Glad you agree on the disclosure mat-
ter. I think the only way to do it is in
person, don't you? We might write up a
short biographical sketch of her book's
author along with some historical con-
```

text, and send it to Ms. Tiptree in advance of a meeting. To prepare her
for...well, there's no other way to put
it...our more upsetting revelations.

Cheers, and Lang sends best—

Horace

Chapter 10

*Clean old window hardware
with paint stripper,
a wire brush, and steel wool.
—Tiptree's Tips*

Waking up after you've been hit over the head, I can report
from sad, hideously vivid personal experience, is a matter of the spirit being willing but the flesh being the consistency of loose Jell-O.

"Jake, are you all right?"

I moaned, tasted blood, and shifted painfully on the cold ground
outside the cottage.

"Jake . . ." The voice faded in and out. Blackness dissolved to gray again, a static-filled roar in my ears. My vision was like a snowy TV screen.

"Easy, now . . ." Eastport police chief Bob Arnold put his big hand between my shoulder blades, supporting me.

Ellie was with him, her face gray with anxiety. Somewhere nearby, Leonora whimpered, then let out a howl they could probably hear all the way across the lake.

Pine needles stuck to my cheek. I brushed them off and put my hand to my scalp; my fingers came away stickily wet.

"What hit me?" But it was coming back to me. I sat up; the world spun only a few times.

"Hey," Bob Arnold cautioned, "watch out for that first step."

I managed a grim chuckle. I could speak and understand okay, my gut wasn't in upchuck mode, and I wasn't sleepy or woozy. So I probably hadn't suffered a concussion; having a brain surgeon ex-husband, even a dead one, came in handy sometimes.

I had, however, been clobbered by someone. "Where are the dogs? Are they . . . ?"

"They're fine. Ellie's got 'em." The next thing I knew, I'd been helped into Bob's squad car and he was driving me away from the cottage. Then I remembered the other thing:

Jemmy. I stiffened, sending a sudden bolt of pain crashing through my skull. Simultaneously another question that had been floating around in there solidified. "How did you find me?"

Bob maneuvered the car around the potholes and rocks. "Ellie called me. She said she thought you ought to be back home by now and that she had a funny feeling about you."

"I see." He misjudged a pothole; the resulting bump in and out of it only made my skull scream in agony a little bit.

"So," I managed. "She had a funny feeling and on account of it you dropped everything to drive her up here."

He glanced over at me. "I had a feeling, too." By now we'd reached the smoother paved road, for which I was so grateful I could've knelt and wept. "Remember how it happened?" he asked.

I started to shake my head; bad choice. I waited until the stars cleared. "Yes. I heard a sound and then somebody hit me."

He didn't comment. A warmish trickle ran into my eye; a head wound, serious or not, bleeds like the devil. Without taking his eyes from the road, he pointed at the tissue box on the dashboard.

Minutes later we pulled into the hospital's emergency room parking area and Bob spoke again. "You know a guy named Mudge?"

The hospital was a low yellow-brick building with an asphalt parking lot. Two sliding glass doors with EMERGENCY stenciled on them in big red capital letters led to a small waiting area.

Bob Arnold wasn't supposed to know anything about Mudge. "What about him?" Feet on the floor, check. One foot in front of the other . . . well, I was working on it.

"Ellie heard from Bella, who heard it from somebody in the IGA, that a fella with a strange mustache got muscled into a car on Water Street this morning."

The world did a weave and a bobble. "That's Mudge. Who saw it happen, did Bella say?"

"Yup. Bert Merkle." Bob took my arm steadyingly as we crossed the waiting area and through another pair of double doors toward the examining room. I guessed he must've called ahead to say that we were coming, because no one stopped us.

Bert Merkle, I thought despairingly as a hospital aide went by the cubicle Bob led me into and did a double take. Glimpsing myself in the mirror over the washbasin, I saw why; my face with its short, dark hair, high cheekbones, and unremarkable mouth—a lipstick-free zone—looked as if I'd been beaten up in an alley.

Merkle was the guy Ellie and I had seen out on the fish pier just before we'd met up with Jemmy Wechsler. Merkle, the UFO nut and grand-prize winner of Eastport's Least Likely to Be Believed About Anything contest . . .

Bummer, as Sam would've said. Dried blood caked my eyebrows and an area in my scalp was split wide.

"I'll be back," promised Bob Arnold. "Hospital's been having some trouble about cars getting swiped for joy rides from the employee parking lot; I'm going to chat with the Calais cops in case the offenders turn out to be from our neck of the woods."

Then Ellie arrived. "I'm okay," I assured her again, though I wasn't yet certain of it. "What's this about Bert Merkle being the one who spotted Mudge getting grabbed?"

"It was him," she confirmed unhappily. "Ranting about it now to whoever'll listen. Which most people won't but he doesn't seem to mind that."

Correctamundo; another Sam-ism. Oh, why did it have to be Merkle when just about anyone else was more credible? "How'd Bella know it was Mudge?" I asked.

"She didn't. She described to me what she'd been told, about the mustache, and I realized. So now all three of them are . . ."

"Yeah. Trish, him, the baby." Vanished. Jemmy too; not good. "What else?"

Because she looked even more miserable than I felt. "Lee's got an ear infection. It started when George was at the pool with her. So I'm going to have to drop everything and . . ."

I'd thought that howl at the lake sounded even more glass-shatteringly loud than usual. "Of course you are," I told Ellie. "To take care of her, the poor little thing. But she'll be all right?"

Ellie nodded. "I left her with the nurses for a minute down in the pediatric clinic. She'll be fine. But . . ."

"But you're sticking close to home for a while," I agreed.

She nodded resignedly. "I know it's a minor thing . . ."

"Don't be silly. Listen, when Sam was little I used to agitate for the pediatrician to give him antibiotics just to have his fingernails trimmed, I was so cautious."

Which the pediatrician wouldn't, of course. But I understood Ellie's feelings completely. "You just go on. Really, it's okay," I insisted.

She looked relieved. "We might hang around your house. Your dad's got George working with him so he can . . ."

Get the job site ready for the really *expensive workers to do their stuff on it,* I finished her sentence silently. But I tried to put a good face on it.

"That's even better. George'll be with you, and you'll be there to keep track of me . . . if you hadn't come looking for me I'd still be up at the lake, you know, lying there unconscious."

Just then the X-ray technician arrived. "Merkle say anything else?" I asked Ellie as the technician waved for me to seat myself in the wheelchair she was pushing.

I knew the protocol better than to insist on walking. Ellie shook her head. "No. I guess I'll go, then. See you at home. You sure you'll be all right?"

"Absolutely," I told her calmly as the tech wheeled me away. My confidence, however, remained secretly a little shaky, since when you have a potentially serious head trauma they X-ray you first, before stitching your scalp, on account of no one's sure yet that they won't have to open your skull up with a bone saw.

Immediately. Because a possible complication of head trauma is hematoma, which is when a blood vessel begins leaking like a pipe down in your basement: slowly at first, then faster until it reaches your brains's fuse box.

Whereupon it starts putting your lights out.

●   ●   ●

As it turned out, the doctors didn't have to use the bone saws, and on the way home an hour and a half later I told Bob Arnold the whole story.

Or almost all of it. Praying that I was doing the right thing, I kept my mouth shut about Jemmy. Bob listened silently until I was finished.

"Little scrap of cloth," he repeated, surprising me.

I'd confessed to him that I'd touched Cory's body as it hung in Henderson's barn, and that in doing so I'd dislodged and lost what I now thought might be evidence.

Then Bob surprised me again: "Nice haircut."

"Sheesh." I glanced in the squad car's vanity mirror, cringing at the two-inch-wide shaved strip bisecting my scalp. The sutures at its center gave it flair. So did the dark orange stain of the cleanser they'd used before putting in the stitches.

"It'll grow back," Bob said comfortingly. "Listen, you sure what clobbered you wasn't just a chunk of birch blowdown?"

"Bob, don't you get it? I'm trying to report three missing people and an assault."

"You know, that dead stuff real high up in the trees," he went on, ignoring me. " 'Specially birches, a big wind breaks it off, it comes down and—"

"There was no wind," I interrupted. "Big or otherwise."

He drove stolidly, the city's old Crown Vic devouring the road without fanfare. "Okay. So maybe it broke yesterday, didn't fall until today," he said.

I let out an impatient breath.

"And that bit of cloth you say you lost," he continued. "Now you feel guilty, you feel like you've got to follow up in case you really did ruin evidence."

"Bob," I began; he held up a silencing hand.

"I'm just saying, that's all, Jake. There are lots of possible explanations for things. And sometimes the way things look to us at first, that's not the way they turn out later."

I said nothing.

"There was nobody at the cottage, Jake. Only you. Just a broken branch and an old birch tree, lot of rot high up in it. Right next to where we found you."

Of course there was no one, because Jemmy had vanished. But I couldn't tell Bob that. Going into custody willingly was one thing, but being taken in—even by cops looking for Jemmy in an attempt to save his life—was another.

And once any cop learned that Jemmy had warrants outstanding, there'd be no choice. We passed the cottage turnoff. "My car," I said, remembering that I'd left it there.

"Ellie drove it home. She came up with me."

"Oh. Sure." We sped through the series of patched-blacktop curves running along the shoreline. I pushed away the thought of Ellie traveling this same way in the Fiat, her foot so thoroughly made of lead that you could've anchored a tugboat with it.

At least somebody was having fun. "Some folks," Bob remarked conversationally, "b'lieve Bert Merkle when he says little green men with big eyes are visitin' his junkyard on a nightly basis."

"Right." I leaned back. My head hurt like a son of a bitch. Heart, too. Because now I was alone in this.

Bob glanced sideways. "Jake, don't go all sullen on me. You can't expect me to drop everything and go looking for people who haven't even been reported missing."

I felt a pang of guilt. He'd already spent half his day taking care of me. "Yeah. I guess. And Trish Trow has been reported to the Canadian cops. But Fred Mudge hasn't and now there's nobody *to* report him."

His neighbors would take a while to notice. And he'd told Ellie that he'd canceled several puppet shows and taken time off to be with Trish, so nobody was going to miss him at work.

Bob sighed as we reached the marshes of the Perry inlet, crossed the old Maine Central rail bed, waited for a couple of noisy tractor-trailers, and took the turn toward Eastport.

"I'll put the word out, all right?" he gave in finally. "On the county's squad radios, their descriptions, both of 'em, Mudge and Trish, your standard lemme-have-a-word-with-them stop and check. The baby, too," he added, before I could do so. "Anyone spots 'em, they'll give me a holler." *Haul-ah:* the Maine pronunciation. "And I could call the St. John folks, say I'd like to know if anything develops on their end. Okay?"

"Yes," I told him gratefully. "More than okay. If the St. John police know you're taking it seriously, then *they* might. . . ."

Not that it was going to do any good. But at least I wasn't out here on the high wire all by myself. "Thanks, Bob."

Minutes later we pulled up in front of my house. "I want you to go in and take care of that head," he said. "Lie down, relax. No running around chasing after something that . . ."

That probably didn't even happen, I finished silently, and got out. He was humoring me but I knew he would do what he'd said he would, and it was the best I was going to get.

"Okay." Lights burned in the kitchen and parlor and the Fiat was in the driveway, having survived Ellie's (no doubt) excellent adventure in it.

"Thanks again," I said sincerely, and Bob drove away, secure in the knowledge that I would follow his orders: sane, sensible.

Uh-huh. Sure I would.

•   •   •

An hour after I got home I was down at the Bayside watching Ann Radham set up for the gig she'd mentioned earlier in the day. What I wanted was to go to bed, especially after all the fussing Ellie and Bella had treated me to the moment I'd walked in. Soup, pillow, ice pack, a blanket over my feet . . .

George had even wanted to call the Coast Guard, have Wade helicoptered in from the freighter repair. But I put the kibosh on that, protesting that all I wished for was the shutting down of the house for the night.

Finally Sam kissed me on the cheek—wine on his breath, I noticed sadly—and they departed, Bella with another half-dozen old mystery paperbacks tucked into her satchel. Ellie said the housekeeper had pounced on them and begun devouring them the second she'd spotted them, between working on her usual steady diet of crosswords and Sudoku.

Now strings of twinkly lights crossing the Bayside's low ceiling mingled with the glow of vintage lamps to give the place a dim, 1950s-era jazz club atmosphere. I stood in a corner, a cap pulled on over my shaved head, unnoticed among cheerful groups of casually dressed folks with drinks in their hands.

The other act on the bill was an acoustic trio, two guitars and a stand-up bass already performing on the small stage. As they swung into "A-Train" I stepped up behind Ann, who sat at one of the crowded tables with her back to me.

Leaning down, I whispered into her ear. "You're going to get me in there again and you're going to stand watch for me. *Smile*," I ordered, my fingers digging into her shoulders.

She stiffened, but managed to produce the requested facial expression. Smart girl; the way I felt, I'd have had no problem moving my hands a few inches upward and twisting her head off.

"Why should I?" Ann demanded when I'd marched her across the seating area and through a set of French doors, leading to a hall with the restrooms at one end and the fire exit at the other.

"Because if you don't, I'll tell Jen you've been stealing from her," I replied.

I knew nothing of the kind. I just knew rich people always suspected something like that. This time the jab hit home harder than I expected, though. Ann's pixie face blanched guiltily.

"Hey, I don't care how far into her pocketbook you are." I took her arm; she didn't resist and I walked her out through the emergency exit, down the gravel-paved alley to the street.

"Fifty bucks here, a hundred there," I persisted; might as well have her good and scared. It would make her obey me better.

But her answering look said I'd underestimated: not fifty or a hundred dollars. More, maybe a lot more. I aimed her at the Fiat, which I'd left at the curb. She gave a little sideways hop to avoid stepping on a crack in the sidewalk, got in and slammed the door.

As we were pulling away she looked yearningly back at the warm wash of light spilling from the Bayside's window. "I've got to be back in time to—"

"Yeah, yeah." I gunned the Fiat. "You'll be there in plenty of time to play your second set," I told her, heading out County Road to the Henderson place.

Not that I cared if she was. "So, are they home?"

"No. Listen, I hope you're not going to tell—"

"That you're a sneak thief? Depends how the evening goes." I drove past the small wooden houses on either side of Marble Street. Inside, folks were watching television or sitting down with their knitting or taking hot baths; peaceful endeavors.

Maybe if this girl had been more forthcoming earlier, I'd be doing one of those things, too, instead of nursing a head bump the size of an ostrich egg, complete with a laceration big enough to let the ostrich out.

"From here on out I'll ask the questions and you'll answer. So where are they and how long d'you think they'll be there?"

"Jen and her dad?"

I made a face. "No, Tweedledum and Tweedledee. Come on, Ann, let's not get off on the wrong foot. You won't like the result."

She nodded, replied hastily. "They're at the ball game. The girls' team here in town. Jen's pitching."

"Daddy's watching?" Another grudging nod. And sure enough, as we passed the ball field at the edge of town, tall banks of white lights glowed over the diamond.

I happened to know the girls' night games didn't start until eight. That gave me about two hours; plenty, unless something went wrong.

More wrong, I mean, than things already had. I kept shoving Jemmy's disappearance to the back of my mind, along with all the worst possible explanations for it.

But it kept popping up again, grinning like the clown from a scary jack-in-the-box.

"S-so what d'you want me to do?"

The closer we got to Henderson's place, the more nervous Ann grew; you'd think she'd been raiding Fort Knox. We pulled up in front of the gates. Lights from the house winked intermittently through the trees. "You can get in, right?"

Faced with actually doing it, she balked. "Yes, but . . ."

That's the thing about unwilling co-conspirators: they take so much goading. "So you are ripping her off, aren't you?"

Her expression darkened but she said nothing, the gold four-leaf-clover earrings winking in the reassuring glow of the Fiat's dashboard lights. "What is it, a credit card scheme? Or does she keep so much cash around, you can just dip in whenever you want without her noticing?"

Sulkily Ann drew a keypad from her bag, pressed buttons on it. The gates swung open. "Shut up about me, okay? Just do what you came to do. And for your sake, I sure hope you know what that is."

If I hadn't been so mad, scared, and practically on my knees with the headache I still had, I'd have burst out laughing at the thought of me knowing what I was doing. I mean besides *looking*: all over the house, the grounds, and in the barn, in case Jemmy was here alive and I could get him out before Henderson murdered him.

The others, too, of course: Trish, the baby, and Mudge. But mostly Jemmy, because when I said I'd be dead if it weren't for him, I meant it. The gates closed behind us.

"So *did* Jen tell Cory what her dad does for a living?" I asked as we approached the big house.

I still thought she had and that Henderson had killed Cory on account of it. Then he'd snatched the others who might betray him believably—because Cory might've told Trish, and she could have told Mudge—before homing back in on his original target: Jemmy himself.

"What he *did*," Ann corrected me flatly. "*Did* for a living. He's been retired for a couple of years now."

"Aw. That's sweet. Took a pension, did he, got a gold watch? They gave him a party, then he magically turned himself from a paid killer into a harmless old duffer who wouldn't hurt a flea?"

The paved driveway transitioned to that dratted pea gravel. The crunching tires-on-stones sound was *loud*. The yard lights were on, too. The porch in particular looked like a trap. But at least no ravenous dogs appeared, and the lights inside the house had that motionless look: nobody home.

Ann scowled. "You're on the wrong track, you know. The whole idea of Jen telling Cory anything is ridiculous. Do you have any idea how much trouble she'd get in if she—?

"What, then? What *is* the right track? What do you know that you're not saying?" But at this the girl fell stubbornly silent, her narrowed eyes and tight, angry mouth letting me know she thought I was being really mean.

"Oh, please," I told her. "Wipe that snotty look off your face. Like I give a rat's ass about your opinion of me."

The scowl vanished, replaced by resignation. "Pull the car around to the rear, you'll see a place." Behind us the driveway remained empty, no headlights moving on it.

So far. I eased the Fiat around to the side of the house, into the dark.

"I don't know why you even think any of this is any of your business, anyway. I mean, you stick your nose in, stir up a whole lot of trouble, maybe even get *me* in trouble–"

"Ann. I'm losing patience with you. Maybe I'll just go back to the ballpark and tell Henderson that you–"

"Okay, okay." Trapped, she put her hands up in a surrendering gesture.

As we left the car behind us in the shadows, it struck me that I was out here looking for three full-grown adults plus an infant, and the Fiat was for all practical purposes a two-seater.

But it was too late to worry about that now; if I found them all, and I should be so lucky, I'd just have to put the top down and they could sit in each other's laps. I doubted they'd object.

Ann let us in. I scanned the hall leading to the living areas and back to the kitchen; there I glimpsed the glowing green "ready" lights on the panel for the alarm system. A couple of empty duffel bags sat on a bench against the wall. I eyed them questioningly.

"Jen's leaving in two days for a couple of weeks of practice with her new team," Ann explained. I glanced around a final time at the deluxe interior of Henderson's trophy house; over it all hung the smells of cedar and beeswax, lemon oil and camphor . . .

Eau de cash, my dead ex-husband Victor used to call it. "So are you just going to stand there?" Ann prodded.

"No. Where would he hide somebody?"

Her dark eyebrows went up in surprise. "I don't think . . ."

"Good. Just show me." *Hope springs infernal,* Jemmy always said. Or used to say; Ann led me to a door leading off the hall.

"Goes to the cellar." I paused in front of it. The doorknob sported a Block lock, the kind it takes heavy explosives to open if you don't have a key, and when I tapped experimentally on the door it made a heavy, metallic noise like the door to a vault.

The cellar was a safe room, I realized; of course Henderson would have one. There was a light switch by the doorway; Ann flipped it and reached past me to open the door. A clean, well-built set of varnished blond oak steps led down between pristine white-painted walls.

Silent, clean, empty. At the bottom of the stairs a green tiled floor stretched vacantly away into what resembled an office corridor with white walls and white fluorescent fixtures recessed into the acoustical-tiled ceiling.

Doors lined the corridor, three on each side. Suddenly I didn't want to go down there where I might find Jemmy's body . . . or more. "What's in the rooms?"

"Nothing." I'd heard of that, never experienced it. Any time my own cellar wasn't full of water it was full of things we would never use again but couldn't quite bring ourselves to throw away.

My least favorite was Victor's treasured set of surgical tools. But now I was glad I'd kept them. If my headache got any worse, I planned using them on myself when I got home. The knit cotton cap atop the scalp stitches had been a particularly bad idea. Ann's eyes widened suddenly as footsteps sounded on the pea gravel outside.

"Oh, shit," she muttered in heartfelt tones. Swiftly she shut the light off and closed the cellar door, leaving me on the wrong side of it.

But first, with the speed of a snake striking, she pushed me.

Hard.

● ● ●

Well, of course Ann had pushed me. The great and terrible Walter Henderson was coming home, and there I was sneaking around his house with her help. It made perfect sense that she would want to get me out of sight fast, so I was more okay with her action than I might have been. My question was, would she tell him I was here?

Probably not. It was in her interest for me to get away so that (a) she wouldn't be asked about my presence and (b) I wouldn't betray her thievery against Jen in a (no doubt futile) bid to save myself.

What I really didn't like was the darkness. I'd had my hand on the rail when the shove came, so instead of toppling down the steps, I'd more like scampered down them. But the only light came from an-other grid of glowing LEDs at the end of the corridor.

Slowly my eyes adjusted so that by the light's faint gleam I could see the walls and doors again. Footsteps crossed the floor over my head, moving to the kitchen. Next came a *chunk!* of the big refrigerator door closing and a clatter of ice from the ice maker.

He was fixing himself a drink. So Ann *hadn't* told him about me. That gave me breathing room; not much, but a little. And to go with it I had a scrap of information, the kind of stray fact you learn by acci-dent, never thinking it will do you any good.

Like this: Once upon a time you could move to Eastport, buy land, and construct anything you wanted on it. Those times were gone, though; nowadays you had to obey the building code, many de-tails of which I knew due to my own house requiring another building permit approximately every ten minutes. And the building code said a cellar had to have a door to the outside.

True, cellar doors were usually locked. But if I'd had a safe room like this one in my cellar, I'd have put in a quick way to exit it from the inside. Creeping down the corridor, I paused to open each door and briefly switch on every light in each of cellar rooms. As Ann had said, they were empty except for one that held winter sports gear: skis, poles, skates, hockey equipment.

Jen's, I supposed. As I went along I tried not to remember that each room also had a small, high window at ground level; that build-ing code again. If Henderson looked out he'd see those lights going on and off. But there was no help for it.

Five rooms opened, one to go; no Jemmy, no anyone else. Metal strips were inlaid into each door frame, making me wonder again about that alarm system. Even if I couldn't hear them, they should be going off somewhere. I'd seen the system's panel of "ready" lights in the kitchen.

The green lights down here belonged to a backup panel, showing the system still activated and featuring a big red panic button. Another safety feature; you could press the button, summoning the cops.

Still, by now I'd done about a dozen things that ought to have set the alarms off and nothing was happening. Which meant the alarms were disabled, either because they'd malfunctioned or because they'd been shut down; so much for summoning help via the panic alert. Switching out the final room light, I made my way to the end of the hall; time to pray that there really was an emergency exit.

The cellar doors I'd hoped would be there actually were; oh happy day. As I reached eagerly for them, however, lights blazed on. "Looking for something?" Walter Henderson asked, smiling as he descended the stairs toward me.

Biting my lip in sudden terror, I shoved the doors. But they wouldn't open and a heavy metal rattle from outside told me why; a chain had been thrown over them and fastened.

Probably with a padlock.

*Keep small disposable foam
brushes on hand for quick
paint touch-ups.
—Tiptree's Tips*

Brush-cut silver hair, faded remnants of a Florida tan, eyes like
iced sapphires coldly focused on me . . . casually strolling down the
basement corridor at me, Henderson kept smiling.

Carrying a thick black leather-gripped assault baton in one hand,
he slapped its lead-weighted business end into the palm of the other.

Oh, my aching head. There was nothing I could say and I was too
scared anyway to speak. He stopped a few feet from me, still slapping
the baton.

"You would be looking for . . . ?" he asked fake-helpfully.

Looking for trouble, was what I'd been doing. And I'd found it. Yes indeed, I'd found a great big heaping helping of . . .

"Jemmy Wechsler." Henderson answered his own question. "Your old pal and compatriot. As you can see, he isn't here."

Annoyance seized me and with it my voice returned. "I've noticed that." Because what did I have to lose? Alone with what amounted to a serial killer—

I meant let's face it, when you added up his numbers the fact that he got paid for them was pretty much beside the point, wasn't it?

—who was getting ready to bonk me. Maybe to death. And there was nothing I could do about it. So yeah, I mouthed off a little. My final words.

So sue me. "You son of a bitch," I pronounced carefully.

It was a good bet I wouldn't get to say any of this again. Or anything else either, for that matter.

I wanted to make sure he understood me. "You murdered that kid because he was in your way. You made it look like suicide so you could go on with your main plan. Killing Jemmy."

A bolt of guilty sorrow pierced me. I'd been wrong even to try searching here; Jemmy was already dead. The others, too, even the baby.

Because standing here with him, I understood something about Walter Henderson that I hadn't before: that when you confront a guy like him and ask the age-old question about how could a person do such things, you're ignoring the obvious.

The fact, I mean, that a person couldn't. That no matter how civilized he'd been able to make himself appear in the past, this wasn't a person but a hideously clever facsimile like one of Fred Mudge's puppets. One that in Henderson's case possessed flashes of human feeling; he cared, apparently, about his daughter.

But it was the way he expressed his feelings that revealed his true nature: murder, mayhem. That was why I was so shocked when he reached past me and unlocked the cellar doors.

The lock was a simple push-button affair, not a chain on the outside; in my fright I'd simply missed it. The doors swung open onto a set of concrete steps leading up to the night sky.

"Go on," he said, waving outward, apparently so I'd know in which general direction I ought to remove myself.

"The bodies are in the barn, aren't they? You've got them in the barn," I said from outside the cellar.

Because of course they were all dead. Henderson looked up at me, his dark shape silhouetted in the lights from behind him. "Would you like to look?" he invited.

The barn's high roof loomed against the sky: dark, silent. From his confident offer I knew it would be empty. He'd found somewhere else to stash them.

As I turned he spoke once more. "I've behaved with restraint so far, as I'm sure you will agree, Ms. Tiptree. But . . ."

He didn't have to finish. I knew a threat when I heard one. Gathering my courage and what few shredded tatters remained of my dignity, I turned my back on him.

Two minutes later I was gunning the Fiat out through the gates, weeping partly in relief because they actually opened and partly because my head was killing me.

Seriously killing me. But mostly I wept because Henderson *had* murdered Jemmy and the others by now; I was certain of it. That was why even in the face of my invasion of his home he'd been so cool and contemptuous: his mission was accomplished.

And he was getting away with it. And as if all that weren't bad enough, when I got home all the house lights were on.

Wade was back.

● ● ●

At two in the morning the stitches in my scalp woke me by the simple, efficient method of feeling as if they'd been lit on fire. Wade slept deeply, dead to the world as I slid out of bed. Once he'd heard the story of my evening and of the past couple of days, he'd read me the riot act I deserved, then offered an idea.

"Maybe she works for him," he said, meaning Ann. "Maybe she deliberately met Jen in one of those city clubs. On his say-so."

"Oh," I breathed, seeing the sense of this. "Because if he knew Jen was going into Manhattan and hanging out in places where she might . . ."

"Yeah, get in all kinds of trouble. And he might realize he couldn't stop her. So he'd get her a minder."

That explained why Ann had taken me out to the house when I demanded it, too. Not because she was really guilty of something but to learn what I was looking for, on Henderson's behalf.

Whether she'd then told him I was there or he'd discovered it himself hardly mattered. "Get some rest," Wade had ordered finally, and I'd promised to.

But I couldn't sleep. The way I'd failed Jemmy was making me crazy; that and the fact that I was never going to see him again. In the bathroom I fumbled for the switch, squinted at the sudden flare of light, and decided not to look at myself in the mirror as I opened the medicine cabinet.

Pawing through old bottles of remedies for ailments we no longer had, plastic bags with only one cotton ball inside, and other pharmaceutical flotsam and jetsam, I found a tube of Xylocaine ointment and another of antibacterial gel originally meant for the dogs.

I'd sent the bacitracin home with Ellie. Smooshing a generous amount of what I did have in the palm of my hand, I put the mixture on my scalp, hoping the numbing effects of the Xylocaine would stay on the surface while the anti-infection gel sank in, and not the reverse. Because I already felt stupid but that was nothing to the way I felt when I turned around.

"Hi, Jake."

It was Victor, standing in the bathroom doorway looking the way he did before he got sick—i.e., snotty and superior.

"Damn it, what the hell are you doing here?" I snarled, taken aback. Even when he was alive a visit from Victor was no big joy-fest, and at the moment I was in no mood for it.

"Beats me," he replied with a disarming shrug. "I think I missed getting the instruction booklet," he added.

I blinked; there was an instruction booklet?

"But since I am here—or maybe I only seem to be—anyway, I'm sorry," he said.

Now I was sure I must be dreaming. He'd never admitted not knowing something in his life, and as for feeling sorry . . .

"Yeah," he said, seeming to read my thought. "Not much like me, is it? But you know, it's different here."

"Really?" I peered closer at him, intrigued in spite of myself. "How different?"

He seemed to step back from me but the funny thing was, his feet didn't move. More like he was near to me and then he was—

Farther. The effect was startling; I let out a little gasp of fright.

"Sorry, sorry," Victor repeated, telescoping away from me. Now he was halfway down the hall and sort of dissolving; I could see through him all the way to the linen closet. Did he mean sorry for frightening me? Or for something else?

"Victor," I managed, weeping again but this time without tears. You always suppose that if somehow you could talk with the dead, you could communicate.

"*Sorry* . . ." The word hung in the air, whispery.

Or imaginary. He shrank to a pixel and winked out.

● ● ●

When I first came to Maine I thought my old house might end up being too huge for me, that after Sam grew up and moved away I might end up rattling around in it like a marble in a box. But when I got up the next morning, I found the whole place so crowded you'd have thought my home was an airport waiting lounge, especially with the roaring noise coming from above the attic.

It sounded as if something was trying to land up there and not having a good time of it. "Hey," Wade said, getting up from the kitchen table to embrace me.

"Hi," I said. Just breathing made my head ache; being hugged made it feel as if the top of it might pop off.

"Mom," Sam began anxiously from where he stood loading his

laundry into the washing machine. His eyes widened at the sight of my injury.

"I'm fine," I assured him as Wade handed me coffee. A couple of fellows I didn't know were there, too, standing at the kitchen counter finishing their own cups. Wade had apparently put Prill's mind at ease about them and vice versa; the big red dog lay relaxed in her dog bed, half asleep.

My appearance, however, was a different story; when they saw me, the strangers vamoosed. They were the carpenters, I realized, come to help my dad do the tricky stuff on the roof. But the way I felt, I didn't care if they were all up there planting explosives.

"Never mind," I told Sam wearily when he tried to question me. I'd taken a gander at myself in the hall mirror, too, and as a result the carpenters' hasty exit didn't surprise me.

Because the surgeon who'd worked on my scalp was no doubt very accomplished at gallbladders and appendectomies. But he wouldn't be winning any awards for fine stitchery anytime soon; I looked like an unhappy cross between the Bride of Frankenstein and a sewing machine demonstration. "Where's Bella?" I asked.

"In the dining room," said Ellie, who stood at the stove warming up a midmorning snack of macaroni and cheese for Lee. The latter was in her playpen—the ear infection was better, I gathered—amusing herself by grabbing Monday the Labrador's nose whenever the animal pushed it between the bars to tease her.

Cat Dancing observed scornfully from atop the refrigerator. "Reading," Ellie added.

The notion of Bella reading while the kitchen looked as if a tornado had struck it was astonishing, but I was too beat to pursue the topic. The roaring from upstairs continued. Occasionally the sound was punctuated by a heavy thud, as if somebody was lopping off the ends of big beams with a power saw.

"He's lopping off the ends of big beams with a power saw," Wade said.

"Oh, goody." Taking a deep breath, I let myself notice even more unaccustomed mayhem. Besides all the dirty dishes and Sam's bags of dirty clothes, the kitchen also contained a duffel bag lumpy with the laundry Wade had brought home from the freighter; I recognized it by one of the red socks sticking out at the top.

Also: a sorry-looking heap of kitchen rugs Bella had been meaning to shake out and wash, the countertops littered with crumbs, plus a basin and a clean rag for her standard daily routine of wiping down everything in the whole house that didn't actively try making its escape.

The basin was empty, the rag dry and unused. A crash came from the attic; I wondered if possibly we ought to evacuate, but no one else suggested it and I was too tired, not to mention too damned bone-deep miserable.

"Bella's on the last chapter of another one of those mystery novels we brought home," Ellie informed me. "And she doesn't seem able to stop."

Thus the undone chores. "Good for her," I muttered. A tear slid down my cheek just as another hellacious crash from above made everyone flinch.

"There was," Wade informed me gently, "even more demolition work needed up there than your dad thought."

I nodded, unable to trust myself to speak. "You sure you're okay?" Wade asked. I nodded—ouch—then went through the phone alcove to peek into the dining room.

"Bella," I said, hesitating for fear of startling her. I'd seen her concentrating before: while distributing Cat Dancing's flea powder so evenly into her fur, for instance, that you'd have thought it had been put on grain by grain with tweezers and a magnifying glass. Or bleaching a stain out of a sink.

But I'd never seen her so *absorbed,* sitting in a dining room chair with a book open on the table before her, gobbling it up with her eyes.

"Hah!" she exclaimed suddenly, finishing the last page and slapping the book shut. "I knew it!"

Tossing it aside—several more, their covers ranging from 1940s noir to 1990s Miss Marple reissues—littered the table. She reached for another from the box at her feet, then saw me.

"You see," she began, "they put in clues. And if they do it right and you read 'em careful, you still won't know who done it. But you'll think you should've."

Her big grape-green eyes shone with enthusiasm. "*And* in the books, the bad one always gets his in the end," she finished with just the right amount of lip-smacking satisfaction.

The right amount for my purposes, that is. Because she was correct; in books, the bad guys always got theirs. But another thing often happened in those books, too: a revelation scene, in which the participants gathered for the unmasking of the culprit. And on account of that I was getting a new idea.

"Punishment," she breathed; just the frame of mind I wanted her in. That plus her fascination with puzzles and her obsessive need to clean up messes could do me a lot of good.

And Henderson some harm. Bella's face clouded guiltily. "Oh, my," she remembered aloud in dismay. "All them dishes still in the sink and I never did get to the laundry or the carpets . . ."

From upstairs came a final-sounding crash, followed by the slam of the attic door. Footsteps descended the stairs.

My father, I supposed. "No, Bella," I said gently. "That's all right." In fact, compared to her usual manic activity this was a relief. But it wasn't why I urged her to sit and select another book.

It wasn't the reason at all.

●   ●   ●

"Well," said Bella indignantly a little later after the men had gone—Wade down to the freighter terminal, my father to the hardware store for another saw blade, and the hired carpenters on lunch break—and I'd told the story about Victor showing up in the upstairs hall the night before, then vanishing. "I call that plain rude," she declared.

"I call it indigestion," said Ellie. "Or those pain pills you got at the emergency room."

"I haven't taken any pain pills," I retorted. "Or anything else." The

Xylocaine seemed at last to be doing the trick on the stitches; I still had a significant headache but I didn't want to take anything for that in case it made me feel dopey.

Victor was death on over-the-counter medications for head injury anyway. He said they messed up your clotting ability and if you were going to have a brain bleed you should have one on account of your primary trauma, not some rinky-dink drugstore item that probably wouldn't work. For pain he'd liked morphine, especially at the end, when he'd needed so much of it himself.

"Jake, do you really think he'd hurt a little . . ." Ellie's voice trailed off. *Baby,* she'd meant to finish.

"I think it's a mistake to underestimate what he'd do," I replied grimly. She was right, the idea was ghastly. But . . .

"So what's the plan?" Ellie eyed the stack of blank cards and envelopes on the kitchen table. I hesitated to tell her; it sounded more rinky-dink even than the drugstore remedies.

But at this point it was all I had.

"We're going to invite him. And bamboozle him," Bella said with quiet ferocity; I'd told her my idea already.

"Henderson," I explained. "I think maybe if we get everyone together, Henderson too, and explain everything that's happened right in front of him with Bob Arnold there listening to all of it, he'll—"

"Talk?" Ellie asked disbelievingly. "Jake, are you nuts?"

"Oh, he'll talk, all right." Bella addressed another envelope and plopped it down on top of the pile. "Because we'll poke his weak spot. That's what villains in books always have. An ah-shilly's heel."

Achilles, she meant; probably Miss Marple had mentioned it. "Hmm. His fatal flaw," Ellie said thoughtfully. "But . . . why won't he just deny it all? Since after all you don't have any . . ."

Proof. Yup, that was *my* ahshilly's heel. Which meant I could either give up or go on.

Try again. Even in the face of almost sure failure, because it was a chance if not to stop Walter Henderson—probably, I realized again with a pang, it was too late for that—then at least to get him caught and punished.

"Why," Ellie inquired reasonably, "would he agree to be present for this at all?"

"Good question. Especially since he's not only going to be present, he's the host. I want to gather everyone right there in his barn, which he'll have to give permission for or I can't even do this thing in the first place."

"We," Bella corrected me firmly, "can't do it in the first place. Only we can, because—"

"Because I'm a pain in the neck," I finished for her.

Ellie gave me a look. "To Henderson," I added. "But most of all I'm a danger to his daughter. Or I'm going to make him think I am. And Jen is *his* Achilles' heel."

Bella addressed another envelope. We weren't putting stamps on them; we didn't have time for postal delivery because we were doing this tonight. Bella was going to hand all the invitations to people or put them in their mailboxes.

"I see," Ellie replied. "Accuse Jen of killing Cory, make it look as if she might even end up being suspected officially . . . But Jake, if she didn't do it—"

"That doesn't matter. We only need to trump up a good enough story so it's reasonable for Bob Arnold to think she might've. It shouldn't be difficult, after all. She's strong enough, she could have lured him over there with that cell phone she gave to him, and most of all she's got no decent alibi."

I breathed in deeply, trying to ease my aching head. "So Henderson could be made to think an official investigation *might* be opened, you see. But we need to do it fast, because Ann Radham told me Jen leaves town tomorrow."

And once his daughter was gone, any threat I posed to her would seem a lot less worrisome to Henderson. Bella sealed the envelopes.

"Good thing he didn't know birch logs rot practically the minute they touch the ground," I added, touching my stitches gingerly. "Or he'd have hit me with oak."

Ellie frowned. "What if they don't get their invitations? Maybe you won't be able to deliver all of them personally. And if you just put them in mailboxes, you won't know for sure whether or not—"

"Yes, we will," I assured her. "We'll know."

Because Bella had devised a plan for that, too. As methodical in preparing the invitations as she was in pot scrubbing or window washing, she'd begun each card by inscribing the thing they all had in common at the bottom of each: *RSVP.*

• • •

While Bella delivered the cards—I told her I'd take Walt Henderson's to him myself but she wanted to get a look at him—all I had to do was think some more about how to make the plan work. But the way my head felt, doing that was like peeling my scalp off with a paring knife.

So to distract myself from the pain I'd gone over to Sam's house to unplug a sink drain, an outcome I can usually achieve by plunging the daylights out of it with a plumber's helper.

"Mom?" Sam asked.

But not this time. The only result was a low *glug-glug* from under the bathtub.

"What?" I snapped back impatiently. "And what do you use to brush your teeth with—concrete mix?" That was what it seemed he had been putting down the drain, to judge by the clog.

Sam sat on the side of the tub watching while I lay on the floor with my head under the sink. I squinted up at the underside of it, looking for the place where the drainpipe met the basin. After the plunger failed I'd tried loosening the trap, but when I twisted it with the pipe wrench it threatened to break off.

So I thought I might try removing the whole basin. But now it was clear that wouldn't work either; the nut holding the basin atop the pipe was too big for even my largest pipe wrench. Also there was the problem of getting the basin detached from the wall without demolishing it.

The wall, I mean. "Maybe I'll go into rehab," Sam said.

I sat up so suddenly that if he hadn't stuck his hand out I'd have smacked my head on the sink; as it was I just got dizzy for a moment.

"Because nothing else is helping," he added.

"Well, if that's your decision you know I'll support you in it. We can . . ."

But I stopped at the flash of panic in his eyes. "Not yet," he stalled. "I'm still thinking about it."

He avoided my gaze. And there was no sense pushing this, I knew from experience. With an effort I got to my feet and grabbed the plumber's helper.

"Give me a hand here, will you?" The *glug-glug* under the tub was coming from *somewhere,* and if plunging the sink made it happen then the sink drain must be *connected* to the . . .

"Here." I pulled a washcloth from the towel rack, soaked it under the tap, then twisted it nearly dry and gave it to him.

"Press this over the drain hole in the tub," I said, "while I try plunging the sink once more."

Because the thing is, the usefulness of a plumber's helper depends on applying it to a closed system. Which this one wasn't, I'd suddenly realized, on account of that open bathtub drain. I would have to block it somehow.

"Press hard," I instructed, so he did while I ran water into the sink again and plunged it again, even harder than before.

"I can feel it sucking on my hand," he marveled, sounding as pleased as a grade-school kid whose classroom science experiment is working.

"Yeah." As I'd thought, the two drains led into a single pipe somewhere. I plunged some more, until suddenly . . .

Blonkglonkgloinkglugsluggleuggleuggle . . . *slurrrrupp!* All the water swirled triumphantly down the drain with a final *glunk!* and a hollow-sounding *dunkdunkdunk.*

"Hey!" Sam exclaimed, slapping me a high five. Because we'd fixed the thing and we hadn't even had to take the sink off the wall to do it. But once the first fine flush—you should excuse the expression—of happiness wore off, I felt ineffectual again.

"Listen, Sam," I said when we got back to his kitchen. Like the rest of the place it was a shambles of dirty dishes and empty refreshment containers. "About what you were saying . . ."

"Don't rush me, okay, Mom? All I said was, someday maybe I might try it."

It wasn't what he had said. But I knew better than to argue, or to ask if just possibly he'd seen his father around anywhere lately either.

Because his father was dead and Sam was about the last person to need any reminding of it; still, that rehab idea had resurfaced from somewhere. "Good. I'll be in your corner if you do," I told him instead, ignoring the smelly can full of unemptied trash by the kitchen door.

His eyes said he wanted me to go now; I was making him feel uncomfortable. I mustered a smile. "Listen, I could use your help again tonight, if you're free."

I explained the scheme for the evening, and a ghost of his old, enthusiastic self enlivened his expression. But then his face fell.

"Maybe," he muttered once more, meaning he'd probably be too loaded by evening. I told him I'd see him later if he felt up to it, and continued out into the thin, chilly sunshine.

Out on the bay a speedboat bounced fast across the sparkling waves. Watching, I wished hard that I were on it, racing away, and I wondered whether after tonight Sam would want me doing more home repairs, or trying to find him a rehab place. Or anything else.

Wade might not think I was so great anymore, either; maybe even Ellie wouldn't. Because somewhere between the sink drain and Sam's chronic troubles, the rest of my mind had continued working on my plan for the gathering this evening. And it had come to the sad conclusion that what I had so far wasn't sufficient.

As a result, the rest of what I meant to do wasn't in the clever endings of any of Bella's books. I still intended to put Jennifer Henderson on the hot seat, since that part of the scheme was crucial to hitting her father where it really hurt.

But for it to work, my own credibility needed a kicker. So in the all-important who-did-what-when portion of this evening's program, I mostly intended to accuse myself.

• • •

After I left Sam I walked on down Water Street toward the harbor, where the year's first big bunch of spring tourists was piling off an excursion bus in the fish pier's parking lot. Wearing thin jackets, they shivered in the onshore breeze, gazing at the fishing boats in the harbor and the old storefronts facing it while hanging on to their hats.

The green-painted park bench where I'd first seen Jemmy only a few days ago—it felt like years—was vacant. I turned away from it, feeling a punch of sorrow; wishing I could go back, do it over. But instead I walked on, pausing to gaze into the shops as if I too were a lighthearted visitor to Eastport.

A newish enterprise called Captain's Cargo was crammed with attractive stuff, good soaps and specialty foods vying for space with Maine-authored books, leather-bound sketch pads, and quality sweatshirts of the kind those tourists would buy if they stayed around much past lunch.

I stopped next at The Commons, spotting the good silk hand-dyed garments Henny Trow had mentioned she was sewing: gorgeous in deep jewel tones with ferns and gingko leaves stenciled on them. At the Moose Island General Store, I went in for a coffee and a cruller, explaining the stitches in my head—unable to bear the tug of cloth on them any longer, I'd taken off the cap—by saying I'd bumped it.

"Oh, too bad," the woman at the counter replied kindly, but when I offered no further details she didn't question me. People in Eastport can be as silent as tombs when they want to be, and nobody takes offense; talking or not is regarded as a choice here, and if you don't do it no one pesters you or thinks any the worse of you for it.

Carrying my snack, I went on past the post office, admiring the newly painted windows and freshly repointed granite blocks. A grant a year earlier had provided cash for this and several other downtown improvements, all more or less successful; the new sidewalks in particular were fine and the set of sculptures—abstract, fire-engine red, and made of metal, the pieces were locally known as "fruit roll-ups"—were admired by many.

Past the post office I dropped my cup and cruller wrapper in a trash bin, then went into the beauty salon called the Ship's Snipper and begged the hairdresser there for twenty minutes of her time. If she couldn't help me, I told her, I intended to buy a razor.

"Oh, my," she replied, horrified. The way I looked, she probably thought I meant to cut my own throat. "I'm sure we can do better!"

I sat obediently in the swivel chair by the shampoo sink, letting her wash carefully and then comb out my remaining tresses with hands gentle as an angel's. "There," she said when she'd finished. "It looks," she added hesitantly, turning me so I could see, ". . . stream-lined."

Um, sure. Like a bullet is streamlined, especially if the bullet has been sewn together haphazardly and has an orange stripe painted down the middle; she'd managed to avoid getting the stitches wet, so the Betadine cleanser remained.

What I resembled most was a refugee from a punk rock band, mi-nus any possible musical talent. Stepping back outside, I felt the breeze touching portions of my neck that hadn't seen daylight in twenty years; she'd buzz-cut it up the back and snipped the bangs off into tiny wisps. It was a boy's haircut, really, and it made me feel unrecogniz-able.

But I still recognized myself. I wondered if, after what I planned to do and say tonight, anyone else would. Thinking this, I turned my steps toward Bert Merkle's place in South End; maybe the old crack-pot would be able to remember something more about Fred Mudge's kidnapping, I thought.

Besides, I needed to fill the afternoon somehow. Ellie had taken Lee to her own pediatrician for a follow-up visit, and as for starting on any more home repairs, I'd as soon have taken a hammer to my head.

The rotting brown stubs of wharf pilings stuck up through the green water of the inlet at half-tide, below the foliage of early lupines massing along its banks. The fresh air helped my headache for a while; climbing the final hill between big new houses rich with custom windows and terraced gardens, I felt almost normal.

But the throbbing in my skull roared back with an awful

vengeance as I knocked and waited for Bert Merkle to come to the door of his little trailer. It sat on a flat quarter-acre of land in a warren of narrow streets, surrounded by so much junk—cars, barrels, crates, and unidentifiable stuff—the place looked like a hazardous-waste facility; his neighbors, I decided, must be about ready to commit murder themselves.

"Who's there?" his rough voice demanded from inside. The door creaked open and Bert peered narrowly out at me, the watery blue eyes in his craggy old face suspicious.

He was wearing a tinfoil hat. From behind him on a table piled high with booklets and newsletters, a shortwave radio let out a series of squeals and crackles.

He observed my wounded head without surprise. "Got to you, did they? I keep sayin' that. Sneak right up on you, burrow right in. Split yer skull wide open sure as if they were usin' an axe."

At the moment, that was just what it felt like. "Can I come in?"

He backed away from the door. "Sure, sure. Always glad to help out a fellow sufferer. You shoulda had one o' these." With a nicotine-stained index finger, he indicated the foil headgear. "Siddown, take a load off. Want a beer?" Without waiting for an answer he opened the trailer's tiny refrigerator.

"No, thanks. Really, I shouldn't . . . well, all right." It was a root beer. I pressed the icy-cold bottle to my temple, sighing, before draining half of it while Bert looked on with satisfaction.

"Hits the spot, doesn't it?" He sat across from me, twiddled a dial on the shortwave. The squeals faded. "Now, what's up?"

The booklets and flyers were all about government plots to hide The Others Among Us, plus related topics.

"I was wondering about that guy you saw getting shoved into a car on Water Street," I began.

Now that I was here, asking Bert about it seemed . . . well, let's just say that in person he appeared even less reliable as a witness. But I didn't have much else to talk about with a man whose reading material included a book called *Our Alien Visitors* and a paperback entitled

Ray-Proofing Your Own Home: A New and Improved Guide to Keeping Them Out of Your House and Head.

Thus, I supposed, the hat. Bert got up and rummaged in the refrigerator again, turning his back on me. Besides the tinfoil beanie, I noticed wires from a metal box the size of a cigarette pack in his shirt pocket leading to tiny earplugs in his ears.

Turning back, he saw me looking at them. "Don't ask," he said resignedly, and I decided not to. Keeping Them Out of Your Head, apparently, required equipment.

"The fellow," I reminded him, "with the mustache."

"Right, right." He sat again. There was barely enough room at the table for two, especially because the walls of the tiny trailer were covered with bookshelves. Scanning them, I expected more crackpot material.

But the books were mathematics texts. "Saw him coming down the street, saw the car pull up. Fellow got out, grabbed the one with the mustache, shoved him in. Drove away." He shook his head, frowning. "Not sure what else might've happened. Not certain-sure, anyway. Tires spun, I remember that. Not much else, though," he added in apology.

"Really," I replied evenly. "Do you remember anything else about the fellow? The one with the mustache. Tall, short? Blond hair? Or dark?"

Bert Merkle made as if to scratch his head thoughtfully but when his fingers encountered tinfoil he let his hand drop again. "Nope. Can't say I do. Blond, maybe. Tall fella. Real tall, and he was wearin' a puffy jacket. Pale blue. My memory isn't what it used to be, though."

"I see." I regarded him silently. In return he offered a big smile and another root beer.

"No, thanks." I got up. "I won't take any more of your time. I can see you've got a lot of reading to do."

At this his smile grew knowing. And forgiving, as if I were the one lying through my teeth. The thought hadn't occurred to me before that maybe the story about Mudge getting grabbed on Water Street really was just as unreliable as the rest of Merkle's tall tales, that it might be a crock like Merkle himself.

But now it did. Except for the table full of literature, the trailer was neat and clean though obviously impoverished. Bert's clothes, threadbare and patched, didn't quite fit him, the frayed thrift-shop sweater too large and his shoes worn at the heel. One trailer window was broken, the hole filled with bloopy orange goo of the kind usually used to stop water leaks.

I looked at the bookshelves again. Several of the texts bore the author's name on the spine. The titles were in English but were as incomprehensible to me as ancient Greek, and one of them actually had Greek letters in it, or something like them.

Bert smiled, ducking his head briefly as if I'd caught him at something. "In my old life," he explained, waving at the shelf. It was his name on the textbooks; he'd written them. "I was a mathematics professor once," he added. The one good chair in the place was a Harvard chair, black with the school's emblem in gold on the backrest. It barely fit in the fake-wood-paneled corner by the junky lamp he'd set up next to it.

A flat footstool held a chessboard. An old pair of reading glasses lay on the board, whose chess pieces were set up in the middle of a game, awaiting the next move.

They were my father's spare reading glasses. I recognized them from the strip of blue painter's tape he'd used to repair them. At the sight of them, suddenly everything about Bert Merkle seemed to mean something different than it had a moment earlier; for one thing, my father suffered fools so ungladly you'd think there was a bounty on them.

I moved to pick up the glasses, to bring them home. But Merkle shook his head. "He'll be back," he said, meaning my dad. "He's two moves from checkmate. So he thinks," he added.

I stared at him. "So," I managed, "what's with the act?"

The whole nutcase-with-the-tinfoil-hat business, I meant, because it was obviously false. Bert chuckled sadly.

"Maybe I just like the flying-saucer nut character better than the one about the math genius gone awry," he replied with a shrug. "Tragically driven mad by the wild, theoretical reaches of his own abstruse research because . . . some things Man wasn't meant to know," he intoned.

His eyebrows arched sardonically. "In other words, it's *better* to be ignorant."

"I see," I stammered, though I didn't. All I really understood was that there was more to Bert Merkle than met the eye, a story behind him that I would probably never hear all of.

But I was figuring out now how somebody else might've made use of it. "So if a new person in Eastport were to ask a local who the craziest guy in town is—" I began.

He made an ironic little bow. "Yours truly."

His Maine accent, I noticed, had faded steadily as our conversation progressed. Now he was a fellow who'd pahked his cah in Hahvard yahd, even though quite a while ago.

Then I noticed something else. Everything in the trailer was worn and shabby. But the shortwave radio looked brand-new. As if someone had given Bert Merkle some money lately, and he'd bought the radio with it.

Money *for* something. Like perhaps telling a story about Fred Mudge being grabbed up and shoved into a car on Water Street? Suddenly I felt certain Merkle had never seen Mudge at all, grabbed or otherwise. The episode had never happened.

Only I had been expected to believe it because it jibed with what I thought was going on. Only I had been meant to hear the tale and . . .

But what had I been meant to do, and by whom?

"Who paid you to tell that story?" I asked Merkle, suddenly furious. "Who's jerking me around?"

He shook his head regretfully at me. Someone had paid him enough to buy not only the radio, but his loyalty. And to me he owed nothing. "You should take care of that injury," he advised, eyeing my scalp.

A cabinet door in his tiny galley kitchen stood open a small crack, enough for me to glimpse cans of cat food stacked inside. Off-brand cat food. And he didn't have a cat.

On the counter by contrast stood a bag of groceries, some unpacked and ready to be put away. Cheese, oranges. Coffee, and a sirloin steak.

And that root beer. It took money to buy groceries. Suddenly I felt dizzy, and not only because of the headache. He offered me one of the booklets from the kitchen table strewn with them.

What THEY Want was the title.

Good question. Angrily, I went out.

● ● ●

When I got home I grabbed a bottle of aspirin and swallowed three tablets, brain bleed be damned. Then I got my car keys, fired up the Fiat, and took off out of there; luckily my father was on the roof again and Ellie was still at the pediatrician's, or they'd probably have tried to stop me.

And the result wouldn't have been pretty, because Jemmy had lied to me. He hadn't trusted me to get him out of his jam; he'd thought I might decide to hang up on him, old-friendship-wise. It would've been the smart thing to do; if he weren't around, all my troubles were over in the tale-telling-to-prosecutors department.

Permanently not around, that is, because dead men don't tell any. I could've let Henderson kill Jemmy and *presto,* instant crime-free history for yours truly.

Thinking this, I slammed the Fiat into fifth gear and stepped on it, slowing only for the speed trap just beyond the end of the causeway and hitting the gas again once I got to Route 1.

You little bastard, I cursed him mentally as I swung hard through the S-turns in Robbinston. *You little . . .*

On the straight stretch toward Calais, I really let it rip. The Fiat leapt gratefully forward, seeming to elongate as its engine snarled, doing what it liked best. Soon enough the timing belt would break again, or the head gasket would blow, sending the car on yet another flatbed journey to a repair shop in Bangor or beyond. But for now . . . *vroom.*

By contrast the bumpy two-mile dirt road to the cottage was a treacherous tiptoe through the equivalent of a minefield; the Fiat's undercarriage was so low, it would take little more than a pebble to rip the muffler off. While I negotiated it I thought again about Jemmy, and cursed him even more forcefully.

Because now I knew he'd done it all: following me and Ellie, faking attacks, two on me and one on Sam. Faking the kidnapping of Fred Mudge, even, and of Trish and the baby, too.

All to make sure I'd keep trying to put Henderson behind bars. Until Jemmy pushed it all too far and things started happening much faster than he expected. He got Trish, Mudge, and the baby hidden away somewhere, pretending they'd been snatched.

But then Henderson snatched *him.* And Henderson would've wasted no time learning the location where Jemmy had stashed the others. So he now had all of them—Jemmy, plus everyone who might believably have repeated whatever it was that Cory Trow had known about Henderson—and I was fresh out of miracles.

Finally reaching the lake, I pulled the Fiat under a canopy of spruce trees and shut off the engine. In the silence the cooling engine's *tick-tick-tick* was the only sound. Unlocking the cottage I paused, reluctant to go in.

But at last I stepped inside. Sunlight lay in bright squares on the red-checked tablecloth. In a glass jar, a bouquet of forsythia twigs from the bushes I'd planted up here two summers ago was just opening.

I bit my lip. I'd come here hoping for comfort, a moment of peace in the midst of grief, frustration, and fear. But all I got was Jemmy again; his industrious, adaptable nature, his ingenious way of making things workable in almost any setting.

His liking for flowers. I wanted to cry but it would've made my head hurt worse, so I swallowed down my tears and instead went outside, unable to stop remembering the last time I'd seen him. Leaving the cottage, talking about Sam, walking to the car and arguing with Jemmy about how maybe the safest thing would be for him to leave.

Leave and let me help him; the memory made me cringe. Fat chance; Jemmy must have been worried I might *tell* Walt Henderson where he was, after which there would be no more worries about him talking to Witness Protection Program people.

About me or anyone else. A few chunks of birch lay on the driveway, one of them the one that hit me; I could tell by the blood still on it. Picking it up, I hurled the club-shaped chunk as far as I could into the woods.

Finally I walked down to the lake. A hundred yards out still floated the buoy hooked to the dock footing Ellie and I had lost, a red-and-white-striped wooden lozenge bobbing gaily like a flag from a happier time. Watching it, I wondered if Jemmy had ruined the place, if I would ever be able to come here without thinking of him.

And I wondered if after tonight I would still be welcome. Returning to the car, I paused once more to gaze at the clearing where only a day earlier I'd stood so innocently, bickering with Jemmy and watching the dogs as they . . .

Then I stopped short, remembering. Monday had gotten up and wandered down to the water. But Prill the Doberman had remained in her nest of pine boughs, pleasantly relaxed.

Prill, whose suspicious nature made her leap to her feet if a new mailman climbed our back porch. Whose worried snarl could be triggered by a strange voice on the answering machine or an unfamiliar truck driver delivering a package.

Who under no circumstances would've stayed in her bed had anyone besides Jemmy and me been here in the clearing with her. Because she was the perfect alarm system, one I was beginning to understand.

She wasn't vicious, not in the least. It was just that the shock of being a neglected stray was wearing off now, so she was remembering her earlier training.

Guard dog training. She'd have gotten up and threatened a stranger. And . . . no wind had been blowing. I remembered that much very clearly. And no wind blowing meant no branch blown down.

It was Jemmy who'd hit me.

From:hlrb@mainetel.net <Horace Robotham>
To: ddimaio@miskatonic.edu <David DiMaio>
Subj: New info

Dear Dave,

    Interesting find here, and I thought
I'd better let you know right away. In the
course of his local genealogical work,
Lang's come up with a cache of letters.
First glance says they're from a servant
girl in Eastport to her sister in Halifax
and here's the bombshell—she seems to
have worked in the Key Street house.
    At the right time, no less. Amazing, I
know, and I suppose it'll evaporate upon
closer examination, as these too-good-
to-be-true coincidences always do.
    Still, Lang's copying them now and
I'll send them along ASAP for you to look
at when you have a moment. He's terribly
excited about being able to contribute,
but if we're going to have to let him
down, as I fear we will, sooner's better.
    On a personal note, we'll both be aw-
fully glad to see you when you come to
meet the Tiptree woman in Eastport.
You'll stay with us? We've a guest room
all ready—plush as the Ritz, Lang likes
to say and we'll feast together like
kings.
    Really, Dave, you'd like it a lot
here. These Maine Yankees don't miss a
trick, and yet they're immensely kind to
a pair of confirmed old bachelors—that's

what they call us!—like Lang and me.
It's so quiet here, too, peaceful and
safe as houses even when walking alone at
night.

   Which I'm about to do, a couple of
miles through the silent streets. Nightly
constitutional, must take care of my
health, so commandeth the other old
bachelor.

   Watch for the letters by overnight ex-
press. You should have them day after
tomorrow, latest. Best from Lang as
usual.

Horace

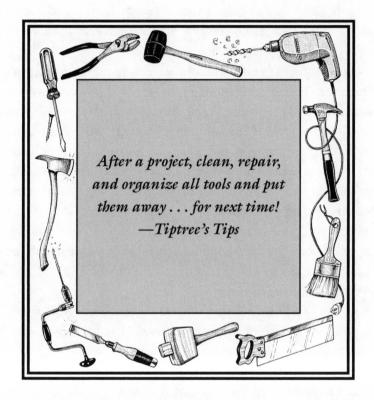

After a project, clean, repair, and organize all tools and put them away . . . for next time!
—*Tiptree's Tips*

$\mathbf{A}$t eight o'clock that night, I wished I were anywhere else, even atop a stepladder. But instead we'd all gathered in Walter Henderson's barn, just as I'd arranged.

The drywall enclosure of the office space Cory Trow's body had fallen into had been removed, the two-by-four framing bashed apart and taken away. Scraps from the demolition work littered the floor in that area. Otherwise the barn looked the same as it had when Ellie and I were here last.

Minus the corpse, of course. I set the podium up, then stood behind it sweating and quaking. I hated public speaking. At least in the
old days when I summoned people for a money meeting, they came
because they figured I'd know what I was talking about.

This time it was more like "what's that madwoman up to now?"
And I still wasn't sure of the answer. All I really knew was that coming
clean about my own past could give me the credibility I needed when
I began describing Walter Henderson's.

Beyond the barn's high windows, clouds raced hectically across a
full moon, its brilliance reflecting in the stars I kept seeing every time
I moved my head. Standing a few feet away from me, Bob Arnold
wore a freshly pressed uniform complete with his sidearm, baton,
cuffs, and all the other cop gear he always kept on his utility belt.

"Hope you know what you're doing, Jacobia," he said, eyeing me
skeptically. His tone made it clear he was here to keep order when this
ridiculous shindig went to hell as it was bound to do.

"Um, yeah," I answered faintly, my heart hammering so hard it felt
as if one of Ann Radham's boomier kettle drums was being played inside my chest. Then Henderson came in looking irritated and aggrieved, and that stiffened my backbone.

The son of a bitch. Minutes after I returned home from the cabin
he'd been on the phone wanting to know what I meant by inviting
people to his place without even asking his permission.

"Just what the card says," I'd replied. Each invitation was headed,
in Bella's harsh chicken scratching, *A Revelation.*

"I'll reveal who killed Cory tonight," I'd told Henderson blithely.
"Or don't you want to know?"

Apparently he at least wanted to look as if he did, since here we all
were. Wearing a black turtleneck, a cream-colored cardigan, and flannel slacks, he flipped the rest of the barn's lights on, revealing the interior in all its fresh pine splendor.

Gardeners' tools, lawn tractors, spacious stalls and feed bins for
more animals as yet unpurchased spread out around us like an elaborate retail display dedicated to supplying a trust-fund-financed gentle-
man farmer with plenty of new toys.

"Might as well have the right atmosphere," he remarked as the fluorescent tubes blazed, "for shedding light on the topic."

His tone was pure sarcasm, meant to convey that he was only humoring me out of patience and the goodness of his heart. My own retort would've touched on the scarcity of those commodities; his true intention was to make a public fool of me and get rid of me forever.

Ellie approached me. "Everyone's here."

My heart's tempo notched up another couple of beats. With Bella's help we'd set up folding chairs to accommodate the invited audience; besides Bob Arnold, Ellie, and Bella there were Henderson, his golden-girl daughter Jennifer, Ann Radham the self-described hipster-sidekick musician, and Cory's mother Henny Trow with her frizzy hair, lean face, and pale complexion.

Henny looked better than when I'd seen her—less devastated, more composed. According to Bella she'd already begun clearing out her house, getting ready to move back to Boston for good. But watching her take her place now, I couldn't help remembering that bit of blue fabric that had first given me an inkling of possible murder.

Feeling my gaze, she glanced briefly at me, then touched the corner of her eye with a tissue. I wondered who she was trying to convince—me or herself?

Behind her stood Wade, George Valentine, and my father; like a stand-up comedian trying out a new act, I'd wanted to look out and spot at least a few friendly faces. Wade caught my eye, gave me a nod of encouragement and the ghost of a kiss.

Friendly for now. Last came Sam, clean-shaven and showered, in clean clothes and with his curly hair combed. He was shaky and sick looking, his complexion the color of pistachio ice cream, but he was obviously sober. That he'd come at all felt almost unbearably poignant to me.

"Hey, Jake," Bob Arnold called, tapping at his wristwatch. "Let's get this show on the road."

"Right," I said. "I'll just be a minute." Nervously I tried marshaling my thoughts but my headache kept scattering them. Ann Radham shifted in her chair impatiently, wearing a green T-shirt with a long tan sweaterish garment over it, and tan corduroys.

The fluorescent lights did nothing for her appearance; under them she looked ten years older than she had at the Bayside. Although alongside the vibrant, toned-and-tanned Jen Henderson no one's looks had a chance; tonight Jen wore a fluffy V-necked cashmere sweater the same hue as her eyes, white slacks, and leather sandals. A scarf was knotted loosely at her throat.

The sweater had short sleeves, showing her tautly muscled arms. And the scarf was silk. Blue, and even from where I stood I could see the tear in it, letting a bit of the sapphire sweater peep through. Her gold hair fell warmly over the silk like sunshine on water.

It was the same scarf, I felt sure, as had been used in the murder; had she worn it deliberately? Or did she not know? Fixed on me, her astonishing eyes were full of hatred.

Fair enough. I wasn't a fan of hers either. And she'd like me even less when I'd finished.

As would everyone else—inhaling deeply, I rehearsed it all in my head a final time—because years ago in the city when I was a hotshot money manager I'd taken cash from enterprises so violent the green-backs should've turned red.

And now I was going to say so as background for the story of who—and what—Walter Henderson really was. I'd known about him all along not because Jemmy had told me about him but because I'd recognized him myself soon after he moved to Eastport.

He'd been on Water Street, just walking along like anyone else. I remember my shock, my disbelief that anything from my old life could even be real here. The last time I'd seen him had been in my office in the city, where he'd been a client of mine.

And out of that relationship I was pretty sure the Feds could make a case for accessory after the fact.

Multiple counts. In short, since I couldn't get anyone in authority to investigate Henderson for Cory Trow's death, I would offer . . . myself. For my own crimes; the whole shootin' match, as Wade would've put it.

And then I would drag Henderson into it, just as I'd feared Jemmy would do to me. "Good evening," I began, "and thank you all for coming. We're here tonight to talk about Cory's Trow's death. His *murder.*"

My voice didn't even shake; so far, so fine, I thought. But then I saw the bulge in Henderson's sweater pocket and suddenly my whole plan was worse than folly.

He could shoot me before anyone could do anything about it. Bob Arnold was armed but I doubted he'd be a match.

Henderson meant to kill me. That he'd never get away with it was no longer an obstacle; he didn't care. People didn't do things like this to him, his eyes said; they just didn't.

No matter what. I looked around for an exit but he stood by the door. Only about ten seconds had passed but it felt longer.

A lot longer. "Jake?" Wade spoke up gently. "Are you okay?"

My mouth felt dry. When I looked up to the loft, I saw where Cory must've stood in the moment before he took a last unknowing step. And . . . something else.

A thin rope or wire was tied to the iron hook where Cory's noose had been knotted. The length of it was strung out tautly over all our heads, ending at one of the barn's massive support beams.

If you were a stunt person in a harness and you wanted to slide down speedily, you'd clip the harness to a wire like that. I blinked at it, trying to understand what it meant.

"Jake?" Wade said again.

Irritably I shook my head; the room tilted disconcertingly, then settled. "I'm fine," I muttered, peering down at the notes I'd made, just a few talking points scrawled on the back of the Bayside flyer Ann Radham had thrust at me the day before.

The letters swam indecipherably and focused. But . . . I peered at the paper. These weren't my notes. I was looking at the wrong side of the page, the *front* of the flyer.

Really looking at it, I mean. Seeing it clear and knowing suddenly that I'd been wrong all along. Henderson took his hand out of his pocket, withdrawing a cigar.

Smiling at my confusion, he lit it. I stared again at the flyer. There'd been *two* musical acts at the Bayside the night Cory died; Ann Radham played twice, once early and again at the evening's end. In between, the guitar duo had appeared. The result was an alibi with a hole big enough to pilot a tugboat through.

And I'd missed it. But even as I thought this a muffled sound came from the loft, like something soft was being dragged across its floor very slowly. Everyone looked up as the trap door creaked open; Bob Arnold's hand slid to his sidearm.

"Jake," Wade said, getting out of his chair.

Something long and bulky fell through the trap-door opening. The noose around its neck tightened hard as the weight hit the rope; then the bouncing thing whizzed down the wire at us.

I just stared. It was Cory at the end of that rope; still dead. In fact after a couple of days in a morgue drawer and with the roughly made catgut-stitched autopsy scar across his forehead and down his middle, I'd have to say that when he slid to the end of his run on the wire he was even deader than when I'd seen him the first time.

His eyes opened. A small, uncontrollable *glurk!* of fright escaped me. Probably if it had happened a little differently, Ann Radham wouldn't have reacted the way she did, either.

But it all went so fast; even Henderson took a startled step back. "Ann," the thing said, its low voice thick with menace like an echo out of a bog, just loud enough for me and Ann to hear.

Up in the loft I could see someone moving now. Bob Arnold spotted it, also, and headed for the steps, gun drawn.

The spiky-haired girl staggered back. "No," Ann whispered to the grisly thing hanging there. "You're not here. Not real."

Her voice dropped to a whisper, until only her lips moved. Just then Bob Arnold glanced back, so he saw what I did:

I watched you die, she told the thing inaudibly, struggling for control of herself. *I watched . . .*

Henderson saw it, too, and reached out furiously for her but she was too fast for him, suddenly seeming to recall where she was and what danger she was in. Straightening, Ann swung around.

"Federal officer," she announced. "Chief Arnold, hold your fire," she added without looking at him. "Get back down here and stand with the others where I can see you, please."

Head up, feet apart in a classic firing stance, both hands on her weapon: a .38 automatic, and where had *that* come from? No matter; she had us all incapacitated with it.

That is until Bob Arnold apparently decided *To hell with this,* raised his own weapon in a smooth decisive arc, and fired.

A bright bloom of blood appeared on the shoulder of Ann Radham's tan sweaterlike garment. And I don't care what wounded people do on crime shows; when you get shot like that, you drop.

Too bad I did, too, her shocked white face suddenly replaced by a view of the barn's high rafters. Flat on my back, I watched them spin.

Faster. Until they spun me away.

•   •   •

I regained consciousness in the ambulance and regarded this as fortunate until we got to the hospital; having a hole drilled into your head while you're awake is not a procedure I recommend, in the yikes-that's-scary department.

On the other hand it didn't hurt, partly because soon after I reached the emergency room they shot enough novocaine to stun a rhinoceros into my scalp. Also, the brain bleed I was having had begun depressing some fairly important functions.

Noticing things, for instance. And caring about them. What did bother me was the sound: a bone-crunching, whine-of-a-power-tool snarl as the surgical drill bored into my skull.

I felt it pop through and my headache vanished as if by magic; *that* I cared about a lot. But not much more; for a couple of days I was as dopy, unreasonable, and hard to control as . . .

Well, let's just say that during my convalescence everyone at the hospital behaved very professionally, while *my* post-operative behavior gave them plenty to be professional about.

Bedpans, for example, were a subject of controversy, as was pill-swallowing. I have it on good authority that several times Wade had to hold my nose just to get me to open my mouth. Though in my own defense may I simply say right here that in my opinion, the sheer indignity of a stay in the hospital is enough to kill you even if your original ailment doesn't.

Still, ten days after the events in the barn, everyone convened for a party at the cottage by the lake to celebrate my survival. Heaven, I imagined, was a day just like today: sun shining, birds singing, and a little breeze blowing so it wasn't too hot. The new dock stretched out over the water in pristine, solid-as-a-rock glory, finished by Wade and George as a surprise for me upon my homecoming from the hospital.

Ripples lapped peacefully around it as Bob Arnold and I sat on it together. "Jemmy still says he didn't hit you?" Bob asked.

"Yeah." My old pal had insisted a dozen times already that the birch-long-on-the-head incident really had been a blowdown, and not another of his attempts to motivate me.

"Honest, Jake, I was long gone when it happened," he'd told me. "I did mean to vanish while your back was turned, I'll admit that. But hit you? Come on, I wouldn't do such a thing."

I wanted to believe him. "And the brick through the truck windshield?" Bob asked now, putting his glass of seltzer down on the deck's bright new surface.

"Jemmy says he meant it to hit the hood of the truck, not the glass. He says I must've sped up just as he let go."

Mm-hmm, Bob's skeptical look said. "What about the car things? Sam's accident, your near miss on Sullivan Street . . . How's he explaining all that? How'd he even get cars at all?"

"Well, he *was* the best vehicle booster-to-order in the tri-state area, once upon a time," I confided. And there'd been that little problem with cars going missing from the hospital parking lot.

"I see," said Bob. "That explains it, then."

Jemmy had known about the cockamamie plan to gather everyone in Henderson's barn because he'd been lurking outside my house when Bella left to deliver the invitations. He'd followed, wondering what all the envelopes could mean, and when she dropped one in

Henny Trow's mailbox he'd waited for Bella to leave, then scampered up and read it.

"What would he have done if you'd spotted him spying in the days previous?" Bob asked. "Or if Walter Henderson had?"

"I'd have been no problem. He could've just said he hitched a ride to Eastport to visit me. He did work up a disguise for any daylight car trips," I answered.

Jemmy had told me about this part with some embarrassment. Having to disguise himself from me was pretty sneaky, he felt.

As if the rest of it weren't. "And meanwhile Henderson really was waiting for the Cory Trow dust to settle before he did anything to Jemmy? But now Henderson doesn't want to kill Jemmy at all anymore?" Bob asked.

I nodded. "Jemmy outed the spy in Walter Henderson's camp. Saved Henderson's bacon. So they're even now, Jemmy says. And I believe him."

The spy being Ann Radham, who really was a federal officer. Bob Arnold had been debriefed pretty thoroughly by her superiors, who were of course rather annoyed at the injury he'd inflicted on one of their number.

They'd gone to a lot of trouble to get her situated where she could acquire evidence on Henderson, Bob had reported later to Ellie and me, although once they heard his story they'd agreed he had little choice but to shoot Ann.

Just as she, from her own point of view, had been forced to kill Cory. His big mouth could've torpedoed her plan to get the dirt she needed for a Henderson arrest. The bottom line was that she'd meant to let Walter Henderson kill Jemmy; then she'd gather evidence of the crime and nail Henderson with it.

But not if Cory blabbed about *her*. If that happened, Ann's big career triumph went kerblooie, along with any plans she might have had for celebrating her next birthday.

So she'd murdered Cory. High over the lake an osprey sailed, wings outstretched. "Where'd Jemmy hide Trish and Fred Mudge?" Bob wanted to know.

"Their place." As I'd suspected, someone *had* paid Bert Merkle to concoct the kidnapping story: Jemmy again.

"Even after you talked to the St. John cops," I went on, "they still figured the likeliest thing was that she'd taken off and he was hunting for her. So Jemmy loaded Fred and Trish up with supplies and they kept their heads down. Or she did," I corrected myself. "Jemmy had an assignment for Mudge."

Jemmy had chuckled while describing this part, his surgery-smoothed face wrinkling into a smile. "God, Mudge is talented," he'd marveled. "All I had to do was describe what I wanted and show him a picture of Cory Trow."

There'd been one in the library's copy of the high school year-book; snipping Cory out of the group shot was yet another of Jemmy's recent misdeeds. "When I told him I needed a full-sized dummy of Cory," he'd said, "Mudge stitched it up in a couple of hours. Pretty lifelike, wasn't it?"

Or deathlike, more to the point. Getting Mudge to trust Jemmy had been easy, too; once Jemmy told him the plan, Mudge's creativity had kicked in and the rest had been smooth sailing.

"I got him a connection in the city," Jemmy had added proudly. "On Broadway. Fellow I know there handles designers, craftspeople. Guy's gonna have a career."

Terrific, I'd thought, and Trish would be happy also since it meant Mudge would be in New York, while she and the baby meant to stay with Henny Trow in Massachusetts. Their first meeting had gone swimmingly and the infant Raj's future would be financed by the proceeds of Cory's insurance policy, the issuing company having already reversed itself on the matter of benefits payment.

I leaned back on the dock, soaking in the spring sunshine. "Was Ann really stealing from Jennifer?" I asked Bob, because I still wondered about her reaction when I accused her of it.

"No," he said. "But you scared her pretty good when you threatened to say that she had. See, she was getting automatic deposits, her FBI pay to a checking account in New York. Under another name, and she didn't access it much. But if Henderson ever dug into her finances in any serious way—say, if he had someone follow her around when she went to the city—"

"He'd find it, and the jig would be up," I finished for him. "That makes sense." Something else still didn't, though.

I just couldn't quite put my finger on what. Bob smiled reminiscently. "Sure wish I had a picture of the look on her face when that dummy came zipping down the wire," he recalled. "And what the hell did it say, anyway, did you hear?"

"No. I mean . . . maybe. I'm not sure." Short-term amnesia was common after an injury like mine, the doctors had said, a mental blurriness that would clear on its own with time. But right now, remembering the episode in the barn was like trying to touch something with the tip of my tongue and not quite being able to.

"I asked Mudge but he said he didn't remember," Bob added. "In all the excitement he just blurted out something, he told me, too busy throwing his voice at all to think about what he said."

"Is that so?" I replied evenly.

"Jemmy said he didn't hear, either," Bob went on. "Didn't even have a plan for what would happen after the dummy appeared, according to him. Just figured he'd try something radical. If it didn't work, no real harm done, but shaking things up might speed matters along, he thought."

"Uh-huh." It was what Jemmy had said when I asked him, too. Exactly what he'd said, word for word.

Bob finished his seltzer. His gaze traveled to the lake's farther shore where, among last year's pale broken reeds, Sam sat motionless in a kayak with the paddle across his knees. "Hope *he* ends up okay."

Me too, but somehow I no longer believed I could do anything about it. Suddenly I felt exhausted. "I'm driving back to town," I said, getting up. "I need to get a head start on a good night's sleep."

"Want me to take you?" Bob offered.

"No, thanks. I'm fine. Just tired, that's all. You stay here and relax awhile."

It was what I told Jemmy as well when I encountered him after retrieving my car keys from inside the cabin.

"Okay," he agreed, smiling vaguely while swatting at a pesky mosquito.

It was the second last time I ever saw him.

Fix what you can.
Call the rest authentic.
—Tiptree's Tips

I **didn't ask you to do this for me,"** I said.

It was past eleven that night when I walked back to where Jemmy sat at a table in the rear of the Bayside Café. Despite my earlier intentions I had not gotten a head start on a night's sleep, and what I'd thought about while I tried wasn't pleasant.

Because as the doctors had promised, my memory was clearing. And as a result it seemed to me now that as often happened, Jemmy had been so impressed by the cleverness of his own idea that he'd taken it too far.

"You killed that kid just as sure as if you put a gun to his head," I told him.

Jemmy looked unsurprised. This was the way we used to meet years earlier when we both knew we still had something to talk about: local place, end of the evening, no appointment required.

I hadn't been sure he'd come tonight, though. "You'd decided you were either going to turn yourself in, which you didn't at all want to do, or you needed Henderson neutralized," I said. "So you came here and hatched a plan."

A good plan, too. But he'd made one mistake: After the Cory thing slid down the wire at Walter Henderson's barn, it spoke.

And I remembered now what it had said: "Ann." Which meant Jemmy hadn't only been trying to shake things up with the thing's sudden appearance, as he'd insisted. It meant he'd known.

"Ann Radham killed Cory Trow because he knew who she was," I went on. "But there was only one way he could've found that out—the same way *you* knew who'd killed him. Because you arranged it. You set the whole thing up right from the start."

"Sit down, Jake," he said. He kicked out a chair.

He was drinking a Rolling Rock. "I don't want to sit down with you. You told Cory that Ann's identity was fake. You clued him in to what she was really doing here, too."

Just walked up to him on the street and told him, probably; that's all it would've taken. Once Cory had gotten a rise out of Ann with the information, he'd have known it was true.

Too bad he didn't realize just how big a rise he was going to get. "You knew by then that he was the kind of kid who'd use anything he could, and that he needed some leverage."

I took a deep breath. "Because he was going to jail if he didn't come up with something to keep himself out," I added. "And on top of it all you nearly killed me."

Because that was another thing: blowdown, my Aunt Fanny. It really was Jemmy who'd hit me out at the cottage. That way I'd go on thinking someone *else* had, so I'd continue snooping not only to find Trish, the baby, and Mudge, but with the added incentive that now Jemmy needed rescuing.

Jemmy, who'd saved my life. Not that he'd known I was going to spring a brain-pan leak. But he'd been willing to risk it.

"How come *he* trusted you?" I asked. "Henderson, who was so hot to kill you?"

Without letting Jemmy answer I rushed on. "But you and Mudge got all that stuff into his barn, the dummy of Cory and the wire it slid down on and I don't know what all."

They hadn't sneaked in with it, that was for sure. "So how'd you convince him to let you . . . ?"

"Hey, Jake? If you don't want everyone in the whole place listening to you, you'll sit," he interrupted mildly.

I looked around, saw I was beginning to have an audience at the tables around us, and sat. Jemmy nodded approval. "Fine. Now look friendly," he instructed. "People like anger. Friendly bores them, they'll look away."

I forced a smile. They did. "I didn't know she'd kill him," Jemmy said quietly as soon as they had. "I thought she'd tell her superiors, the way they're supposed to when anything like that happens."

Like Cory finding out she was a cop, he meant. Whereupon her bosses would pull her off her assignment and somehow Jemmy would take the credit for it with Henderson, for getting rid of her . . .

No. It didn't wash. "Why didn't she?" I demanded. "Instead of running off the rails she might have been able to find some other way to salvage her situation. Or worst case get yanked off the job, you're right," I conceded.

But instead she'd gone straight to premeditated murder, and Jemmy must've had an idea she would. Because to cut any ice with Walter Henderson—enough for the information to save his own life or keep him out of federal custody—Jemmy would've had to *show* who Ann was, not just have her up and vanish.

"Come on, don't try to kid me anymore. You knew all about her before you even came here," I told him.

He said nothing. "Well, didn't you? Don't tell me you just blew in without getting the lay of the land."

When he didn't answer I recited for him. "Ann Radham was a cop, she got close to Jen Henderson on purpose, cozied up to Jen in the clubs Jen liked to go to so she could spy on Jen's dad. But Ann was also a loose cannon, she already had a reputation for it, didn't she?"

A reputation Jemmy's federal buddies would've discussed with him. Because at Jemmy's level, the cops and crooks talked to one another . . . and that was the only way *he* could've known about her; that her own bosses had told him.

For the first time he looked uncomfortable. "Yeah, she was a real ladder-monkey," he admitted. "Someone who doesn't care about anything but the career," he translated when I looked puzzled. "I figured I'd have a better shot at Henderson without her, is all."

I made the face he deserved at him. "Oh, don't give me that, either. You've never killed anyone in your life."

Jemmy was a money man; it would've been dumb for the guys he'd worked for to let him kill anyone. If he got caught for it, he was in a position to betray too much.

Just like me. I leaned across the table at him. "You knew there was a very good chance she'd kill that kid if he threatened her," I said. "So you made him do it, you practically forced him into it."

I grabbed his Rolling Rock bottle, swallowed some. "You told Cory Trow that Ann Radham was an FBI undercover cop," I repeated my accusation.

"Next step was, he threatened her with the information just like you knew he would. He told her she'd better help him out of his jam or he'd tell Walter Henderson what he knew about her."

Still nothing. "After that Ann Radham did what you figured *she'd* probably do, based on what you knew about *her:* she tried to go it alone."

He listened with mild interest. "Instead of reporting what had happened with Cory to her higher-ups, risk being called off an assignment that could really help her career-wise, she decided to keep silent and take care of it herself."

And now came the heart of the matter. "So she made her own plan, prepared the equipment, the rope and so on. She had access to the place, of course, and she knew the alarms were off because that was her job, keeping an eye on Henderson and his doings."

Jemmy nodded, added a little background for me. "Henderson was actually planning on killing the kid already," he confided. "He didn't know Jennifer had broken up with him for real. She'd been sneaking out to the Bayside at night just to get out from under the old man's thumb, but he thought it was to meet the boy in the barn, like she had been.

"He found the body," Jemmy said. "Had no idea who did it. But the trap door was shut, he figured the kid hadn't reached up there and closed it himself."

No kidding. "That must've been a shock."

"Yeah. For once in his life he didn't know what *he* should do next."

"Really," I said, taken aback. The idea of Henderson being unsure about anything was a new one on me. But so was what I now knew about Jemmy.

That he was the kind of guy, I mean, who if somebody had to die to save him or a friend, somebody did. Even if the somebody was an innocent bystander.

Like Cory Trow. "So Ann picked a night when she'd have half an alibi and called him on the cell phone Jen had given him," I went on with my own recital.

The phone hadn't been there when we found him; Henderson must have recognized it and taken it along with the scarf, after opening the trap door and faking the note.

"She lured him there by telling him Jen wanted to see him," I said. "Then she waited, had the rope all nice and knotted ahead of time. Wore Jen's perfume, probably, kept it dark in the barn, put that scarf over his eyes for good measure."

The one that had left a tiny blue fabric scrap hooked on his finger-nail. The beer tasted bitter.

"Timed it all so she could bike out from the Bayside and back during the break between sets," I went on. "Anybody saw her, so what? She did it all the time, there was no reason for anyone to mention it."

As for handing me the Bayside flyer for that night . . . had it been a mistake? Or had she been so sure of herself, so certain I'd never catch on, that she could afford the taunt?

I might never know. But now Bob Arnold's phone message about the autopsy came back to me and suddenly it too made sense. "She got him up to the loft, dropped the rope over him fast. The final shove she gave him was probably with a drumstick, of all things. Made a tiny bruise on his back, no one thought anything of it."

Closing the trap door had definitely been a mistake. But as it turned out, that hadn't mattered. "Once she'd killed him," I said, "you knew I'd think Henderson did it, start poking around the way Ellie and I always have."

I took a breath. "You got lucky when Bella turned out to be Henny Trow's friend; if you got a little luckier, I'd stumble onto the truth. And you meant to be around for that. Participate in it so you'd come out the hero in Henderson's eyes."

As Jemmy had. The result: he was free without having to kill Henderson, which he no more knew how to do than I understood how to jump off the roof of my old house and fly.

He took a sip of beer. "She'd done it before, you know. Got in a situation, shot her way out."

"Ann Radham did?" I asked, and he nodded. I must've looked curious; he made a face of distaste.

"The details don't matter. But they called it justifiable," he said. "Even though it wasn't." Which gave Jemmy what *he* wanted: an Achilles' heel, something about her he could use.

"She said her folks were government workers," I mused aloud. "FBI, maybe? Got herself legacied into the Academy that way, then turned out to be a nut job?"

If in fact she was too well-connected to fire, this could've been a plot to get her to flame out. But Jemmy wasn't telling. "Once I got here I kept my head down," he said instead. "Listened to the talk in the bars and so on."

Not getting in touch with me, though. Not yet. He must've been around for weeks; it was the only way he'd have known Sam was going to be in Cooper the night the Fiat went off the road.

"There turned out to be plenty," he continued. "Once I knew the nuts and bolts of the story . . ."

The Cory Trow *vs.* Walter Henderson feud, he meant. That part he hadn't arranged, of course, just used it the way he found it. "You're right, though," he added, "I knew if the kid got killed you and Ellie would look hard at Henderson."

Especially if Jemmy primed me to believe it, as he had. I'd cooperated in the whole thing, too, by keeping *him* in the know on every detail. As for getting the cooperation he needed from his enemy on the night I'd gathered everyone in the barn:

"I called Henderson, told him if what I had in mind for your party didn't end up helping him out big-time, I'd stand there and let him put the bullet in my head." Jemmy put his beer down. "And Henderson agreed. Honor among thieves, and all that."

In a pig's eye; by that time Henderson had wanted something also: someone to take care of Ann Radham permanently for him in a way that didn't require him to commit the ultimate no-no: killing a federal cop.

Because don't tell me Jemmy hadn't passed Ann's identity along in the course of the conversation. Whereupon Henderson had seen the benefits of doing a little adapting himself.

Jemmy looked around; it was late and the crowd in the Bayside had begun thinning.

"You traded Cory Trow's life for your own," I said.

And for mine. Just the way he'd planned. "Jemmy?"

Even then I wanted him to deny it but he didn't seem to have heard me. Instead he gazed past me to the front of the room where a jazz quartet was playing the hell out of a tune I didn't know.

"Yeah," he said finally. "That's it, the whole ball of wax. You're wrong about one thing, though," he added. "It wasn't about you. It all was about me, start to finish."

He turned back to me. "Now look me in the eye and tell me that in my place you wouldn't have done the same thing yourself."

I got up and walked out.

•   •   •

"**You get everything** straight with Jemmy?" Wade asked.

He'd still been up when I got home from the Bayside, on his hands and knees in the back parlor with a steel-wool rubbing pad. Ellie and I had stripped the varnish off the floor over the past winter, using liquid stripping solution and scraping the old finish away one three-foot-square section at a time.

Underneath lay maple hardwood milled into flooring so fine-grained, it resembled the feathers on a bird's wing. The stripper took off the varnish but not the stain it had imparted, a golden glow that seemed to radiate up through the floor instead of only from the surface of it.

"Hi," I'd said, not answering his question. "That's great what you're doing there."

Fine steel wool polished the surface. Next we meant to apply polyurethane; the result would be a floor so richly finished that it would look as if you could dive into it.

One look at my face, though, and Wade had put the steel-wool pads away, packed up the cooler, then started the truck and aimed us back toward the lakeside cottage, just the two of us.

Now we sat at the end of the dock in the midnight darkness, a blanket over our shoulders and his arm around me. Under a blue-black, star-filled sky the red beacon on the new tower across the lake winked steadily like an eye opening and closing.

"Jemmy set Cory up," I said. At the edge of the water, frogs emitted rhythmic bass notes and treble trillings. "There's a lot more to it, though."

"I see," said Wade when I'd told him all the rest.

Almost all. Good thing Jemmy wasn't here now; Wade sounded ready to rearrange my old pal's new face for him, and his way was a lot faster than plastic surgery.

To the moon, Alice. The old situation comedy line echoed in my head along with the canned laughter that usually accompanied it. But this wasn't funny. And a punch in the nose wouldn't fix my buddy and savior Jemmy Wechsler.

Nothing would. "People change, I guess," I said sadly. "My trouble is, I'm wondering now if maybe he didn't."

One of my troubles. "If maybe he was always that way and I just never caught on until recently."

Or if I'd known all along and just wouldn't look straight at it until I had my nose rubbed in it. After all, I'd agreed when Ellie said he was a sociopath, and what had I thought she meant?

Wade squeezed my shoulder. "All you did was take whatever help you could get back then. So if some of it was from a guy who wasn't so decent in other ways? That's no big crime."

It wasn't all I'd done. If it had been maybe none of this would've happened. "And if Jemmy's not your idol anymore," Wade added, "well, that's what idols do, isn't it? They break."

We sat a while longer listening to the frogs. Bats swooped unseen in the darkness around our heads. Then:

"Anything else comes up, we'll deal with it," Wade said. "If it does."

The weight of the world lifted suddenly off my shoulders, but I couldn't quite let it go that fast. "Confession is good for the soul?" I hazarded, letting him hear the question in my voice.

Wade just laughed, bless his heart. "Only children believe the world works that way, Jake. And you know it."

And that's where we left it. He got up. "But listen, there's something else you need to hear about. Sam's gone."

"What do you mean? Gone where?" A dozen possibilities raced through my mind, each worse than the one before.

"Rehab," Wade said. "After you left here earlier, he came in off the lake and told us."

"But how'd he get . . . ?" Anxiety seized me.

"He asked George to take him to the airport in Bangor," Wade said. "George said he would, and they went."

So that was what all that sitting on the lake in the kayak had been about: gathering his courage. "Do you think he might go through with it this time?"

Wade shrugged. "Your guess is as good as mine. But he had a funny look on his face when he told us what he had planned."

A coyote yipped lonesomely in the darkness beyond the lake's far shore, where people lived year-round and the pickings were better: chicken bones from trash cans, the last few french fries tossed out a car window, unlucky house pets.

"I think something's made an impression on him; he's heard or seen something that's made him want to try again," Wade said.

The lump in my throat felt as big as a fist. "He'll call us?"

"George will. As soon as he gets there and he's handed Sam over at the rehab place, he'll leave a message for us at home."

He put a hand on my shoulder. "And there's an envelope for you, came in today's mail. From that fellow in Orono you sent the old book to, I forgot to mention it."

Exhaustion swept over me. "I can look at it tomorrow."

Or next month. I had no expectation whatsoever that Sam's latest effort would work, and I could already feel myself starting to cling to that attitude, not wanting to jinx my son.

"I'm going in," Wade said. "Don't sit here too long, you'll get a chill."

"Right," I agreed, making my voice sound okay. But as soon as the screen door finished closing, I put my face into my hands. So it wasn't until I looked up again that I realized someone else was there with me.

"Hi, Victor," I managed, but he didn't answer, only smiled sympathetically before vanishing again . . . almost.

A brownish him-shaped print remained as if he'd burned his outlines in the air.

Then it too was gone, maybe even for good.

From the *Bangor Daily News:*

ROBOTHAM, HORACE L. Suddenly at Orono, May 21, 2006. Mr. Robotham was founder and co-owner of Horace-Langley Rare Books & Papers in Orono. Born in Rhode Island and a graduate of Miskatonic University, he authored numerous scholarly papers on manuscript preservation. He is survived by his friend and business partner Langley B. Cabell. There will be no services.

ABOUT THE AUTHOR

SARAH GRAVES lives with her husband in Eastport, Maine, where her mystery novels are set. She is currently working on her eleventh *Home Repair Is Homicide* novel, *Killer Driller*.